VID STAR

A MINA KANE NOVEL:
BOOK FOUR

AMANDA CARLSON

VID STAR
A Mina Kane Novel: Book Four

This book is a work of fiction. The characters, events, and places portrayed in this book are products of the author's imagination and are either fictitious or are used fictitiously. Any similarity to real persons, living or dead, is purely coincidental and not intended by the author.

ISBN-13: 978-1-944431-27-3

Email: amanda@amandacarlson.com

Published in the United States of America.

Apparently, vid stars need CIU NannyBots in 2105.

Secret Agent Mina Kane's prime objective is to help a friend who's running from a powerful corporation hellbent on keeping him quiet. While doing so, she finds herself inside a lollipop shop at the edge of the outskirts. After receiving a pleading request, in a place where she has no jurisdiction, Mina finds her hands are bound in purelock.

Things take a turn when she and Agent Adams are assigned to investigate a threatening message received by a vid star. They're hoping for light duty, but the op quickly morphs into full-blown extortion. When none other than Vincent Kramer attends the vid premiere, things go from flying under the radar to being launched into full strato. After an attempted murder, Mina and company transport their spoiled celeb to the edge of the outskirts where everything coalesces into a moon shot of a case.

Maybe highly trained colonels from France can be of some use?

Other Books by Amanda Carlson

Jessica McClain Series
Urban Fantasy
BLOODED
FULL BLOODED
HOT BLOODED
COLD BLOODED
RED BLOODED
PURE BLOODED
BLUE BLOODED

Sin City Collectors
Paranormal Romance
ACES WILD
ANTE UP
ALL IN

Phoebe Meadows
Contemporary Fantasy
STRUCK
FREED
EXILED

Holly Danger
Futuristic Dystopian
Danger's Halo
Danger's Vice
Danger's Race
Danger's Cure
Danger's Hunt
Danger's Fate

Mina Kane
Futuristic Thriller
Total Enhancement
Perfect Plant
Cupid's Bow
Vid Star
Code Teal

Chapter 1

"I HAVE ZERO recall on this, and it's bugging me. I watched *A Crafty Planet*, like, two weeks ago. It vid-starred that one guy." Kaylee snapped her fingers. They looked enormous on Mina's sleep room wall screen. In her half-awake state, she'd accidently ordered Veronica, her home sim, to place Kaylee at one hundred percent. "What was his name? Paul—no, too normal. Pica? Prancer? *Crap.* It's completely escaped me." She shook her head, straight black hair skimming her shoulders. It was seven thirty a.m. Kaylee was already dressed and ready to start the day. Mina snuggled deeper under her soft, silky sheets. "All I know is it was something weird and vid starry."

Mina giggled as she tracked Kaylee's hands, which her pal and fellow CIU agent kept moving animatedly in between snapping.

"What?" Kaylee frowned. "So I don't know vid stars? You try and name one. Honestly, if there's not a dolphin frolicking or a marmot munching on a nut, you rarely pay attention."

Mina laughed. Marmots didn't eat nuts. Did they? See? She didn't know everything. But Kaylee was right. She did have a terrible attention span when it came to watching vids with people in them. Naturecasts were her fave.

"I mean, his name could've been Pez or Posty. But come to think of it, maybe it was Petra. Yes—it *was* a girl. Petra Pebbles! That's it. What a ridiculous name. Vid stars take the printed frosting when it comes to identity-chipping themselves after dumb things like rocks and fingers."

Mina snorted. "Fingers? Come on."

"Cuticle Cantrell. Knuckle Knot. Or maybe it's Cuticle Knot and Knuckle Cantrell?" Kaylee swished a hand, then leaned forward, shaking her finger. It was the size of a small child on Mina's huge screen. "And if you don't stop that annoying hyena cackle, I'm going to drone over to your super-lux suite in the sky and give you a five-fingered knuckle sandwich. Honestly, it's the only time we should ever use the word 'knuckle' in a sentence." She balled her fist and fake-punched the air.

Dag, her dog, jumped up and barked, thinking Kaylee was going to throw a ball, which was his fave.

Mina had to wait a few seconds to catch her breath.

She hadn't laughed this hard this early in the morning since she was in elementary programming and woke up from a rowdy girls' sleep party. "I'm not laughing because you don't know vid stars. I promise. I'm laughing because I found you the perfect partner, one you can hone to a nice, sharp point. You're going to love her."

"No, I won't. I despise mentoring."

"She's a snapper and a waver. She's a hydro-cracker,

and you're going to love her. There's no one else in the entire agency she should be paired with."

"Our department hires new recruits, like, every six years or so," Kaylee chuffed, waving a hand. "Maybe in six years, I'll be ready to wrangle a baby."

"McAllister offered her a job."

Kaylee sat back in her chair. "Offered *who* a job?"

"Harmony Biggins. Strum Littlefield's daughter. I forgot to tell you. With all the jumping-off-the-ship stuff and getting-detoxed-from-a-chemi-swim stuff and all the...other stuff, it slipped my mind."

Other stuff was Vincent Kramer.

Mina was determined to enjoy her peaceful morning, and doing so included not mentioning the colonel-in-arms of the French Protectorate. So she wasn't going to. Until she did. Or Kaylee did.

"McAllister told her she had a job with the department if she could disarm the missile." If she hadn't, the serial-killing group Veritus could've launched it into the city, killing thousands. Harmony deserved compensation, and she'd chosen to take it in the form of a job with the CIU. Not a bad choice. "And because he's hiring her without any formal training, she's going to need a *really* good mentor. So naturally, that would be you."

"Flattery will get you a big, fat data check in the trying-to-froth-me-up column. And, yeah, she did make that happen. She saved a lot of lives." Kaylee paused, becoming uncharacteristically pensive. Good news for Harmony. "How old is she? I never saw her, only heard her through your cuff."

"Almost twenty-two," Mina answered. It was a teensy stretch. Harmony had told them she was twenty-one and a half. Close enough. "She's a Level XIV hacker."

"Level XIV? I thought they just went by *super* after XIII?" Kaylee grinned. "So you're telling me my baby hacker agent is better than your baby hacker agent?"

"Way to spin it." Mina laughed. "I don't pretend to understand their ranking system. But yes, that technically means she's achieved a greater number of hacker points or whatever." Hackers determined their own scoring system, and it remained a mystery to everyone else, just the way they liked it. "Lee's right there, though. He let Harmony and her father do the disarming, even though he could've figured it out himself. The kid's brilliant at code. He just is."

"Is that pride I hear leaking around your cackle?"

"It might be." Mina brushed a few strands of hair out of her eyes and debated tossing off her covers. "Just between us, I'm not sure how I completed some of my other cases without him. He saved my skin on the Tedesco op. I wouldn't have been able to breach the penthouse without his help. He figured out the military security cam switcheroo in, like, thirty seconds. If he hadn't, I shudder to think where we'd be right now. Tedesco would've gotten away with all of it, and Veritus would still be operational."

"Yeah, don't let your brain go there." Kaylee scratched Dag behind the ears as her lovable dog draped his huge body across her knees. "So, in effect, you're saying that having a baby hacker partner makes *you* a better agent?"

Mina chuckled. "I guess I'm saying that."

"Interesting."

"Seriously, you're going to love Harmony. You're almost the same person."

"It'll be up to McAllister." Kaylee shrugged.

"I'm rec'ing you. She needs someone strong and levelheaded. Harmony likes doing things her way." That was something of an understatement. Envisioning the two of them together made Mina want to hyena cackle again. Harmony was going to meet her twin gravitational force in Kaylee. "She's supremely confident, which is an asset, though also a hindrance, especially when she's coming in so green. She'll respond well to your style and therefore err less than she would with someone else. It's the perfect pairing."

"Levelheaded is quite the compliment coming from you. I like to think my lid stays in nice equilibrium during times of crisis," Kaylee snarked. "But the erring part is the problem. That's the reason I don't take on babies. They make a kiloton of mistakes, which in our business can get you killed, and they tend to irritate me when they cry. And from what you're describing, there's a high likelihood I'm going to make this girl cry. Not my thing. No enjoyment there."

"She doesn't strike me as a crier," Mina said. "Don't forget, you're talking to someone who went into mentoring against her will. And I can tell you from the other side, it's not that bad. I like Harmony. She's strong, intelligent, confident, and will benefit from someone who can keep her on track. You won't be sorry. She'll probably end up helping you more than you think possible."

Kaylee started to snap. "So essentiall-*eee*, you're telling m-*eee* that Harmon-*eee* just might b-*eee* a reall-*eee* good train-*eee*?"

"Stahhhp!" Mina laughed, finally throwing off her covers. She couldn't fight it any longer. It was time to start the day.

"Never." Kaylee slid Daggie off her legs and started drumming her thighs. "Harmon-*eee* is my new ment-*eee*, but only if sh-*eee* can face scrutin-*eee*, not my fault if I make her w-*eee*p, she'll have to k-*eee*p...it together." Kaylee giggled as she stood, Dag jumping beside her. "Okay, so that last part needs work." She peered at the screen, moving closer. "Is that a new, shiny cuff? How'd you get another one so fast?"

Mina held it out. "Lee had it droned over last night. It's just like the other fancy Zenith one, but snazzier. I haven't figured out all the features yet."

"It's super delicious. Green envy vibes rolling through my stone-cold green heart right now."

"I'm sure you'll get one soon. I heard all the agents are getting upgrades." Mina rolled to the edge of her platform, lifting a leg over the padded edge. The cush was still too cushy. It was like being stuck in a lux cage.

Kaylee cackled. "Watching you get out of that thing is like watching a roly-poly from *Mars Bots* trying to wobble out of a shallow crater. Just fix it, already."

Mina made it up and over. "I sleep like a baby in that hole." She gestured to the interior of the platform, which was now a rumpled pile of silky modal goodness. "I don't want to mess it up. But trying to get out each morning is becoming an issue. I think it quietly swallows me a little more each night."

"Can't you just raise the interior? I'm pretty sure that platform is top-of-the-line. Everything on it is adjustable. Not just the cush."

Mina glanced quizzically at her bed. "Huh. I never thought of that. Veronica, raise platform base eight centimeters." Her home sim was connected to all of the operational tech inside her residence. Most everybody's sim had similar compatibilities, if they chose to pair them. People had been living with this convenience for over fifty years. Hard to imagine life without it.

Almost immediately, the interior of Mina's platform began to rise.

"See? Told you," Kaylee said. "What would you do without me?"

"Sleep later." Mina tested it by sitting on the edge, bouncing twice. "Hey, same cush, new height. And look, I can slide right out." She scooted off. "You're a genius." She headed to her closet. "Why'd you tag me so early, anyway?" she called from inside. "I forgot to ask."

"*A Crafty Planet* popped into my head. Not Tedesco's ship you bounded off of yesterday, but the actual vid it was named after. Then I decided to check on my bestie. You emotional drone-coastered pretty hard last night. First, you thought you were working on equal eurofooting with your childhood pal, then he pulled a double cross that almost blew the entire op into the strato."

The Vincent Kramer seal had been broken.

At least Mina hadn't been the one to break it.

The colonel had indeed held back vital information that could've gotten a lot of people killed. He'd definitely compromised the op.

"Plus, I was curious—okay, downright insanely piqued—to see if the colonel-in-arms, after all this drone-coaster drama, had the guts to show up last night."

"Here?" Mina came out of her closet holding a pair of mustard-colored tuck pants and a black tunic over one arm. "He can't get to this level without authorization. So I'm not sure if he had the guts or not. I've got his calls on mute. Deliveries shut down. Veronica even added him to what she called my 'excrement list' last night without even being asked. So, no, he didn't show up."

Mina probably wouldn't have let him in. The fact there was a *probably* irritated her.

Kaylee hooted. "An excrement list! That's hilarious. Poor Kramer. Though the man's basically royalty. He could get up there if he wanted to." She shook her head. "Don't look at me like that. It's true. He goes where he wants. But he zapped himself into a black hole with his glaring omissions."

"'Omission' is just a fancy word for lie."

"Agreed. However, he could have a perfectly excellent explanation for what happened. Like the ancient sun god Ra said he'd roast his firstborn alive if he didn't save the world or something."

"Why are you so intent on pushing Team Kramer?"

"Because he makes you happy. I saw it before you could tuck it away. I like you happy."

"I like me happy, too. So that means Kramer stays on the excrement list."

For now.

Kaylee chuckled as she rubbed Dag's ears as he tried to lick her face. "We're going out soon, you big lug." To Mina, she said, "I'm going to have Kevin make a stinky list, too. Preston Jazz Hands is definitely going on it."

Preston Jazz Hands was Kaylee's nickname for a short-lived boyfriend who'd tried unsuccessfully to embezzle from her.

"I can think of a few more who would be right there at the top," Mina said.

Kaylee's finger came shooting out, waggling. "Do *not* say Porcupine Jones. Do not."

Mina mocked running a finger over her lips. "I'm sealed. I will not bring up the weirdest guy you've ever dated."

"I went on *one* date with him. There was no wisp of a relationship. He doesn't even qualify for excrement. You and I vowed a long time ago that we wouldn't bring him up, and here we are wasting air on him. Let's move on. What's your plan today?"

"Not sure," Mina replied. "McAllister debriefed me about Veritus and his meeting with Ambrose Bernard and Kramer last night, but he didn't give me further instructions. I'm planning to follow up with Norm and Harri first thing. Harri got fired. Bliss Corp is spying on him. If they're experimenting with Plush on unwilling people, they will try to keep that a secret at all costs." The implications there were vast and scary.

"Norm is keeping watch over him until I figure out the next move."

Norman Webb was a former federal marshal, and Mina trusted him with her life. Harri had worked at a Pleasure Emporium until yesterday, when Mina had gone to interview him.

"That sucks for him."

"I know. Unfortunately, the Plush case won't become a full op for a while." Likely a long while, since big-time corporations had their elbows locked with the federal government. "I'm assuming I'll get a new op designation at some point today. Have you received one?"

"Nope. Still waiting," Kaylee replied. "McAllister said he'd get a hold of me soon."

Mina changed into her clothes behind her closet door, poking her head out. "I'm kind of hoping for a case with a little to no drama. Maybe a nice extortionist or an elderly thief."

"Yeah." Kaylee chuckled. "Running down an airchair is a lot easier than commandeering a gigantic ship in hot pursuit of notorious serial killers. But don't count your moon rocks before they arrive. Speaking of which, I need to order some. I've got a cousin who goes crazy for them. Her birth-year celebration is coming up, and I happen to know a moon cultivator who owes me a favor."

"Of course you do."

Mina's sim announced, "Vid chat request coming in from Norman Webb. Do you wish to accept?"

"Yes, hold," Mina told Veronica. To Kaylee, she said, "There's Norm now. I have to go."

"Gotcha. And if Kramer tries to crawl back, don't be too hard on the poor puppy. Deep down in his black heart of hearts, he meant well." Kaylee threw Mina a three-finger salute. "By-*eee.*"

Mina snorted as her friend disappeared.

Meant well and *did well* were two entirely separate things.

CHAPTER 2

"Veronica, screen on," Mina ordered from her position on a stool at her meal counter.

Her wall remained dark. No Norm.

Just before Mina could inquire as to what was happening, Norm sputtered, "This is a code teal. I repeat, this is a code *teal*."

Mina's brows furrowed. "Norm, I can hear you, but I can't see you. What's a code teal?" That was not a designation she was familiar with. It must be a marshal term.

"Dang it," Norm swore. "Just a minute. I'm on one of those tiny handhelds. I swear the hot zones have gotten smaller with each iteration. Pretty soon, they're going to be so nano-sized that a mouse couldn't even turn one on."

Mina refrained from commenting that he could use his voice. Instead, she said, "I have faith in those golden fingers. They can do anything they set their mind to."

Norm popped on her wall.

Mina leaned forward. "Where are you?" The room behind him was poorly lit, the furniture sparse and cheaply printed.

He glanced over his shoulder, his image bouncing around as he lifted his handheld and placed it somewhere in front of him, finally evening out his image. "We're at a pay-a-day. Had to zoom out fast. They turned up the heat during the wee hours."

Mina didn't have to be told who *they* were.

"Don't want to talk on an open channel," Norm said, "even a secured one like yours. Kid's in the sprayer. We snuck out, dropped down from the roof. They tried to follow, but they couldn't keep up. Nobody can catch ol' Norm. I got an address for you. I'll shoot it straight to your cuff. It's a lollipop shop. Touchdown a full kilo. We'll be waiting in thirty." He popped off. Or tried to. His hand reached out, fumbling with the handheld for a few seconds before he grunted, "Don't be late."

Her wall went dark.

She sat back, digesting. A lollipop shop, in agent terms, referred to a secured area where agents could swap information. Lollipops used to be exchanged between friends before the advent of meal printers, which had been before Mina's time. Touch down a full kilo meant to land at least a kilometer away and walk in on foot while watching closely for a tail. A pay-a-day was nothing more than a rented sleep room containing the barest of necessities and usually required actual currency instead of borrows for a stay.

A second later, Mina's cuff vibrated.

The address Norm sent came in coded, which wasn't a surprise. She chuckled as she noted that Norm had used not one, but three different federal decipher codes, all bunched together. So very Norm.

It took Mina four seconds to deduce where she would be heading. *Damn.* The location, as far as she could tell, was on the border of the outskirts, or quite possibly inside, as Mina hadn't been to that area for quite some time, and the outskirts were constantly expanding.

No wonder Norm had evaded Bliss Corp. If they'd followed him and Harri to that location, they would've been spotted by anyone with eyeballs, and in the 'skirts, everyone saw everything. If you had anything usable—information, physical items, images, vid—it was up for grabs.

Norm knew exposure like that would be risky for Bliss Corp. That's why he'd chosen that location. Mina had entrusted him to keep Harri safe, and he had.

She stood, heading back to her sleep room to change. Mustard tuck pants weren't going to cut it today. "Veronica, send this recording to Lee Adams. Mark as urgent. Lee, it's Mina. Just got a call from the spider. He's left the web." Apt in more ways than one, since Norm's surname was Webb. "We rendezvous in twenty. Pickup a block south of your residence at the public landing area. I'll be in an unmarked. Wear"—she hesitated—"something that says you can throw a few punches?" She posed it as a question, because was that request even possible for him? Punching was iffy. Though Lee did have a solid over-the-knee move. She knew he didn't have a clothing printer in his place, but she couldn't worry about that now. He'd figure it out.

"Sending audio," Veronica confirmed.

Mina changed and walked briskly back into her living area. "Veronica, tag Director McAllister for vid chat. Label as urgent. Display immediately at thirty."

Ten seconds later, her director appeared on her wall. "Report, Agent Kane." He was at headquarters.

Guess it wasn't so early after all.

"I just received a call from the spider," she informed her boss. "He was forced to shuttle his query underground sometime in the early morning hours. He relocated successfully without a tail. He's requested a meet at a lollipop shop and sent me coded coordinates." They talked on a secured government line, but Mina was careful not to divulge any specific details over the connection, just in case. Her director followed along just fine. "The location is on the border of Peach Street." Agentspeak for the outskirts. "How would you like me to proceed? Keeping the civilian safe is of the utmost priority to me."

"For me as well," McAllister confirmed. "We're going to need more intel before I can decide on a next course of action. Interesting things have been filtering down regarding multitrillion corporations and their involvement inside our government. I have full ears out. I'll do some digging while you are at your meet. I'm assuming Agent Adams will accompany you?"

"Yes. I contacted him already."

"If the corporation in pursuit does not desist, I will arrange a safe house for him."

"I trust the spider's take on this. If he thinks there's continued danger, that will probably be the best option. They're at a pay-a-day, which might add up on a government tab, but it could end up being more under the radar than an official government safe house." Bliss Corp definitely had reach within the government. How deep that went was an unanswered question. People talked.

"I'll decide once we have the complete story. Did the spider say anything else?"

"He said something about it being a code teal."

McAllister rubbed his chin. "A code teal means tread with caution, bodily harm expected. At least that's what it used to mean. It's an outdated term."

"Bodily harm?" Mina rubbed her face. "I should've known that was a possibility from the beginning. We're dealing with a very powerful entity, and I droned into their home base and placed my friend squarely in their sights."

"You went there to question him, on my orders, about a harmful reaction to a drug they're peddling illegally. This simple information-seeking interview should've, by all accounts, remained private. It's clear they were spying, or at least had an understanding of why you were there, which is highly illegal under the Civilians Privacy Act of 2085. No corporation, no matter how big, is allowed to spy on its customers without their consent. If they were smart, they would've done nothing but keep their ears open. However, by reacting without thought or consequence, they've shown their intent, and that will work in our favor. You've already read Mr. Hampburg his rights. He's a protected government asset in this case, even though it remains unofficial at this time. I plan to make it known loud and clear through every channel available to me where the federal government stands on our protection of Harold Hampburg. I will not capitulate to any form of intimidation. It will not be in their best interest to pursue Mr. Hampburg for much longer. You can count on that. If they do, they'll pay the price in high court, and exposure will be unavoidable."

Mina believed her director. He would make things right, and he had the power to do so. They were up against a greedy megacorporation with infinite resources, so they were going to have to work diligently to uncover all the facts they could find.

She sighed. "I didn't think cases got much bigger than Veritus. Taking down a serial-killing ring that wreaked havoc for over twenty years was big." The biggest Mina had ever been involved with thus far. "But pinning down a multitrillion-dollar conglomerate that may or may not be testing drugs on innocent people without their permission may prove to be bigger and far more elusive."

McAllister's expression mirrored Mina's, flashing both wariness and anger. "I don't expect to get authorization to investigate this on a federal level for at least a year, maybe more. During that time, we will gather evidence, verify it, and keep moving forward. The levels at which Bliss Corp is entangled within the government will take time to unravel. An unmarked drone will be at your residence in five. Attach a weapon to your belt.

Report once the meeting is over, or before that if you run into any issues."

"Will do."

⸺◆⸺

"Whoa," Lee said as he boarded the craft. "You look..." He blushed, his owl eyes darting away from her before making their way back. "You look...tough. I don't, you know, have any syn-leather." He cleared his throat. "I thought this was okay for the punching stuff." He glanced down at his outfit skeptically.

"It'll do," Mina told him. It would have to. At least the rookie had donned dark colors. He had on basic black slacks and a navy pullover with tight sleeves. He still looked young, but he didn't look like his usual earnest self.

Well, not as much, anyway.

Mina was decked out in the syn-leather pants she'd worn when she and Kaylee had posed as the Ford twins when they'd contacted Jordan Maybach, the superhacker Tedesco had hired to zap his files. She'd opted for a black suction shirt paired with a black cropped jacket with titanium studs running along the shoulders.

Going full syn-leather would've been overkill and too eye-catching. She had to look like she was ready to take somebody on, but not stand out as a federal agent.

Her gem laser was attached to her waist in full view, like McAllister had ordered. To add more sass, and to keep her cover, she'd worn a temp hair alt in vibrant red that fell just below her ears. The kohl around her eyes was smudged on purpose, and red lip dye finished the look off.

Mina crossed her legs, her scissor-heeled boots bobbing. "Have you been to the outskirts before?"

"Are you kidding?" Lee's mouth gaped open. "I mean, as teenagers we got close on dares and stuff. But no one in their right mind just wanders into the outskirts. That can be deadly or worse."

What did he think could be worse than death? Mina wasn't going to ask.

Unfortunately, an outskirts-like area surrounded every major city in the entire country. These were areas where people were forced to go when they had no borrows left to their names. Places of stark survival. Mina wasn't looking forward to visiting and was grateful Norm had remained on the perimeter.

The craft sim announced, "Setting down in three minutes and thirty-seven seconds. There is no public landing zone available near your destination. Do you wish to exit at street level, Agent Kane?"

"Street is fine," Mina confirmed. "Do a pedestrian sweep first. Wait until it's clear before setting down." There shouldn't be much foot traffic, but she wanted to be sure. "Stick to the original destination." She'd programmed the craft for a hard landing one-point-two kilos away from the address of the lollipop shop Norm had given her. On the satellite feed Mina had used, it had appeared to be a back alley of some kind, so hopefully the craft wouldn't look as conspicuous setting down there.

It would be impossible to go in unnoticed, but it was the best they could do.

McAllister had sent a beat-up unmarked with decals on the sides to indicate they were a private company that inspected water lines.

"Confirmed," the sim said.

Mina turned her attention back to the rookie. "There's a very slim chance we'll encounter a serious threat. People, even on the border, do their fair share of shaking down anyone they think might have currency or something of value, but they're going to think twice before engaging with us." Syn-leather bottoms and titanium shoulder studs said as much. "I trust Norm to have picked a place that isn't too dangerous." Just dangerous enough. "Did you bring your maxi?" Lee had used his maxi stunner to bring down another criminal.

"Yeah," Lee answered. "Plus this acorn laser I was commissioned a few days ago." He slid a small—more like super puny—laser out of his pocket. The front was round and scalloped like the nut with a straight stem. A long handle came out of the point at the bottom. It shot a short burst of hot light from the cap, just enough to sting, but not to kill. Unless you went for an eye. Almost any laser could kill if you shot it directly into the eye socket. A hit to the brain through soft tissue was always deadly.

Mina nodded. "Palm them both. Set the maxi on stun. We're not here to make any noise." Or any more than necessary. "Once we're on the ground, follow me. We're heading to a lollipop shop." Lee flashed his confusion, which she'd been expecting. She was ready with a short definition. Mentoring. "Before the invention of meal printers, it was a custom for children to exchange lollipops as gifts to express their friendship. Lollies originated hundreds of years ago, I'm not sure where, and are basically hard sweets stuck on the top of a stick. But the exchange practice began around 2045, after the Global Climate War. They were seen as a symbol of peace and were usually decorated in vibrant shades and colorful decals. Anyway," Mina continued, "a willing exchange of friendship is where the term came from interdepartmentally. If Norm is offering this place up as such, that means he's familiar with the location, has likely scouted it, knows the owner, or all of the above. It should be safe to rendezvous without any trouble." Mina left out the *code teal* and *bodily harm* stuff. No reason to worry the rookie more than he was already worried.

Lee nodded. "I got it. My mom used to go to a specialty printshop around special holidays to buy me the old-fashioned lollies, though these were printed. They were really good. I don't know if any more of those kiosks exist, but they should."

The sim voice intoned, "Setting down in thirty seconds. No pedestrians on the ground within a twenty-meter mark."

The craft eased down between two buildings. As they dropped from the sky, the light outside got darker and darker.

Chapter 2

THEY WERE HALF a kilometer in when Mina noticed the tail. She glanced at Lee to see if he'd picked up on it, but the rookie was focused on the crumbling facades all around them, his head angling around. "This place is just so… unfortunate. There are piles of junk everywhere. Doesn't the government come in here and do a sweep once in a while?"

Mina didn't glance behind her. Whoever was following them wasn't being quiet about it, and they were gaining. "No. They don't. They justify it by claiming that no one here pays taxes, so they somehow don't deserve cleanup services, among other utilities. But honestly, it's a good thing they have rats with really long tails to help them control the mess."

Lee's head jerked toward her, and his eyebrows quirked as he tried to figure out the meaning of her strange non sequitur. He was about to ask her what she meant, but she cut him off, emphasizing, "They have really long *tails.*"

Mina had to physically grab his arm so he didn't crank his head around to check for a tail and give them away. She kept her hold on him, guiding him around the next corner.

Once there, she directed their backs against the wall, bracing a forearm across Lee's chest to indicate she wanted him to stay where he was. She wasn't ready to pull out her gem. Yet.

It didn't take long for the tail to make the turn. Mina was ready. She swiped out her foot as she slammed the palm of her hand into a chest. The small, petite body tumbled backward instantly, landing on its backside and skidding half a meter before coming to a stop.

Whoever they were wore a helmet.

Mina stood, legs apart, arms crossed, waiting.

Finally, the small human reached up and tugged off the head covering. Long, dark hair spilled down around a pair of skinny shoulders. Her face was smudged with dirt, her locks unsprayed, her clothing, from what Mina could see under a dark jacket, frayed.

She was maybe eleven or twelve.

"Why'd you do that?" the girl spat.

"You're following us." Though Mina didn't have to explain the obvious. This girl knew exactly what she'd been getting herself into by coming after them. It likely wasn't the first time she'd skidded to a stop on her backside.

The girl shrugged, then stood, whisking the grime off her pants with one hand. Pants that were several sizes too big and were cinched at her waist with carbon fiber.

"Why *wouldn't* I follow you? You set down in a fancy craft in the middle of Pormal and walked out like you own the place. Figure you're good for something."

Mina wasn't going to touch the fact that this girl thought the banged-up unmarked was a *fancy craft.* "What's Parmal?"

"*Por*mal. Short for Poor Man's Land. See? I knew you weren't from around here." She lifted a finger and dragged it up and down in the air, tracing Mina's body. "Nobody wears stuff like that or has big lasers banging against their hip like that. That's for the 'skirts, not for Pormal. Most people here don't want trouble. We've been pushing off the 'skirts for a-ons." The girl made a show of looking up at the small two- and three-story residences. "Even though it looks pretty desti-lute"—Mina followed her meaning despite the creative pronunciations—"we can still cobble together some borrows here and there for essentials. Nobody wants bad stuff to go down."

"Except you." They weren't going to lose this girl as a shadow unless they came to a mutual agreement. The girl hadn't bothered to keep her pursual of them on the down-low, when Mina had no doubt she was capable of doing just that. There was a chance she was a runner for someone powerful. The helmet looked newish, and even though her clothing was frayed, it wasn't in tatters. She had some means.

Mina couldn't have this girl spreading information that they were here. She hadn't been familiar with the term *Pormal,* and she also hadn't been aware that people could *push back* the 'skirts. And honestly, she was happy to find out they could and hoped they kept it up, despite Lee's dismal view of the area.

"What's it going to take to forget you saw us?" she asked.

The girl shot her a petulant look. "I don't need nothing from you." She rested the large helmet under one arm, her small hand barely dangling around half of it.

"Because you can get it from somebody else," Mina countered. "By telling them where to find us." She took a step toward the girl, a scissor heel clacking loudly. "You think maybe if your boss takes us down, you'll get a cut of something better. But I'm here to assure you that's not even close to the truth. Instead, you'll be in the zero-particle zone instead of ahead of it. Deal with me now, and you get something. Later? Nothing. I'm sure you know how this plays."

The girl appraised Mina, eyes narrowing. The urchin was still unsure. She knew her world and only her world. Mina was certain that federal agents didn't come here very often. Certainly not the PPF. People were on their own. It was grim no matter how you microsliced it.

"I told you I don't need nothing." She tilted her chin up, puffing out her chest.

Mina needed to hurry this along. Norm was already in position. Clearly, this girl wasn't going to take anything freely. She preferred to make a grab over forging a deal with someone she didn't trust.

"Okay, let's do this another way," Mina suggested. "How about you provide us a service, and in exchange for that *service*, you get paid?" At least that way, she'd be within Mina's periphery until they vacated the area.

"What kind of service?" Mina heard curiosity, but also wariness.

"Nothing you're not already qualified to do. We figure you know this area pretty good, right?" Mina looked at Lee, who nodded along helpfully. "Probably born and raised. We're looking to get to 410 Renault. We need to get there without picking up another tail, if you catch my drift."

"Biters? You're going to Biters?" She squinted, cocking her head. "You know Quaz?"

Biters? Quaz? "Yep," Mina answered smoothly. "You lead the way, and you'll get a reward."

The girl's demeanor changed. She relaxed by a few degrees, and her face went slack. She popped on her helmet, whipping up the visor. "Why didn't you just say so?"

"Listen, kid, you're the one who followed us. We haven't had time to get to know each other." The girl began to walk, and Mina followed, beckoning to Lee, who was half a step behind.

"If Quaz knows you, then you're good," the girl tossed over her shoulder.

It didn't matter if Quaz knew them or not. "What's your name, anyway?"

"Noy-B."

"That's a nice name," Lee offered, his voice upbeat and cheerful.

Mina elbowed him as she addressed the girl. How did the rookie not know that was short for *none of your business*? "I realize your name is noo-B"—*none of our business*—"but we are, in fact, in business together as of right now. It would be nice to know who we're dealing with." It was a bit strange to think of this girl being a valuable asset in the future, but she very well could be. If federal agents ever had business in this area again. It wasn't out of the question.

The girl stopped abruptly, turning on her scuffed heel. "You think I have a bunch of crater rocks where my brain should be." She tapped the side of her helmet. "And that I'm stupid like a baby. But nobody stays little around here for long. You stay young with a head full of crater rocks, and you don't survive. Our business part-nor-ship is on a need-to-know basis until I say so. Clear?" She began to walk again.

Mina was impressed. "Clear."

"Quaz doesn't like you, you're out anyway," she mumbled.

Out had a few different meanings.

Likely, this girl figured Quaz would have the power to toss them out of his house if they hadn't been invited. Then, once they were out, it would be broadcast that Mina and Lee were freshly printed treats available for sampling. Worked for her.

"We aren't getting tossed out," Mina assured her. "No need to worry all those pebbles bouncing around inside your brain."

She grunted. "Why did you set down so far away if you're going to Biters?" She crossed a pedestrian roadway with zero pedestrians on it. Mina had no idea if people stayed inside all the time to be safe, or if they had a network to let them know when strangers were in the area. Probably the latter. "He's got the only landing pad in about five kilos in front of his place. Would've been less con-spit-uous that way. Occasionally, he gets customers from outside of Pormal."

If Biters was the lollipop shop where Norm was meeting them, he hadn't wanted them to set down there. Mina trusted the ex-marshal. "Have you ever heard the term 'flying under the radar'?"

The girl openly scoffed. "That's old-timesy. Nobody flies here either. You mean crawling under the foil zone. Not many places to hide around here, but we got our share of tossed foil. Mostly from old craft. You crawl under there, and you can't be seen from the sky. Nobody knows you're there." She tossed a simpering look over her shoulder, aiming it squarely at Mina. "If you were trying to sneak around, you're bad at it. At least fifty people saw you set down in that alley. Word's already out far and wide you're here. Lucky we ain't too far from Biters."

The girl crossed another pedestrian walkway. The automated people conveyors had shut down long ago and were busted out. The girl stopped to jump up and down on one of the belts a couple of times.

Even though she didn't believe it, she was still a kid.

Something in Mina's heart broke for her. But she also

knew that this girl, because of her situation, had learned how to handle herself. She had people in her corner looking out for her. She appeared well fed, had clothing, had supreme confidence—enough to tail them in the open, even though it could've been a very bad idea. Maybe this Quaz was one of the adults in the area making sure she survived and thrived.

Not everybody in the 'skirts—or, in this case, just outside of the 'skirts—stayed there forever. Some people made their way out. They found jobs, they earned back borrows. It happened.

The girl rounded a corner. As they followed, Mina pulled up short.

In the distance, a lone cinder block building stood out from the others around it. A landing pad encircled the entire single-story place. A junk craft was parked off in one corner. Otherwise, no other drones occupied it. A plume of smoke came billowing out of what looked to be an old-fashioned chimney set squarely in the middle. Possibly how they kept the place warm, or they needed it to vent something. There were no windows, solar catch or otherwise.

"What are you waiting for?" The girl stopped, glancing back at Mina. "We're almost there."

Lee leaned in, whispering, "What is it?"

"I've been here before."

Earlier in her career, Mina had been assigned an op in the outskirts. She'd gone after an illegal-goods trafficker by the name of Barker, a highly dangerous individual whom she'd successfully bribed with a literal hoverbus full of physical currency. He hadn't gone down willingly. It'd taken several SWAT teams to subdue him. He was currently in a box doing serious time.

The government chased criminals into the outskirts only when they affected life on the outside, which Barker had. He'd been ripping off large companies and funneling goods.

As usual, being a CIU agent meant you were responsible for a small piece of a much larger, much more complicated puzzle. Mina had been the sparkly gemstone that had gotten Barker's attention. Once the deal had been made, the Department of Goods and Services, aka DGS, had taken over. Barker had been apprehended after an intense standoff not far from this location. After his capture, information had trickled in that Barker's enterprise had been much bigger than the intel had initially reported, and Mina taking him down had caused a lot of problems, in-fighting, and break-downs within the community.

Mina had met Barker inside this building once to do business, going in through a lone entryway from the 'skirts that had been coded to her for that specific meeting. The place hadn't been called Biters then, and she'd never known its physical address. She had walked, because, as the girl had said, no one flew a craft around here. If she remembered correctly, the place had been owned by Barker's brother back then.

Lee was concerned. "Is it going to be a problem?"

Mina shook her head as she started forward, cursing herself for not making the connection when she'd seen the location on satellite. All the buildings here looked the same from above, but she should've spent more time examining it. "I don't think so, but from here on out, we stay on high alert."

"Um, I kind of already am."

Mina flashed him a look, eyes in their standard upward roll toward the galaxy and beyond. "An eleven-year-old almost got the jump on you. If I hadn't been here to knock her down, who knows what would've happened? When I say 'high alert,' I mean I need you *on*, Lee. Take in everything. Listen, watch, read the situation. Anticipate what you think will happen, and then be ready for it."

"Okay." He nodded rapidly. "I got it."

Mina dragged him by the sleeve. "Come on. Let's do this."

Chapter 4

IT DIDN'T TAKE them long to traverse the expanse. There wasn't much else around. Residential housing had ended a block prior, and the buildings that remained were empty for the most part, as far as Mina could tell. The official border of the outskirts was just a few meters to the north. Barker had considered this a safe zone to conduct his business dealings. He'd never called the area *Pormal*, but Mina could see that this space was neither the outskirts nor an inhabited area.

It was neutral.

Apparently, it'd stayed that way after all these years.

Ahead of them, the girl ducked inside the building through a small door in the back, likely to tell Quaz he had visitors and to rub her little mitts together, hoping for trouble. Mina contemplated contacting McAllister, but at this point moving forward was a must. She had to help Harri. She owed it to him.

Mina turned to Lee. "I look different than I did five

years ago, and thankfully I put on a hair alt and smeared black around my eyes this morning, but there's a chance the guy inside is the brother of someone I know. If he recognizes me, things could turn. If you sense anything is heating up, place your hand on your shoulder like this." Mina set her right arm across her chest and gripped her left shoulder.

"The brother of someone you know?"

"Old case. One of my first ops," she answered as they walked. "Guy named Barker. He was an illegal-goods trafficker, very powerful in the 'skirts. When we took him down, things got messy." *Messier.* Since they were always messy here. "The woman responsible for putting away the man who peddled goods in these parts to people who needed them will not be welcome." Quite the contrary, in fact. "His brother used to run what's now Biters, though I don't remember his name being Quaz. It was something like Garwin, and this place used to be called Reds. They served a lot of red food. Don't ask me why. I'm going to have to convey all this to Norm without saying it outright. If he thinks this is a safe harbor, and he thinks PPF and feds are welcome here, there's a reason. I need to know what that reason is, or we bounce out."

The girl hadn't reemerged, so Mina and Lee made their way around the building. The main door, manual with a large handle, sat squarely in the middle of a bland cindercrete wall. No windows, no welcome sign, no advertisements. It looked barren and uninviting. Mina didn't have to check the address on her new, spiffy cuff, which was hidden under her jacket sleeve, to know this was the right place. This was likely the only public meeting place near enough to where Norm had scuttled Harri.

Mina didn't bother to knock. She took hold of the lever, yanked the door open, and walked in, allowing her hand to slide down so it rested near her gem, her fingers tapping her thigh.

The ultras were low, if they were even on at all. Hard to tell. It took a second for her eyes to adjust, which was the point. Before everything came into reedy-light focus, she heard Norm clear his throat. She turned toward the sound, zeroing in on a small compartment that held a single table and two benches, surrounded by a short polycarb wall to keep privacy between other patrons—if other patrons had been here, which they weren't. The entire building had been printed an *a-on* ago.

The compartment Norm and Harri occupied was one of about a dozen in the building. Back before this place became desolate and too close to the encroaching 'skirts, it would've been advertised as a "printed, themed diner."

When meal printers first came into fashion, they revolutionized restaurants, making anything attainable in their overfarmed, low-pollinated world. Old themes came tumbling back into style. Mina was pretty sure most diners had specialized in hamburgers and french fries a hundred years ago. When the place had been Reds, everything had been fairly tasteless and tinted red. That was the theme. Red stuff. Mina wasn't expecting much more now. Hard to get slurry, elemental or otherwise, when you weren't piped into the main line.

Mina slid into one side of the bench. Lee followed.

"What took you so long?" Harri huffed, spreading his arms wide. His dark, curly hair was disheveled, but clean. His eyes darted back and forth. "I feel like we've been in this place for hours."

"It's been five minutes, boy. Calm yourself down." To Mina, Norm said, "He's rattled. I don't blame him. We had to blast out fast last night."

Before Mina could get down to business and figure out what Norm knew about this broken-down, printed, themed diner, a throat cleared beside them. The man was dark, from the top of his hairless head to the tips of the strike boots that Mina had no doubt he wore. He was formidable and held a full-size crystalline board in his hand. It looked like a mini because he was so large.

"You come into my place, you eat. There's a minimum per person, hard coin only. I can print whatever."

Mina kept her eyes pinned on Norm, who looked the opposite of Harri, his ice-blue diffracted eyes clear and his short, steel-colored hair in line. "I'll take a breakfast roll and coffee."

"What do you want in the roll?" It was almost a challenge. Almost.

"Surprise me."

Lee shifted in place on the bench next to her. "Um."

Please don't ask what's on the menu.

"What do you have—"

A scissor heel landed squarely on top of Lee's ecoslide under the table. She gave the rookie credit for not crying out.

"I'll have a breakfast roll, too," he said quickly. "And a bubbly. I don't care what flavor."

The man grunted. Mina didn't meet his gaze, which she knew lingered on the table. She was certain the girl had given him, and whoever else was back there, an earful. The young girl hadn't materialized yet, but Mina expected her to show soon. She wouldn't be able to help herself.

After the man left, Mina leaned forward, her voice low. "Why'd you pick this shop? It's a drumbeat for me."

Norm's eyebrows rose as his head craned around. "Here?" His disbelief was apparent.

Mina said nothing, only nodded.

"Packard's ex-mili." Norm used his thumb to indicate the guy who'd just taken their orders. "This area is considered a safe zone—"

"What about a guy named Quaz?"

Norm shook his head. He didn't know anyone by that name. The way the girl had made it sound, Quaz was in charge, not this Packard guy.

"What's going on?" Harri asked, his voice quaking. "I don't understand what you're saying. Are we safe?" He turned a shaky glance to Norm. "You said we'd be safe here. You *promised.*"

"Keep your voice down," Norm instructed. "Nowhere is going to be perfectly safe until we shut the Corp down for good." Norm raised a finger toward Mina, then thrust it toward the kitchen. "I trust Pack. We go back. This place is *known.* I've used it a few times. Once you're in, things are sealed up tight. No physicality allowed of any kind."

"How long has Pack been in res?" Mina asked, searching to see if she could spot any mics or amps. They were likely there, but whoever had installed them had been skilled. Nothing caught her eye.

"A couple," Norm responded. "He lost his borrow ability and was brought on as muscle no more than two ago."

Mina's op had been five ago, so he wouldn't have been here when she met with Barker.

"We eat," Mina said, "then we beat." This place wasn't shored up as tight as Norm thought.

Harri began to complain again, and Norm settled a hand on his wrist. "Trust goes a long way, kid. We take this to the next spot. No worries. You'll stay safe, and things will get handled. You can hold on for a little longer."

It was hard to ignore Harri's distress. Mina had inadvertently gotten him fired by Bliss Corp, a multitrillion-dollar corporation, and worse, they'd come after him. His life had been hurled straight into the stratosphere without his permission. Mina just had to keep it from being sucked into a black hole for good.

She was about to placate him and tell him that they'd go back to the pay-a-day, which should have fewer ears than here, and figure out the next move, when Pack came back to the table, two plates in his hands.

He set them down abruptly in front of Norm and Harri. They had both ordered a standard breakfast of eggs, bacon, and potatoes. Everything was a similar drab color, and the bacon didn't come close to being Lee-style crisp.

On a scale of one to edible, it was a two or three.

Mina didn't miss the perusal Pack gave her, his keen eye missing absolutely nothing. She wasn't getting out of here without words being exchanged. She just hoped the only thing exchanged *was* words.

Lee leaned toward Mina. "Where's the girl?"

The rookie also had the vibe that they weren't getting out of here without some sort of payback. He was catching on.

"What girl?" Norm asked, his voice just above a whisper.

"We collided with a runner on our way in," Mina told him. "Treaded loudly, no fear, her turf. Once we told her where we were going, she seemed relieved, agreed to lead. Disappeared through the back. Told her she'd get paid, so we'll see her yet."

Norm eased back in his seat, his beefy arm reclining on top of the wall ledge, his eyes critically perusing the place. There wasn't much to see, but the opening from the booth gave full view to a long counter that would've once held diners and double doors with high windows that pushed back into the kitchen.

The only thing back there was likely a single printer, a grinder, and a dish sprayer, if they reused items. Back when the diner was first printed, there would've been lots of windows. No windows now. They'd been pried out a long time ago and replaced with cinder block. Anything with value was stripped quickly around here.

Harri picked up his fork and halfheartedly poked at his food, not brave enough to actually put a bite in his mouth.

Mina didn't blame him. She wasn't planning on eating either.

They all waited for the inevitable.

Mina brushed back her jacket sleeve to reveal her cuff. Her fingertip hit the edge, and a holo keyboard popped out. She wasn't expecting serious trouble, but she had to let McAllister know an issue might be brewing and that she was in drumbeat territory of the Barker op. Drumbeat, in agentspeak, was an echo of an old op. For undercover agents, visiting old places could be compromising. If these guys had cams positioned around the restaurant, they might be able to see what she was typing, so she used code. They could crack it if they had talent back there, especially if Packard was ex-military, but it would take time.

By then, Mina and company would be gone.

McAllister's response was swift. A word popped up on the display, floating above her wrist.

ONE.

"What does that mean?" Harri asked anxiously. Mina made sure everybody could see, including those who might be—were almost surely—snooping.

"I hit one finger anywhere on my cuff, or say the word, and backup arrives in under two." Mina announced it loudly. That meant McAllister would be sending teams out now so they'd be in close proximity. It was a little sticky, because Mina and Lee weren't on an official op, but it was necessary for their protection.

Mina figured McAllister would summon Kaylee. She was the right agent for the job, as she knew the Barker op well, via Mina's debriefing, and would be an asset.

The kitchen doors banged open.

They all glanced that way. Nothing was visible above the counter line until a small figure with long, dark hair appeared around the corner, carrying two plates. The girl's smirk could light up a room.

She delivered the two crappy meals, dumping the plates in front of Mina and Lee. No drinks. The breakfast rolls rocked back and forth. The "pastries" held a greenish tint. Better than red? Possibly. But they still wouldn't be ingested.

"Quaz wants you in the back," she announced, jamming her thumb over her shoulder. She didn't have to specify that she meant only Mina, because she was boring holes straight into her soul, ignoring the rest of the table. "And if you don't come, there's going to be trouble." Her eyes sparkled. She was hoping for that outcome. Not a surprise.

Norm made the motion to rise from the table. Mina shook her head. He sat back down.

"You assume Quaz gets what he wants," Mina responded. "But he doesn't. Send Packard back out here. I require a little chat first."

"I don't haveta do what you say." She sliced her hand down in a defiant motion. "I told you where you need to be. So get up off your lazy—"

"Suli, get back in here!" a voice shouted from the unopened kitchen door.

Listening, indeed.

The girl, whom they now knew as Suli, looked as though she might not follow that direct order. Mina watched as her expression switched to resigned as she tossed over her shoulder, "*Fine.*" She stomped back around the counter. "But you said to get her back there no matter what. So I was just doing what you said—"

"Enough!"

The girl disappeared through the kitchen doors.

"We've got two secs to make an ouster," Norm said, rising off his bench in anticipation. "Your call."

Mina shook her head. He sat once again. Sending out a child to do their bidding was a clear signal to Mina. This wasn't likely to get violent. Mina was also curious. They risked a lot by ordering her back. There was no way they were in the dark that she was a federal agent by this point.

"What's going on?" Harri asked, his voice wavering all over the place, accentuating his frazzled state. He was at the end of what he could handle. "Why do they want you back there? You can't go back there! What if you don't come back?"

Lee decided to field this one. "Don't worry, Harri," he reassured the civilian in a nice, measured tone. "I have full confidence in Agent Kane, and you can too. She's going to handle everything, and we'll be out of here in no time."

That was true. Mina was going to handle everything.

She pierced Norm with a look. "What's the quotient?"

"Ten plus," Norm responded without hesitation.

"I'm going to trust in your very high number." Norm had just vouched that Packard had his trust more than tenfold, which was as high as it went.

"His answers will be true. They will let us leave without a draw." A draw meant each party drawing weapons.

"This has to do with my drumbeat. I'm almost positive," Mina said. "They've seen and heard everything that's gone down since we arrived. They're not willing to take the government on, but they want something from me."

To punctuate her statement, Packard literally punched through the kitchen doors, using his fists as pile drivers. The doors swept back and forth like birds flapping their wings.

He reached their table, his face set. He glanced at Norm, then at Mina, then back at Norm. "An exchange of information. Nothing more."

Norm shrugged, giving the air of casual indifference, when Mina knew he was a twitch away from sweeping them out of there. "It's up to her, not me."

"It's up to the head," Packard proclaimed, crossing his arms.

"It's actually not," Mina interjected. "But tell him I'll be back there in two." Packard frowned, turning away from the table. Before he got far, she added, "Anything goes awry, and we shut it down. *All* the way down."

He smirked, mirroring Suli frown for frown. He didn't believe Mina had the power to shut this place *all the way down*—meaning the government would raze it to the ground. She couldn't let him or anyone else back there think they had the upper hand. That would be unfair, because they didn't.

"I can and will call a paradox."

Packard stopped.

Mina hadn't been sure this man would pick up on the reference, but she'd taken a chance since he was ex-military. Seemed he had. After a moment, he continued into the kitchen without looking back.

Norm whistled low, leaning over the table. "I knew you had reach, but I didn't know how high until right this minute." Norm had no idea which department Mina worked for in the federal government. He'd never asked because he knew she wouldn't confirm. Most people thought she worked Street Crime, since that was her cover. An agent working Street had no authority to declare a paradox. But an agent in the CIU facing a life-threatening situation did.

"I don't get it," Harri said. "What's a paradox?"

Mina rose from the table as Norm answered, "One word from her, and they come in here and wreak holy-hell havoc. She just told those who are most interested that if they mess with her, their livelihoods will be obliterated just like that." He snapped his fingers.

Even though Mina had the authority to declare a paradox under extreme circumstances, that didn't mean any orders she gave would be executed. It would all be up to her director's judgment. But if anything happened to her, Mina figured McAllister would likely wreak some holy-hell havoc. He was solid like that. So she hadn't *exactly* been bluffing. More like...improvising? Something agents needed to be good at when things got sticky, and this definitely qualified as sticky.

Lee stood, making his way out of the area so Mina could pass. She thought she'd have to give the worried rookie some workable directions.

Instead, he winked, startling her. "I'm *on* it. If anyone messes with you, they'll have to deal with me."

"That's the spirit, Lee," Mina said, genuinely happy. "Keep it up. I'll see you in five."

Chapter 5

Mina pushed her way into the back, her gem bumping against her hip. She hadn't unhooked the strap that held it in place. The interior looked nothing like a kitchen. One industrial-sized printer, dented in several places, sat on a lonely, equally dented, stainless-steel countertop next to a grinder that looked like it coughed up most of its contents instead of swallowing them. Well, that explained the crappy food.

That's as far as the restaurant piece went.

The rest of the space had been parsed into individual workstations with cheaply printed desks and some low-end tech scattered around. Three men, including Packard, stood in an area with a single lounger and two chairs. As Mina moved into the room, they stepped away, revealing a seated man who waited for her, his long legs crossed.

To her relief, he didn't resemble Barker's brother, Garwin.

She figured this had to be Quaz.

Mina hadn't spotted the girl before because the men had been in the way, but Suli stood just behind him. The resemblance was uncanny. Father and daughter was Mina's guess. But they could be siblings. Quaz appeared fairly young, early thirties at most, but the youthfulness could be attributed to enhancements.

Nobody said anything as Mina moved forward.

The man in the chair had the same long, dark hair as his daughter—or sister?—and wore a neutral expression. He gestured for her to sit across from him on the lounger. Mina debated staying where she was, but her instincts told her this guy was worried about something and wanted an audience, that he didn't intend to rough her up or scare her because he thought he could. He couldn't.

Instead, his visage was tight and anxious. His hands were twitchy, and one badly worn ecoslide was busy tapping the dirty floor.

"What're you waiting for?" Suli erupted from behind the man's left shoulder. "He told you to sit. When you're told to sit, you *sit.*"

"I'm going to sit," Mina assured the girl, taking the last few steps to the lounger. "But not because you, or he, told me to. I'm sitting because I choose to." Mina was further impressed by the girl's rock-hard resolve. She didn't even come close to being daunted by Mina, even though Mina had bested her a few times already. "It would be handy if you remembered that."

"You don't get to choose nothing—"

The man's hand rose in the air. "Go clean the waste room."

"What?" Suli's expression exploded into incredulousness, her eyes going wide, her nose bunching up. "I just cleaned it, like, a *day* ago."

"Go."

The girl balled her fists and sulked off, exiting the room through a door on the other side.

"Excuse my daughter," he replied smoothly, inclining his head. "She can be rather...overzealous when it comes to..."

"Defending what's hers?"

"Exactly." He seemed pleased by Mina's response.

"I don't blame her," Mina offered. "Though you might need to give her a few lessons on treading a bit lighter. I had no idea she was a child before I saw her, and if I hadn't gone easy on her, she'd have much more than a bruised backside right now."

"She has no reason to tread lightly here. Everybody knows she's my daughter. She has certain..."

"Privileges?"

"Yes, of course. *Privileges.*"

"Why am I here?" Mina glanced at the ceiling, which was peeling who knew what in more than a few places. "I don't have to point out that you took a large risk summoning me back here. When I came into your shop, I wasn't even a little bit curious about what was going on behind those dented doors." She waved casually behind her at the entrance. "I came in to talk to a friend. We're patrons enjoying your fine establishment, nothing more. Now"—she inclined her head—"you and I are creating a different story, and I'm hoping it will be one with a happy ending."

She paused. "For you, anyway. I know what my ending will look like."

He leaned forward suddenly, his eyes bright, his tone cutting. "I know who you are."

Mina shrugged, waiting.

She didn't have to wait long.

His voice came out as a growl before he could tone it down. "I'm Quaz. I run this place."

"Figured." Mina gave him scraps. He was visibly agitated. It wouldn't take long.

"Barker was my brother."

She showed no reaction, not even a flinch. This place had stayed in the family. Not great news, but workable.

"You put him away. You're the girl who sauntered in here five years ago pretending she was something."

"Wasn't pretending."

His eyes sparked. "You *owe* us."

Mina reclined back, clasping her hands together across her waist, the picture of ease. "How do you figure?"

"I *figure* because when you took Barker away, you took everything we had with him. It's been years, and we still haven't recovered our losses. Things only got worse."

"I'm not responsible for your losses. Putting *dangerous* people in boxes is my job, and I happened to be good at my job." Barker had, in fact, been dangerous. Not only had he been an illegal-goods dealer, but people who'd worked for him had turned up missing quite often, never to be found again. Once he'd been taken into custody, he'd been given Babble, a powerful truth serum reserved for only the worst offenders. He'd admitted to more than forty-seven murders.

That was not a small number.

Mina hadn't known Barker's penchant for ending people's lives at the time, as their intel had been laser-focused on his big-time goods operation, and even that had been thin, but she would've gone in anyway. She just would've been better educated about the threat she'd been facing.

One look at Quaz, and Mina knew he knew exactly what she was talking about.

The man in front of her began to physically organize himself, making an effort to tamp down the anger swirling behind his eyes. Watching him go through the motions told Mina a lot about his character and who he was. Life had dealt him a suck-hole of a hand, and he was actively trying to do something about it.

He cleared his throat finally. "I'm in need of your... services."

This guy was a pro at pregnant pauses.

Mina allowed herself a small snort. "My services...are not for sale."

He was undaunted by her refusal. "My brother had a competitor. He's still in business. He's more ruthless, but he's not nearly as intelligent as Barker. Up until now, we've been able to beat him back from our rickety border. But things are coming to a head. There's rumors of a big event going down very soon. Like, tonight. It's something that's supposed to boost his gain. Something that will give him the edge and all the power he needs to blow through here. Without the fear of either of my brothers to keep him in check"—so Garwin was also gone, apparently—"this entire area will be firmly situated in the 'skirts in a matter of days. No going back."

Mina recognized the plea for what it was.

His anger had been replaced by compassion and anguish. This man was genuinely worried about the people of Pormal, this broken poor man's land. That commanded respect. No wonder Barker's competitor hadn't been scared off by him. Quaz could pretend rage, as Mina had seen, but underneath he was a decent guy trying to do some good.

"What is it you think I can do?" A reasonable place to start.

He shrugged. "I dunno. Bring the federal government in here and throw his ass in a box like you did my brother?"

She didn't point out the obvious, like needing proof. Or the political, like the actions of this guy—whoever he was—had to have affected something major within city limits to catch anyone's attention or interest. Not exactly the world Mina wanted to live in, but it was the one she occupied.

"What's his name?"

"Dominic Nesbit."

"I'll look into it." She stood. It was all she could do.

"That's it?" He sprang out of his seat. "You'll *look* into it? Lives are at stake. You come into my place today without a care in the world. Five years ago, you took away my flesh and blood." He shook his finger at her, his anger ramping up. "My brother may have been a criminal, but he was the *only* protection we had. He brought in resources, which we can't get anymore, and your answer is you're gonna *look* into it?"

A face appeared around the doorjamb. "See? I told you! She's just a good-for-nothing!" A small fist shot through the opening, shaking wildly. "She has that look about her." One eyeball flared at Mina. "All shiny on the outside, but rotten to a stenchy sulfur core on the inside."

Ouch.

Quaz placed his hands on his hips as he tilted his head up to the grubby, falling-apart ceiling. "I told you to clean the waste room." His voice was patient, even though Mina knew he was still angry.

Suli took a step into the room. "It's already clean. I told you. I did it, like, a day ago."

He shook his head, giving up and turning his attention back to Mina. "If you want to know the truth, nobody here wanted me to ask you for help." Quaz appeared weary down to his bones. "It goes against everything we stand for in this place. The government doesn't give a damn about us, so we don't give a damn about them either. We openly oppose everything they stand for. They're not for the people. They're for profit. They're for greed. They're for corporations. But this is different." He gestured toward his daughter. "Her life has value. So what if we can't get bank borrows? We're still human beings. We have rights. If Nesbit acquires this last bit of power and blows over the border like he keeps threatening to do, everything we know here is finished.

Everything. He'll take out anyone he perceives as a threat, and no one will bother to investigate." That meant Quaz and his allies. "He will force others to do his bidding or worse." Mina didn't want to think about the worse. "He'll make everybody's life miserable, and we've been fighting to keep it just above miserable for a very long time."

A continuing story around the nation. Thousands who used to live on the borders now lived in the outskirts. It was amazing Quaz and his crew had been able to hold out this long. Barker had been rotten to his sulfur core, but it seemed his brother Quaz was not.

"Even if you don't care or support our government, you understand how it works," Mina said. "My services cannot be bought. I am assigned an operational case based on proof and evidence, decided as such by the federal government. Without that, I cannot do anything but investigate what might already be on file for this Nesbit guy."

"Packard here said you have the authority to declare a paradox. I'm not familiar with that term, but he is. People who can do that have resources," he challenged. "They have power. Tell me that's *not* who you are. If you do, you can walk out of here, but once you cross that boundary, don't ever come back."

"I do have the authority to declare a paradox, but only if my life is in immediate danger. It doesn't work—"

"If my daughter's life is in immediate danger," he cut in, waving a hand at Suli, who was still glaring at Mina.

He was correct.

This man didn't know her. Didn't know how hard Mina worked to dismantle high crime at the top levels of their broken government every single day. He didn't know that she had a soul and she cared. No matter what Mina felt about this on a personal level, she could not, and would not, go rogue and handle it on her own. She wasn't Vincent Kramer. That's not how she operated.

She would take it through the appropriate channels, whether Quaz understood that or not.

"I acknowledge your request for help," she said. "And I take it seriously. As you said, you are people who deserve help. I've told you that the best I can do is look into Nesbit's file. If he's as notorious as you say, he has a file." It was probably several centimeters thick. "Whether or not it's in my jurisdiction makes no difference. My director can, and will, take what we find and funnel it through the appropriate department so they can take up an inquiry and try to have it declared an official case. But I'm telling you now, being as upfront as I can be, it will move at a nuclear-decay pace."

The degradation of a nuclear atom would probably move faster, considering.

This would be considered an outskirts issue, even though Biters and Pormal technically sat inside city limits, but just barely. Since the people here didn't have official bank borrow accounts and didn't pay taxes, they didn't qualify for city resources. The government pretty much ignored their existence. There was very little chance anyone would be deployed here to take up an investigation anytime soon.

"Nuclear-decay pace won't help us." Quaz expressed his frustration by running both of his hands through his long hair.

"I'll contact my director once I get myself and my party to a secure location," Mina said. "I'm offering you help within my constraints. But this comes *after* the business I came here to deal with."

"How about a trade?"

Mina's eyebrows rose as she crossed her arms. "What kind of a trade?"

"I keep the kid out there hidden and safe so you can be freed up to deal with Nesbit."

"You run the pay-a-day." It wasn't a question. "He can't stay there. It's not secure enough. The entity that's after him is infinitely more dangerous than Nesbit, with currency backing to Mars and beyond."

"I have another place. Very secure. No one gets in or out without my consent. Hard to find. It's set up with decent comforts."

Mina gave him a scrutinizing look. He gave her one right back. He wasn't going to relent.

"I'll check it out," Mina told him. "But I'm not guaranteeing you anything, and this isn't a trade. We pay fair currency for a safe house. You have my oath I'll look into Nesbit's file at my first chance, regardless if we use the safe house or not. That's the only for sure you're going to get. Take it or leave it."

Quaz was pensive for a moment. "You know how I knew I could trust you? Bring you back here and ask you for something we've never asked anyone for, ever?"

"How?"

"When you were dealing with my brother, you stopped to help a kid. A young boy, no more than seven or eight. Not too far from here, but over the border in the 'skirts. Do you remember what went down?"

"I do."

"You summoned a medi-unit. When they got here and saw where they were and what they were getting into, they tried to power-thrust out. You stopped them. You forced them to help that kid."

The child in question had been entertaining a small crowd, doing tricks. He'd been very talented and had obviously been trained to do physical tricks at a very young age, which lots of children did in the 'skirts. You had to be quick and nimble to survive. That night, he hadn't been so lucky. He'd jumped on something that couldn't take his weight. He'd taken a hard fall, broken his arm, slashed his thigh to the bone, and had been knocked unconscious.

Quaz continued, "You tried to do it on the sly, ordered everybody away, waved a weapon around, acted like you were from around here. You didn't think people noticed. But we did. If any of us had told Barker that the girl he was courting had the power to bring a *medi-unit* almost inside the 'skirts and make them *help* someone, it would've outed you." He pierced her with a gaze that went bone-deep. Mina shivered. "We chose *you* and that child over him. Remember that."

CHAPTER 6

MINA PUSHED BACK through the kitchen doors to find both Lee and Norm standing sentinel at the counter, weapons palmed. Surprisingly—or maybe unsurprisingly—Kaylee and another agent by the name of Tyson stood by the door, weapons drawn, both with legs splayed and *don't mess with me* looks on their faces.

Kaylee's eyebrows rose as Mina came around the counter.

"We're leaving," Mina announced.

Lee followed, while Norm went to retrieve Harri from wherever he'd tucked him away in the restaurant.

Kaylee and Agent Tyson exited first, since they were closest to the door.

Mina said nothing as she made her way outside and around the back. The group followed. There were no crafts in sight, so Kaylee and Tyson had been dropped nearby.

Not a moment after Mina and company had turned the corner, Suli stepped out.

To say the girl looked unenthused that she'd been tasked with yet another boring job would underestimate her level of disdain. "If you don't keep up this time," she announced, "I'm not 'sponsible for what will happen to you. I don't care what my dad says."

"We can keep up just fine," Kaylee challenged, arching a brow.

Suli sauntered up to Kaylee, elevating her nose and taking a few exaggerated sniffs. "You got sulfur for blood, too. Just as rotten as the rest of them."

Mina watched Kaylee's face, knowing her fellow agent was respecting the hell out of this kid, but she didn't give away too much. "My blood is not sulfuric," Kaylee replied. "But I guess it wouldn't be so bad if it was. I'd just nick my arm and scare everybody away. Including you."

"Nah. That wouldn't scare me." The girl turned and began to hustle across the landing area. She called over her shoulder, "Only thing that scares me is nutin'."

Kaylee fell into step next to Mina. "So, what? We're just supposed to follow this little monster?"

"Yep." Mina brought her cuff up. "Agent Kane here. What are my orders?" She'd kept her line open. Her director had heard her entire interaction with Quaz.

"Dominic Nesbit has a modest file. He stopped working in our world many years ago." That meant declaring him a priority would be almost impossible. "Check out this safe house and report back. I will continue to investigate on my side."

Mina tapped her cuff, then addressed Kaylee as well as Lee, who was now on her other side. "This area is called Pormal," she said. "Quaz, the guy in charge, is the younger brother of Barker." Kaylee gave a snort, indicating she remembered exactly who Barker was. "He assures me that tongues won't wag that we're here. Offered up a safe place to keep Harri until we figure out our next move. We'll see when we get there. In exchange, he wants me to help him with a shady criminal outskirt named Nesbit, who's looking to bring this area fully into the 'skirts and under his control. Timeline is soon."

Kaylee whistled. "So you came here to get the deets on the runner those two had to take last night"—she nodded toward Norm and Harri over her shoulder—"because a multitrillion-dollar corporation made a very bad decision. But then the guy in that ramshackle printed husk of a dump recognized you as the gal who took out his brother? Then he appealed to you for help?"

"Now you're all caught up," Mina answered.

"Hardly. But I will be soon enough. I'm sticking with you. Orders are orders. Agent Tyson is on his way back to the beat."

Mina glanced around. Sure enough, Agent Tyson had disappeared. "I appreciate the help, as always. But it's not necessary if you have something more pressing to attend to."

"What's more pressing than calling for a paradox?"

She scoffed. "I wasn't *actually* going to call a paradox. I used the resources I had in a sticky situation, as we do. I had no idea who Quaz was or what he wanted. Figured low side would be interrogation, high would be a physical shakedown. Just wanted to give them a heads-up on what would happen if they went high side."

"Makes sense. I would've done the same." Kaylee shrugged. "Likely. Probably not. Paradox is like bringing a barrel laser to a gunfight. No, scratch that. Paradox is like bringing a barrel laser to a NannyBot sing-along."

Mina chuckled. "Next time you have an op in the outskirts, let me know. Paradox will be your best friend."

In front of them, Suli zipped between two buildings into an alleyway that was skinnier than a craft could fit. The area didn't look residential. It was hard to know what these buildings were used for, since there was no commerce here. No shops, no borrows, no real employment. Everything was dark. Mina figured people were around, but they were careful not to be seen. It was likely that prowlers from the 'skirts cased this area on a regular basis. Couldn't look like you had resources or be vulnerable when strangers were in the area.

The girl stopped in front of a nondescript door. She adjusted something on the outside, and a clinking sound followed. Then she pushed it open.

She appeared super bored, her disdain keeping her fueled. "Well? What are you waiting for? Get inside. You're already huge, ugly eyesores."

"Eyesores that no one's going to say anything about, right?" Mina said as she ducked inside the dark space.

"Nobody does anything here without consulting my dad." Pride streamed out around the disdain. "If they do, they find themselves hungry lickety-split."

Mina grimaced. She hoped that dented meal printer wasn't the only source of food for this entire area. That was a fairly bleak thought. "Ultras on," she ordered.

Behind her, Suli snickered. "Everything's manual here. We're not fancy sulfur farts like you."

Kaylee passed through the opening, murmuring, "The kid's got an issue with sulfur. I wonder how that poor gas wronged her."

After everybody crowded into the dark entryway, Suli shut the door behind them with a loud *snap*. She brushed past Mina, flipping levers on a wall.

Pitiful light streamed into a dank hallway. Mina was relieved to see this wasn't the space Harri would be occupying. Harri looked equally relieved. The rapid increase in his breathing started to calm.

Suli marched ahead. Three meters in, there was another door. She held her hand up to a palm plate. The door slicked open. So not everything was manual. Mina chose not to comment.

They all passed through. A few meters more, and a stairway appeared. Suli wound her way down, not stopping for three levels.

Behind them, Norm grunted, "We're heading into a bunker."

"Of course we are," the girl announced. "What'd you expect? Our safe houses are *safe*. They keep everything out. And because there's not a lot of tech, and no signals get in or out, no one can find you." She cackled like a little witch.

"Are you sure about this?" Harri whispered from behind Mina.

"Yes." No signals in or out was preferable.

No door was in sight at the bottom of the stairs, just another landing with one tiny, weak bulb providing all the glow. Or lack thereof. A musty smell permeated the area. It had an underlay of sulfur, quite possibly explaining why the kid had such an aversion to it.

Suli marched toward what appeared to be a dead end consisting of blocks of syncrete hastily painted over in a dead, dirt-smeared gray. She stuck her entire finger into what looked like a random hole in the wall. There was a loud scraping noise as one of the thickest doorways Mina had ever seen creaked open slower than an airchair.

They waited.

Once it was cracked enough, Suli snuck through. The rest of them waited for it to open farther. It didn't. When they didn't follow her, she stuck her head back out. "What are you plasma-rots waiting for?"

"Kid, that opening is ten centimeters wide," Kaylee said. "Us ladies might make it through, but these boys won't."

Norm chuckled. Seemed he enjoyed being referred to as a boy.

The girl rolled her eyes. It was a fairly impressive roll, with lots of height and white showing. "It swings. Just muscle it."

Kaylee moved forward, grunting as she set her shoulder against it. "This swings as easily as a graphene beam set in purelock." She gestured at Lee. "Don't stand there gawking, come and help. It hasn't moved a centimeter." It took both Lee and Kaylee a few pushes to get it to crack open three more centimeters. Kaylee blew out a breath. "I think that'll do it. Now let's follow this little monster down into the depths of despair and hope we get to reemerge with our lives intact once this is over."

They all slipped through, Norm cursing a little as he executed more of a scrape than a slip. They found themselves in yet another hallway, this one narrower, with only the light from the crack in the door illuminating the area. They could all turn on their cuffs and beam light inside this space, but Suli's footsteps came to a shuffling stop. Mina was about to ask what was up when the kid bent over and pulled an inset handle out of the floor, pulling up a trapdoor.

Inside sat a solid sheet of steel.

The young girl then pressed her entire face against the steel. Possibly a crude form of retinal scanning? It took a moment, then gears began to grind. Slowly, the steel rolled out of the way to expose yet another staircase.

"We have to be below water level," Kaylee groused. "What is even happening here? This is more secure than our underground at headquarters. How can that be?"

Even in the low light, Mina could see Suli's petulant expression. "Of course it is. What you have sucks compared to this. My dad wasn't making up a bedtime story. When we say we keep people safe, we *do*."

To be realistic, this urchin had no idea what they had at headquarters. She likely hadn't been out of Pormal more than a few times in her entire life.

"Did that steel plate just perform a retinal scan?" Lee asked, his voice incredulous.

"It appears so," Mina answered. "Full face rec would be tricky on metal. Irises are the most reliable."

Overhearing them, Suli shrugged indifferently. "I dunno. I just scrunch my face on it, and it zaps open." She headed down the stairway, flipping a lever. Better-quality ultras blinked on.

They followed, ducking through the opening. Mina knew Lee would be examining everything as they went.

Mina didn't have high hopes that this place would be habitable, but she was pleasantly surprised when they rounded a corner, and Suli opened a fairly regular-looking door. More ultras popped on. It wasn't modern by any means, but it was clean and efficient, just like Quaz said it would be.

A platform sat in one corner, and a few sleeping pods were arranged against one wall. Pods were cylindrical tubes that could be shut for privacy. They were fairly high tech, though these were older versions. They contained their own illumination, oxygen, and temp settings. Most of them also had screens and other amenities embedded, but Mina wasn't sure if these did. Getting them through the maze of hallways and small openings must've been difficult.

Along another wall, a lounger and a few chairs were arranged. A small meal-prep area was positioned next to them. There was even a cooling unit. Mina eyed the printer, a self-contained model where you added your own slurry to a reservoir on the back. No elemental piping down here. She wrinkled her nose. If the slurry came from Biters, she already knew what the food would look like.

The others meandered around, inspecting things. Harri sat heavily on the lounger, looking dazed. Kaylee pulled a piece of tech out of her pocket. So one of them had been smart enough to bring detectors. Agent Poston began to sweep the area for bugs.

"What is she doing?" Suli asked, her voice piqued with anger. "She can't do that! This is our place. She could wreck something!"

This was when Mina wondered, not for the first time, why Quaz had sent his preteen daughter instead of coming himself or sending one of his henchmen. She hadn't questioned it before, but it was a big question right now. This young girl didn't have the wherewithal to understand what was happening.

Mina decided to be patient with her. "She's not doing anything that will wreck anything. We're making sure your father isn't listening or recording our conversations."

"I told you. There is no signal in or out down here." She stamped her foot.

Mina crossed her arms and took a wide stance, tilting her torso down to look this urchin in the eye. "There doesn't have to be a signal. Your dad could record something on a self-contained unit and retrieve it later. There are myriad ways to spy. Your dad promised me there wasn't anything down here like that, but I don't know your dad. And I don't know you. Trust is built on respect. It has to be earned. You're going to start earning mine by leaving the way you came and opening that hatch back up in thirty minutes. On the dot. Not thirty-one, not twenty-nine. But thirty. Do we have an understanding?"

Suli's eyes darted back and forth. This girl wasn't sure she should be taking orders from Mina.

"Better yet," Mina added, "I want you to run back to your dad. Tell him I told you thirty, and you listen to what he tells you to do."

"If he tells me to, I'm going to leave you down here."

"No surprise there, little monster," Kaylee said as she took her place next to Mina. "You've got that look about you. All nice and pretty on the outside, slimy and stinky like rotten slurry on the inside." Kaylee whooshed down into a crouch. She went quickly enough to surprise the young girl, who took a step back, her eyes widening. "That's right. I do things fast. Including disciplining little girls who don't listen to orders."

"You would never. If you touched me, my dad would let you have it!"

Kaylee's voice tinkled with laughter, then she straightened, almost in an instant, her face set. "Do you *honestly* think your dad would win in a fight against me?" Suli bit her lip. Kaylee hadn't seen Quaz. Didn't know he was a nice guy. "That's right. He wouldn't. Now skedaddle." She lifted her hand and made a sweeping gesture with her fingers. "And make sure you're back here in thirty, like my partner said. If not, I'm going to find a creative way to make you suffer, which will include a lot of yelling on your part." When the girl didn't move, Kaylee barked. An actual bark. Not like a Dag bark, all cozy and yummy, but like...a rabid canine.

The girl took off, racing up the stairway at top speed.

The gears moved as the steel eased back, and a *thump* followed as the hatch door fell into place. Mina couldn't hear her footsteps, but she imagined Suli was still running.

Mina glanced at her friend, shaking her head. "Jeez. I'm going to have to reevaluate your mentorship for poor, defenseless Harmony. It appears you grind little girls up and eat them for breakfast. She didn't cry, though, so that was a bonus credit."

Kaylee brushed herself off, even though there was nothing on her clothing whatsoever. Then she ran her curled fingers up and down her chest and blew on them. "I wasn't being mean or eating anyone. I was modeling appropriate behavior. That little monster is a complete sponge. She's utterly fearless. I saw a ton of me in her. Someday down the line, she's going to use those moves I just showed her and repeat my words, though here's hoping she uses a lot more inappropriate adjectives. She'll do the bark and everything. And it's my greatest hope that it just might save her scrawny little sulfur-filled behind."

Chapter 7

"YOU CAN'T LEAVE me here," Harri pleaded. "You heard what Norm said. They're coming back! They're not going to just forget about me. They know where we went, or at least the general vicinity. They can find me here!"

"They can't. We just went over it," Mina answered. "All four of us believe this is the safest place for you to stay. I have to consult with my director, once I get in signal range, but I think he'll agree with our assessment. You're completely off anyone's dar down here. There's not a government place more off-grid. Nobody—not even Bliss Corp—can get into this area without being seen by hundreds of loyal residents, who all follow Quaz's orders. Word will get to us immediately if Bliss Corp attempts to track you here. Quaz will know how to get a hold of me. It'll be just for a day or two. My director is in the process of sending Bliss Corp a very strong, very powerful message. Once that message is received, you'll be cleared to leave. If Bliss Corp continues to pursue you, a huge federal investigation will follow, along with very public court proceedings. It would be a media frenzy. I can assure you they will *not* go that route. It's much more important to keep this sensitive, and highly illegal activity, under—*way, way under*—the radar."

"How do you know that for sure?" Harri's arms shot up in the air. "They could find me, take me, murder me. No body, no crime. They have the reach and the currency to do it *and* cover it up. The only way there would be an investigation is if they left my dead body where you could find it. And they wouldn't do that. I'd just be dead."

"In order to get to you, they'd have to get through me first." Norm slapped his palm against his chest. "What am I? Chopped liver?"

Mina shot the old marshal a quizzical look. "What in the world is chopped liver?"

Norm shrugged. "I dunno. It was something my great-grandpappy used to say. Honestly, I have no clue. Sounds about right, though. I mean, if it's chopped, it has to be small and inconsequential, right?" He turned to Harri, who had started to pace. "Nobody's getting into this bunker, young man. And if they do, I'll protect you. It's time for you to straighten up that spine. You've got the best of the best looking out for you. If anybody can bring a multitrillion-dollar corporation to their knees, these three can."

That was being generous. Mina appreciated it.

"Listen—" Mina started.

Lee interjected, moving toward the restless Harri. "If you really don't think you're safe here, I can stay. Like Agent Kane said, it's just for a day or two."

Mina was about to protest, in a nice, pragmatic way, or at least a pragmatic-ish way without any eye-rolling-ish. Agents didn't assign themselves duties. That's why they had a director. Lee could request to be assigned here, but it wasn't up to him, nor was it guaranteed.

Kaylee got there first. "Rookie, don't make promises you can't keep." She sauntered up to Harri, hips rocking, her urban boots clacking audibly across the floor, even though they shouldn't technically be making that much noise on a smooth syncrete surface. But she was making it happen. "You know what? You can do this." She placed an index finger in the middle of Harri's chest. It wasn't a Harmony poke, but it came close. "They aren't getting in here." She jammed a thumb toward the ceiling. "Outside, there's a chance. If Bliss Corp can spy on you like a nanny cam stuffed in a soft play toy, don't you think they have spies in the government on the inside? Somebody has their ear to the ground right now, listening for where you're going to end up. If you stay here, you're safe. I've never seen a place like this before, or known it was an option. If I'd known, I would've brought my own people here. If you don't believe me, be my guest." She stepped aside and swept her arm toward the stairway. "Get in line. You can be the first person up those rickety steps when the little monster comes back." Kaylee checked her cuff. "She'll be here in three minutes and nineteen seconds. You have that long to decide if you're going to be stupider than a spy cam stuffed in a play toy."

Kaylee turned on her heel and sauntered back over to

Mina, exaggerating her swagger. Not that she needed to. Her plain ol' swagger was a beautiful thing.

Norm and Lee went over to reassure Harri, likely to persuade him to make the right choice.

Mina leaned in. "Were you modeling behavior to the grown man who's being hunted by a powerful conglomerate?"

"Hell no," she scoffed. "That was him being had by a girl. Should do the trick." She clapped her hands together like she'd just finished cleaning up a huge mess.

Mina couldn't really argue. It was precision work at its best. Kaylee was a master.

"Suli will be here in less than two now," Mina said. "I'm assuming that after a debrief with McAllister, Lee and I will head into headquarters. I want to look over Nesbit's file before we're assigned our next op."

"You're going to be in a tight place with that, but good luck," Kaylee said. "Nobody gives a flying comet streak what happens to these people. It's more than a shame, it's the great downfall of our greedy, icky, bank-based, soulless existence. If we were in charge, we'd set up military squadrons here to protect these people. That would keep that piece of printed excrement Nesbit from encroaching. Hell, we could arm Suli with a barrel laser, and that would likely do the trick. But we can't. Because no one will authorize it."

As if Suli was above them and had heard her name being uttered, gears began to grind at the top of the stairs. A moment later, light footsteps threaded downward.

They were followed by heavier ones. Mina touched the handle of her gem.

Suli rounded the corner, as they'd kept the interior door open, looking a little flushed and out of breath. It seemed Kaylee had made an impression on her. She wasn't willing to be late, so she'd hustled. Good for her. She was upping her own chances of survival.

Her father came around the corner next.

His demeanor was calm with an undertone of anxiety. He scanned the room before his eyes landed on Mina. "So? Good enough?"

"It works for me, but the final decision is not mine. I'm going to step outside and get clearance. What's the pay rate?"

"I told you. I provide protection, you provide tactical defense."

Mina shook her head. "I told you that's impossible. We pay fair currency value for a safe house, then I do what I can on the other end."

He shrugged. "Whatever, then. I'm sure the government doesn't veer much on the price. I'll give you two days, no more. That is, unless you open up an investigation into Nesbit. Then you can stay as long as you want."

"Give me a time frame on spotting and signaling. If a craft lands or bodies enter the vicinity, what are we looking at?"

"Thirty seconds." His expression didn't change. He was barely tolerating this interaction, but knew it was in his best interests to keep this channel open rather than shutting them down.

"Got it." Mina gave a nod to the rest of the group, then headed up the stairs. She wound her way up the stairs and through the hallways, squeezing back through the syncrete doorway. Once outside, she held her cuff up to her lips, speaking low. "Contact Director McAllister. Mark as urgent."

No one else was around, since this area was not residential. Regardless, she made her way to a far corner of the alleyway with no direct doors or windows within six meters.

"Report, Agent Kane." His voice was clipped. He was distracted.

"Safe house is a level ten in my estimation. Four stories underground, no signal in or out. Alert rate in thirty—seconds, not minutes. If anyone is able to find this place, even the best people hunters currency can buy, it would be a miracle. Getting in without authorization would take a hydro-bomb."

"Approval granted. Pay rate typical, unless special circumstances can be cited."

"Cited circumstances would be civilian man-hours, both on watch, physical placement, and as alarm givers. Without that, we'd have to station one of our own here. Equal hours for agents stationed on pay scale is requested, in addition to bunker-level pay."

"Bunker level?" Mina heard curiosity in his voice. "Bunker level is military pay rate. Twice the level of what our department is granted. I'd have to request special approval."

Mina didn't speak, letting her silence speak for itself.

If she couldn't flood this place with agents to help, she could certainly give Quaz and his people physical currency, something that they were ridiculously short on, if they had any at all. With coin, they would be able to purchase some resources to help them in the fight against the encroaching outskirts.

Finally, after her boss stayed silent, she said, "Sir, with all due respect, this place is fortified four stories underground, as stated. The syncrete walls are over a meter thick. It's impenetrable without blowing the neighborhood sky-high. If that's not a bunker, I don't know what is." She continued, "The civilian in charge will take less, and I will make the standard agreement as you negotiate, but it's my hope that you will get military-rate approval."

"You're asking a lot, Agent Kane. I understand your reasonings, and I will do my best. Don't make promises you can't keep."

"Understood. What are our orders moving forward?"

"You and Agent Adams are to head to headquarters. I will be in meetings for the next two hours. You're free to go over the Nesbit file until then. See if you can link any of his dealings within city limits." He'd uttered the last part with bitterness, as he felt the same way she did about the government's lack of interest in these people. "After that, you and your partner will get a formal designation."

"Got it. The civilian we're trying to keep safe is understandably on edge." That was an understatement, but Mina wasn't going to elaborate. "What shall I tell him is happening with regard to his safety and eventual freedom?"

"After this meeting, I plan to secure authorization to make the public statement I specified this morning. I'm formulating it as my department taking up an investigation linked to a recent employment termination of a sworn witness. It won't mention any names, but those who are listening at Bliss Corp will understand its meaning clearly. We will give them twenty-four hours to make their move. I wouldn't be surprised if they offer Harri his job back within a few hours of the statement's release and pretend it was all a gross misunderstanding."

"I haven't told him it'll be a good idea if he leaves. I'm dreading it. He's going to take it hard."

"I suspect he will," McAllister said. "But there's not much we can do on that end. However, it will be crystalline that if anything happens to him—either purposely or accidentally—here or wherever he relocates, a full investigation will be opened, and everything Harri has confessed into the veribox will be exposed during those proceedings. They won't risk it. Going after such a bit player who knows next to nothing about their internal operation gains them very little. My guess is, in an effort to shut down a very small leak, they will admit they took it too far and offer him his job back. But they're regrouping as we speak. They will come back smarter. They will shut down leaks before we hear about them in the future."

Ugh. A smarter, sleeker Bliss Corp.

"I'd like to stop at home and change and grab a bite,

if there's time. I'm dressed in…outskirts gear. Not exactly great headquarter duds."

"That's fine," McAllister said. "Have Lee do the same. In fact, if I'm not mistaken, the rookie has an appointment to tour a high-rise in about thirty minutes."

Mina's eyebrows rose.

Lee hadn't said about anything about that this morning. The rookie was getting a new residence, and he was pretty excited about it.

"I'll make a quick change and get to headquarters," Mina said. "Once I'm there, I'll start researching. Lee can meet me after his run-through."

"Tell Agent Poston that she can resume her scheduled duties. Have her contact me once she's in her craft. There will be three crafts waiting for you two blocks north of your current location."

"Got it."

"And, Agent Kane? Good work. You kept calm under pressure. You negotiated fairly. I'll do my best to secure the pay rate you're looking for."

After a quick pause, she decided to ask, "I'm curious. Would you have enacted a paradox on my behalf?" She knew her director had heard everything that had gone down.

Her director chuckled. "I've only ever had to do it once, during an uprising in Europe after an entire town was decimated. I hope to never have to do it again."

"I'll take that as a no."

"Don't be too doubtful. The lives of my agents are as important to me as the residents of that small town."

Chapter 0

THE THREE CRAFTS were sitting where McAllister said they'd be. "Thanks for the backup," Mina said to Kaylee as she veered to take the one closest.

"Taking care of your backside is a never-ending job. I'm putting in overtime for this."

"No overtime needed. I was part of your regularly scheduled programming today." Mina cackled. She threw Lee a salute. "Hope the high-rise works out. See you at headquarters."

Lee grinned, eyes fully round. "Yeah. I'm sure it will. I mean, anything is better than what I have now."

"By the way, where are you going?" Mina called to Kaylee as her best pal eased her leg into her craft. "McAllister gave nothing away other than saying you were to continue your 'scheduled duties,' which was an odd thing for him to say."

"He was cagey on purpose. You will actually find this very amusing. I'm meeting with Harmony. McAllister wants to see if it'll work. I got the call right after I talked to you this morning. So, yeah, I might get my very own rookie. We'll see. If I make her cry in the first five minutes, I'm blaming you."

Mina was only able to give her a thumbs-up as both of their craft doors closed.

"Destination The Spire, hub level twenty. Do you wish to make any changes?" the sim inquired as Mina placed her finger in the helix slot.

"No." She leaned her head back against the gel rest.

"Arrival time three minutes, forty-eight seconds."

Plenty of time for Mina to focus on how she was going to get Harri out of this mess. He'd agreed to stay in the bunker. Kaylee's swagger had worked its intended magic, but he was battered and emotionally fragile. No matter what she'd said to try to comfort him, he'd remained certain Bliss Corp would find them.

Norm had intervened and finally pushed them out the door.

There was no question Harri had to leave town. Mina knew from their short past together that he was from someplace in Michigan, but she didn't know much more. Or didn't remember. Or whatever. Harri had been a dalliance. It'd taken her director to point out that Mina dallied. She felt a little ashamed that once Harri had been out of her life, she'd pretty much erased him from her consciousness. But wasn't that what people did with exes?

"Place an audio call to Quinn Kane, information on file," Mina ordered the craft. "If there's no answer, leave this message: Hi, Quinn, it's Mina. I have a few questions for you about Harri. Get back to me as soon as you can."

"Calling Quinn Kane," the sim confirmed. Government drones made it easy. Once Mina's DNA had gone into the helix, the software running this craft had known everything about her.

Everything on file, that was.

Not what she'd had for breakfast, which had been a big, fat nothing. Her stomach gave a loud growl. It would be doing much more than that had she ingested the food at Biters. She owed Quaz for the four meals. She'd add it to his tab.

Quinn's voice came through the integrated aural system a moment later. "Hey, sis. What's up?"

"I have a second between jobs and have a few questions for you about Harri if you have a moment," Mina replied.

"Funny you should call. I was actually just going to contact *you* about him. He disappeared. He's not answering my calls, and I'm worried. He never does stuff like that. We were supposed to meet up, and he just didn't show. If he can't meet, he always lets me know."

Quinn and Harri had been friends for the past six years, pretty much the entire time Harri had lived in the city. They talked daily. Mina should've realized her brother would be worried.

"He's fine," Mina said. This was the tricky part. Even though Quinn was her brother, he was a civilian and on a very limited need-to-know basis. "He ran into a few issues after he was fired, and I'm helping him out."

"Fired!" Quinn gasped, then sputtered, "What do you mean *fired*? How did he get fired?"

"It's a long story." Actually, it was pretty short. "It happened after I went to talk to him about Daphne."

"Is *she* in trouble?" Quinn's voice edged toward concern. "What's going on? What's happening?"

"Calm down, Quinn," Mina instructed. Her brother had inherited a much greater flare for drama than she had. Good thing, too, because in Mina's line of work, an abundance of anxiety would not make this job any easier. "No one's in trouble. No one's in danger." Not technically. At least not as much anymore. "What's happening is classified. I'm sure once Harri gets back to his normal life, he'll fill you in. That will be his choice. That's not why I called. I called to ask you some questions about his upbringing in Michigan."

"Michigan? He's not from Michigan. He's from New Mexico."

"Are you sure? I'm pretty sure he told me he was from Michigan."

"Well, he was born there, but he spent most of his childhood years in New Mexico." So, technically, Mina hadn't been wrong. "Then he moved back to Michigan. But he was only there for, like, three years before he moved here."

Mina blew out a breath. "Let's start again. Where is Harri's family located?"

He was definitely going to need the support of his family. Mina knew his parents were still together and that he had three siblings.

"In Michigan."

Why did she feel like they were back where they'd started? "Okay, what town?"

"Why do you want to know? Are you guys getting back together?"

"*No.*" It came out a little more vehemently than Mina had intended. "I'm trying to help him. Just answer the question. I'm on a timeline here. Where do Harri's parents live?"

"Ann Arbor, along with one sister and an older brother."

"Perfect." Mina would have to do a little research about job opportunities in Ann Arbor. She could likely swing something, possibly a job interview somewhere. She could do that much.

"But he's not moving back," Quinn replied confidently. "He hates it there. Too small. He loves the city. Talks all the time about how it changed his life for the better."

Quinn definitely wasn't letting her off easy. "What about New Mexico? Did he like it there?"

Mina was glad she'd decided to tap her brother instead of accessing Harri's life file, which would have given her generic information rather than thoughts and feelings.

"He enjoyed it. I know he still has friends there. He goes back a couple times a year to visit."

All good information. Mina might be able to finesse something in either location and give him a choice. He couldn't go back to working in the pleasure industry. That would be too closely connected to Bliss Corp, but she could try to find him something he would like. "Before he worked at the Pleasure Emporium, what did he do?"

"He held odd jobs here and there. He was a server at a printed restaurant for a while. They had a really cool theme. It was all-you-can-eat tacos out of a porta-grinder."

"A porta-grinder?" Portable grinders ground up biomatter and stored it until you could dump it into an appropriate receptacle to recycle it. "Why would somebody eat something out of a grinder, portable or otherwise?"

"That was the whole catch," Quinn said with a snort. "If you didn't finish the tacos in a certain amount of time, you owed the weight of the elemental borrow once they were ground up. If you ate them all, they were free. Brilliant. Harri said the restaurant piled them in, and most people ended up paying for more than they would've had they just bought a couple on their own."

"Interesting." Mina was certain Harri hadn't loved that job. "What else?"

"He mentioned a job he loved a few times. He worked in one of those hydro-dome atmosphere bubble things. Because of the heat factor down there, they have a lot of those self-contained domes for gardening and living and such. He said it was like a whole town in there. Met a lot of people he liked. He really enjoyed tending the fish."

An aqua gardener. Who knew?

"That's perfect. Thanks for the info. Now I've got to run."

"Fine, but one more thing. Mom and Dad are getting back from their trip to the South Asia islands next week. Mom wants to do a family dinner. Do you think I should bring Daphne?"

"Sure. Why not?" Their parents had left on their scheduled holiday a few days prior. Mina's mother had left her a message, but Mina hadn't had time to listen to it yet.

"Well, you know how she gets. Mom always asks those super-invasive questions. Daphne's still upset about all the Plush stuff and the fact that she doesn't have much family. But"—he paused, likely scratching his head—"I want to ask her because I really like her. I'd like Mom and Dad to meet her."

"I'm sure Daphne is familiar with how mothers operate. If she doesn't feel comfortable, she's allowed to change her mind at the last minute."

"She said if you're going, she'll go," he hedged.

"I get it now." Mina laughed. "You're trying to bribe me." Mina couldn't always attend family gatherings because of work. It was pretty much understood that if she was busy, she'd make it up to them later. Mina and Quinn were fiercely independent because they came from fiercely independent parents. No one got too worked up about anything. "You know I can't promise anything. I'll have to decide at the last minute."

"Yeah, I know. I was just hoping you'd be there. Daphne feels really comfortable around you."

"I like her, too," Mina said. "She seems really nice. But I really have to run. My craft is touching down. Thanks for answering my questions about Harri. He's going to be fine.

He'll likely get in contact with you over the next day or two." As the craft descended, Mina could see through the window that the hub at The Spire was bustling with public and private transpo crafts flying in and out, along with hoverbuses and airtrams and basically anything else that was regulated to fly this high. The transpo hub ran the full width of the megascraper, one of the biggest, active residential hubs Mina had ever used.

"Got it," Quinn said. "Hope to see you later. Bye."

Mina said, "End call."

"Communication ended. Landing at The Spire."

The craft door opened, and Mina hustled out.

Inside, she grabbed a tube up to the three hundred and twentieth floor. In a matter of seconds, the door whooshed open, and she stepped out.

She came up short, her mouth tumbling open. She didn't even try to shut it. That was, until she tried to speak. "What are you doing here?"

The tube door slid shut behind her.

"Hello! How fun to see you!" Suzanne, her mega rep, squealed as she clickity-clacked toward Mina on a pair of champagne-colored heels that had to be at least eight centimeters high. In fact, Suzanne was covered in champagne and sparkles from head to toe. She'd amped her game up to some serious megawatts.

Mina understood why, because standing right behind her was a man wearing a casual black shirt and slacks, but there was nothing casual about him. Even when he was trying to fit in, he stuck out like a gigantic, helium-filled, supersonic, hydro-blimp of an advertisement.

He almost glowed. *Damn him.*

Suzanne came at Mina like a rocket on spindly heels. Mina took a step back and to the side, but she wasn't quick enough. Suzanne latched on to her forearm, her hyperglo nails popping on and off. The mega rep shook Mina's arm excitedly before she exploded, "You'll never guess what happened! Vincent Kramer called me. He actually *called* me. Well, he called me back, because I, of course, left him a follow-up message after our nice conversation the other morning." Of course she had. Why hadn't Mina factored that in? "I figured it would be the professional thing to do." Not really. "You know, to let him know that I would be a *very* discreet rep when it came time for him to take up his new residence here in our very own Spire. Of course, I didn't get a hold of him directly. I left a message with his office. And wouldn't you know"—she leaned in, bobbing her forehead against Mina's like they were in this together, teammates to the death, much to the amusement of the man standing right behind her—"he called me back *personally* and set this meeting up." She squealed again. A real, live squeal. "He said he couldn't *wait* to see the building." Suzanne vibrated with enthusiasm. The woman's teeth were almost chattering with it. Mina felt sorry and excited for her at the same time.

Manic celebrity obsession was a thing, and Mina was getting her first gander of it in the champagne-sparkled flesh.

"I'm sure he jumped right on it." Mina flashed her best stink eye at Vince over Suzanne's shoulder.

He smirked. Not a Suli smirk, but close.

"Mr. Kramer particularly wanted to see a unit on this floor," Suzanne whispered, "even though I assured him he was qualified for the very tippy-top of this mega. The units up there are *oozing* with lux. The soaker can accommodate three people comfortably." Why three? "They have sprayer nozzles placed in a three-hundred-and-sixty-five-degree arc, a dryer with a reclining position, a Magnito Platinum hooked up to every trace element imaginable, and the platform is *enormous*. The sensual gel-filled pillows contour to every part of your body—"

Mina cleared her throat.

Loudly.

Then she began the task of unlatching Suzanne from her forearm so she could step away. "I'm sorry to cut you off, Suzanne. I'm sure you guys are very busy with Vincent's *big tour*"—her voice held enough sarcasm for Vince to catch, but Suzanne remained oblivious—"but can I borrow Vince for a quick sec? There's something I need to discuss with him inside my residence." Suzanne looked stricken, her hand falling away on its own, like Mina had just snatched away the most deliciously printed treat she'd ever tasted. "It's okay," Mina soothed. "I promise it'll only be for a teensy minute." She was using words that Suzanne would recognize and hopefully take comfort in. "Vince and I are old pals, remember? I just need to discuss some boring old friend stuff with him."

Suzanne's hand snaked to her chest, edging up to her neck. "Yes. Yes. Of course. Of course. I'll just be right..."

Vince, understanding what was happening to the poor, discombobulated civilian, swooped in with a wide, comforting smile.

One Mina felt the urge to punch off.

Instead, she tightened her fingers into a ball, then released them. Then did it again.

"I'll just be a minute or two, Suzanne," he comforted. "I'm sure my old friend Wilhelmina here just has some inconsequential news to share." Now she really wanted to hit him. "Why don't you continue on into the unit you're going to show me? I'd like to see how the meal printer works, as well as the sprayers and the grinders. Why don't you set that all up, and I'll be in shortly?"

"Oh. Yes." Suzanne brightened as she glanced up at Vince, her eyes genuinely glazed over, like she'd fallen into some kind of a trance. "Okay. Yes. That sounds fine."

Vincent Kramer, colonel-in-arms of the French Protectorate, took this diamond-honed mega rep by the upper arm and guided her toward the unit next to Mina's, all while murmuring reassuring things into her ear, managing to get a few chiming giggles out of her.

If he actually did commit to that unit, he and Mina would have a shared wall. There was no way he would secure that unit. It wasn't happening.

Mina turned and stomped toward her own door, feeling like she was back in middle school programming, instead of being the grown adult she was. Mina had just negotiated a hostile situation on the edge of the outskirts. She could handle Vincent Kramer.

She stuck her thumb on her smudger and placed her eye up to a micro cutout for a retinal. Her door popped. She was just about to snap at Vince to hurry up, turning to yell something garbled and unintelligible down the hallway, and found him standing right behind her.

Suzanne was nowhere to be seen.

He gave her a dopey grin, one side of his lips arcing upward.

Mina closed her eyes. And wished like hell she was back in Pormal.

Chapter 9

"THIS IS A BEAUTIFUL place," Vince commented as she ushered him through her doorway. He headed straight for her solar-catch windows. "Suzanne wasn't lying about The Spire's virtues. The finishes are top grade, and the view from this high is amazing."

Mina snapped her door closed, knowing her residence was completely soundproofed, and no one would overhear what she was about to lay down. "What in the holy cosmos above do you think you're doing here?" Her voice was full of enough grit to cause Vince to spin around. She didn't wait for him to answer. She moved forward, needing to get closer, but not too close, stopping next to her meal counter and crossing her arms. Unfortunately, her swagger game was not nearly as honed as Kaylee's, but she was wearing syn-leather and titanium shoulder rivets. They helped. "By coming here, you've blatantly put me at risk. This is my building. My sanctuary. Is my job a joke to you? Do you think coming here is some kind of cute, apologetic act? People have seen us together. I had to bribe the very same mega rep who's currently in the next unit over trying to recover from your quick departure into staying quiet. She shouldn't even know we know each other! The first time we were spotted out together was an accident. If it happens a second time, I get kicked out of my agency. I can't work undercover if I'm recognized as a dalliance of Vincent Kramer's. You can see what happens to people when they're around you." Mina gestured toward the wall they definitely weren't going to share. "Suzanne was reduced to a puddle of goo in your presence. People don't forget when it comes to you. They remember. I happen to love my job, and I plan on keeping it at all costs." She felt like doing something completely appropriate for middle-grade programming, like making a face or making a crude hand gesture that wasn't actually crude, but more like a frustrated jab. But she refrained.

Something about being around him made her feel like she was stuck back there again. Like when they were young kids arguing about some game gone wrong. Except this wasn't a game. And she was a grown woman.

Vince's genial smile vanished, replaced by a grim expression that was half determination, half exasperation. "I'm very sorry. Genuinely. I didn't think you'd be here. Or at least not out in the hallway. It was not my intent for us to be seen together. I understand how you feel, and it's fully justified, and I realize now it was a mistake to come here. A big one."

Well, then. "Go on."

"To tell you the truth, I was going a little crazy. You're refusing to talk to me. I've left you half a dozen messages, both audio and vid, and you haven't answered any of them." He reached into his pocket and pulled out a tiny quantum drive. He held it up between two fingertips so she could see. "So I brought this. I was going to distract the mega rep and attach it to your door. See? I put a sticky ball of elastomer on the back." He spun it around. She couldn't see anything from this distance because it was too tiny, but she believed him. "It's my sincere apology." He shrugged, putting it back in his pocket. "That's it. That was my entire motivation for coming here. I would never purposely risk you or your livelihood. I care about you, Mina." He shifted over to her lounger, looking defeated, and sat, placing his head in his hands, running his fingers through his hair the way he liked. Which happened to be the way she liked. "Honestly, I wasn't expecting an opportunity like this to present itself, where we would be able to speak face-to-face. That wasn't the plan. I was caught extremely off guard when I got a call from Suzanne saying she'd gotten word directly from you that I was pursuing a residence here. I just sort of reacted. It was a happy chance. Now I realize it was selfish to follow up in hopes I could stick a drive to your door."

Mina dropped her arms and glanced around her living area sheepishly. "Yeah, about that." She moved forward, gripping her hands together nervously. Why was she nervous? She wanted to shake out her hands, but she refrained. "Now it's my turn to apologize. Suzanne accosted me the morning after we had dinner together. She'd seen a blurry picture of us at À La Carte, and when my director released my first name to the public, she put two and two together. I had to make sure she kept quiet, and you shopping for a residence here was the first thing that came to mind. She's one of the few people who has access to my birth name. I couldn't risk her gossiping about us, so I dangled the ultimate Vincent Kramer prize in front of her until she was so focused on that, it was all she could see." Mina took a seat on a chair across from Vince. "I didn't consider she'd follow up with you. I should've. Not very agent-like of me." Mina blew out a breath. "That's what mega reps do. They sell things. They contact people and follow up with them, do all the reppie things. At the very least, I should've informed you of what I did so you'd be prepared. I'm sorry."

He glanced at her, the beginning of a grin forming on his lips. "I'm kind of glad you didn't. It was a pretty good surprise. She made it sound like you couldn't *wait* to have me close by because our friendship was so deep-rooted and you missed me and hoped I found a place close by. She's quite a prolific seller."

"Please tell me you didn't make the trip all the way from France to drop off a quantum drive."

"No, I didn't come from France. I'm actually staying in the city for the foreseeable future. Ambrose is, shall we say, a little put out with all the events that have transpired with my connection to Veritus. The French have taken a totally different view on my 'heroism'"—he put the word in air quotes—"than the Americans have."

He had been pretty heroic, in Mina's estimation. He'd sacrificed a lot to save innocents from Veritus. In the process, he'd omitted key information that could've compromised the op to a great degree, stripping away a good deal of Mina's trust.

But he'd gone in with a pure heart, as far as she was concerned. Even if his decisions regarding the op hadn't been perfect, he'd been trying to help rectify a really bad situation. "That's too bad, and undeserved in my estimation."

He looked hopeful. "Thanks. French people are a cautious, skeptical bunch, and the French media is spinning it a few different ways. One is that I did what I did without authorization, which is correct. A crazier version is that I'm trying to subvert the government somehow. Another is that I'm a Soviet State spy." He glanced toward her windows for a moment. "Anyway, Ambrose wants me to keep a low profile here while he does cleanup there. I'm still managing some military operations remotely, while continuing to do interviews and put in face time to keep 'optimistic French relations' at the forefront."

Now he looked miserable. Mina felt a little sorry for him. Ambrose Bernard, leader of the Protectorate and Vince's boss, could've easily placed Vince under arrest, or kicked him out of the Protectorate, or any variety of things, really. Vince had broken protocol in a big way. Making him stay in America and do public interviews wasn't the worst. He still had a job, after all. But it was still unfortunate.

"Interviews don't sound so…awful," Mina offered.

Vince gave a short, barking laugh. "Please. If you were in this position, you'd be on the verge of tearing your hair out. Remember that time we were forced to sit and listen to—what was her name again?" He snapped his fingers. "Mrs. Cantor! That's it. She ran those supplemental courses called Youths With Purpose. Our mothers thought it was a good idea to sign us up. They were torture. If I remember correctly, all we did all day for a solid week was interview each other in mock professional scenarios. Well, compared to *these* interviews, that was the best week of my life."

Mina laughed. "I do remember Mrs. Cantor. She always wore corrective lenses perched on the end of her nose and those weird orange one-piece unis, even though vision correction is free at any age, and she could've printed any outfit to wear. Was there a *purpose* to those Youths With Purpose seminars? I never found one. Mrs. Cantor had several mantras that have somehow managed to stay ingrained in my brian. One was, 'You must carry yourself with respect at all times!' And, 'Don't let others do your thinking for you, do your thinking yourself!' What were we? Twelve? Thirteen?"

"Right around there. Even though attending those were tedious, I always had a good time because you were there. I remember we sneaked off a few times and got into a bit of trouble. Nothing major, but you always had some great idea about sneaking onto the roof or dropping an amplifier somewhere."

"Yeah." Mina chuckled. "My mom got called a few times. She usually attributed my negative brushes with authority as me being bored because I was too smart for my own good." Mina remembered being restless during those seminars. "I *was* bored, but it had nothing to do with smarts. It was because people like Mrs. Cantor couldn't teach a class to save her life. She rarely stayed on any topic and had nothing important to impart to our young, impressionable minds. It was just her way of making some quick currency."

Mina stood, brushing off her thighs, feeling a little ridiculous in her outskirts getup. Vince hadn't asked her about it, and she was grateful. Who knew what Suzanne the mega rep thought? Not the typical outfit of a tri-linguist, which was her cover story. But it was time for Vince to go, or Suzanne would start to wonder. They didn't need her wondering about anything else.

Vince reached into his pocket as he stood, following her lead, and moved toward her meal counter. "Your mom wasn't too far off. At twelve, you had the smarts to teach that class, and every kid there would've learned a great deal." He set the quantum drive down. "I'm going to leave this here for you in case you feel like watching it later. I'll take off now. I'm sure Suzanne is pacing in the unit next door. Her heels are probably a centimeter shorter by now. People tend to panic when they think they have something, and then they suddenly discover it's gone."

His eyes found hers and settled there, holding her steady, not breaking for several seconds.

Mina was pretty sure that when she swallowed, it was audible. Perhaps even to people on the ground outside. "Yeah, you should probably go." She resisted sneaking her hand up to her throat. She had to appear as calm and cool as he was. She moved toward the door. "I'm due at headquarters, but I'll try to watch later." She nodded to the drive. "Where are you staying?" She disengaged her door, but didn't swing it open just yet.

"Bellatone Tower." He came closer.

"Nice. I guess nothing but the best for visiting royalty." Bellatone Tower was the second megascraper built in the city, with residential units on the bottom and short-term, high-end luxury stays on the top.

"Not technically royalty." He held up a finger, grinning. "I'm actually required to reside there when I'm in town because they have the best security of any guest accommodations in the city. They have their own guard squad, a combination of bots and air breathers. Other than, of course, securing my own residence here." He inclined his head.

Mina shook hers. "No way. You're not moving in here. Don't even think about it. This is my zone." She swished her hand in a circle. "All of it. The entire Spire is Mina Land. Go find your own mega."

Vince laughed, a full-throated sound. Mina didn't hate it. "I just might do that. But you're going to have to be the one to break it to Suzanne. She'll be devastated that I'm not securing a unit today. She told me I have something called instacredit. I don't have to go through a single channel to get approval. We don't have anything like that in France. Even the cheapest kiosk in the city inspects your DNA swipe like you're going to be disqualified from borrows in a matter of moments. I'm not sure how she knows what's in my account, since I didn't give her authorization to look, but I'm not going to argue."

"Kind of like tacos delivered in a porta-grinder," she mumbled. But exactly the opposite.

"What's that?"

"Never mind. Just a story Quinn told me today." She cocked her head. "I have a favor to ask, if that's okay."

"Sure. Anything."

"Can you lead Suzanne on for a little while? Instead of telling her it's a no-go today, can you let her down slowly, like, say, maybe over the next month? And let her know that you don't want her speaking about our friendship, that it's a private matter to you. That will go a long way toward keeping my cover intact, and I would really appreciate it."

Mina didn't relish repeating all this to McAllister, even though she would. He would certainly have an opinion on the situation.

"I will absolutely do that." He rested a shoulder against the wall and stared intently at her. She blinked a few times. "Thanks for inviting me in and letting me explain. I know it doesn't erase everything that happened between us. I broke your trust. But I'm prepared to apologize until you're ready."

Ready for what? She didn't want to think about it right this second. Especially since her chest was feeling a little constricted and her heart was beating a few beats too fast.

She managed, "I'm relieved you didn't come here trying to find me. I'm also relieved that we won't be sharing a wall. I wish you well with the interviews. I hope Ambrose smooths everything over so you can go home soon."

He gave her a devilish grin. "I hope he takes his time."

Mina opened the door for him. "It was good to see you."

He exited, turning and walking backward. "You know how to get a hold of me." He held up his cuff. "Here's hoping it will be sooner rather than later."

When he turned around again Mina groaned. It wasn't fair that someone could look that good in a pair of pants.

Mina shut the door, placing her back against it, splaying her palms against the cool surface.

She wasn't sure she was ready for any of this. But she wasn't sure she wasn't.

Chapter 10

"Computer, go back fifteen years. Cross-check current Nesbit, Dominic B., files with the name Nesbit, Shauna K.," Mina ordered from her place at a small, serviceable table in a tiny conference room at headquarters. The wall wasn't very large, but the entire thing was a screen. She'd just come across an anomaly with the name Nesbit, and she wanted to take a closer look.

She'd been working for approximately twenty minutes, trying to dig up whatever she could to help the occupants of Pormal.

"Cross-check in progress," the computer replied.

Mina was using a secure, encrypted connection via her own compucase through a microfiber cable so thin it almost wasn't there. This allowed her to have direct access to everything the government had on file. Helpful and much faster than trying to do this work from home, where she would inevitably come across security checks at regular intervals.

A light knock came at the door. Not even a second later, Lee burst in, huffing and puffing, his compucase banging against his thigh. It appeared he'd been running. He looked startled to find her sitting there, staring at him.

He smiled. "Hi. Sorry I'm late." He took a seat at the only other chair in the room and placed his case on the table. "Have you found anything yet?"

"A few interesting tidbits. There's a guy by the name of Dominic B. Nesbit who did time in a box for illegal-goods trading approximately twelve years ago. He's the best candidate I have for the Dominic Nesbit Quaz was talking about. Once he emerged from his box, he pretty much slid completely off the grid. All gone, no DNA hits, nothing. But oddly, the name Shauna Nesbit pops up in tandem with his name in some of these searches, almost like an addendum. It's like she's a close family member, but I can't find any formal relation between the two. They're not siblings, no actual family relation whatsoever. They weren't married. I think it might be a DNA-swap situation, but it's going to take some time to unravel. The records are patchy at best. The official report when Dominic was sentenced doesn't contain many details either, no names of relatives or close associates. It's odd." Mina reclined in her chair, running her fingers through her hair and stretching. It was close quarters in here. "How'd it go with the high-rise? Do you like it?"

"Yeah. It's amazing." Lee slumped back in his seat, taking a few deep breaths, steadying himself as if visiting a possible new residence had taken everything out of him, and he was just now finding a second to breathe.

"The place is totally spec. It's on the twenty-eighth floor." His eyes gave off some serious sparkle. "It has great views. Not like yours, but cool, like of some buildings and stuff. It has four rooms. A good-sized living area, a sleep room with an updated sleep pod that's all decked out." More sparkle. "It even has a wall screen. Like, the whole wall. Not a huge wall, more like a side wall, but it's a *wall*." It sounded like the place had all the techie things his heart desired. "It doesn't have a soaker, but there's a roomy sprayer, a dryer, and *two* grinders, one in the living area and one in the waste room." His eyebrows actually waggled.

Mina chuckled at his enthusiasm.

"It also has a small utility closet, which McAllister said was necessary so I can have extra tech installed."

Mina expected him to flap his arms like a baby chick who was ready to fly into its own nest. He didn't. But she was excited for him. The rookie deserved it.

"That's great. So did you tell them you'd take it?"

"Tell who?"

Mina maintained her Zen. It was a constant practice when she was with him. She even liked to believe she was getting good at it. "The rep, or whoever you were with," she offered.

His face fell. "I was the only one there."

"That's not a problem. They do it differently depending on the residence. In my case, I did the tour virtually. Then I met with my mega rep." Mina wondered how Suzanne had taken the news Vince wouldn't be signing on to The Spire just yet. "Not all high-rises have reps. Depends on who runs it."

"There was just a digilock on the door. I gave my DNA to get through two levels of security, and that was it."

"The next step is to get a hold of someone in the government housing department and let them know you want it. Once you give the okay, they'll start the upgrades. Security, full sim integration, extra elemental valves, everything you'll need. That is, unless you want to see another place. I believe you get to see three or four."

"No. I want this one!" Lee said quickly. Realizing he'd answered at excitement level fifteen, he blushed. "Sorry. It was kind of perfect, actually. Twenty-eight is the day of my dad's birthday. So, you know..." He looked down at his thumbs as he jammed them together. "It felt right."

Well, jeez.

"Sounds like the perfect place. The upgrades won't take very long. Then you'll have a whole new residence."

"Cross-check completed," the computer announced. "There are three areas of intersect between the two names. One, Dominic B. and Shauna K. Nesbit were at the same location at the same time twelve years, three days, twenty-three hours ago. Two, Dominic B. and Shauna K. Nesbit have the same day of birth, different birth year by three years, see dates listed." Shauna was three years younger. "Three, a death certificate was filed for one Dominic B. Nesbit eleven and a half years ago, then rescinded."

How did one rescind a death certificate? Mina had never heard of that.

"No known DNA sample has been taken or processed from Dominic B. Nesbit for twelve years, three days, and twenty-two hours. Shauna K. Nesbit frequents the following locations."

A data list expanded, highlighting multiple DNA hits within the city.

Mina got up and moved toward the wall. "So Dominic disappeared right after he got out of the box and met up with Shauna. Boy, she likes her spa enhancements. Most of these locations are beauty-related. Computer, access Shauna K. Nesbit's residential address."

"No physical address is listed for Shauna K. Nesbit."

"That's weird," Lee murmured, coming to stand by Mina. "Even if you're above borrows and purchase a unit with physical currency, there still should be a record."

"Not if you live in the outskirts," Mina pondered. "She could maintain a residence there and still frequent these places. Look, she visits a known manufacturing mecca south of the city regularly. Why would she go there? Those are completely automated and don't offer any retail experience whatsoever."

Manufacturing meccas were shared land hubs built by multiple corporations in tandem. Each contained a huge mag-lev hub at the center so goods could be efficiently and speedily transported all across the country and beyond.

Mina continued, "It looks like she swipes there at least once a month. The company is called Honeycomb Gelskin Inc. Computer, list company details for Honeycomb Gelskin Inc."

"Honeycomb Gelskin Incorporated manufactures a variety of body-insert shapers, limb prosthetics, alternative fiber hair coverings, silicone hand and foot coverings, eye diffraction kits, skin cement, as well as a full stock of beautification products. The company was established in 2093 by a single owner, name Esther R. Rizzo."

"Details on Esther R. Rizzo, highlight connections to Dominic B. Nesbit and Shauna K. Nesbit," Mina ordered.

"Esther Rose Rizzo, age fifty-three, born in Huntsville, Indiana. Mother, Margaret F. Stone Rizzo. Father, Scott M. Rizzo. No siblings on record. Relocated to this area at age eighteen. No DNA samples received or processed since 2094. No death details on record. One connection to Dominic B. Nesbit. They were both in the same vicinity, location unknown, twelve years, three days, and twenty-two hours ago."

Lots of interesting connections.

"So all three of these people were in the same location right after Dominic Nesbit got sprung from a box," Mina said. "Directly following, Dominic Nesbit goes MIA, then shortly after, so does Esther Rizzo. Shauna is the sole survivor. Computer, complete full lifecheck on Shauna K. Nesbit."

"Shauna K. Nesbit. Birth date May 14, 2070. Nothing else is found." She was thirty-five years old now, according to that data.

"What you mean nothing else is found?" Mina asked. "She's swiping her DNA all over the place."

"No other information is found."

"Where's she from?" Mina prodded.

"No location available."

"What are her parents' names?" Mina asked stubbornly.

"No data available."

"Ah," Lee interjected. "I think I might know why. This is reading like a DNA alias, not a swap. If Shauna's identity is manufactured, there would be no records on file. Obviously, something went down twelve years ago between her, Dominic, and Esther. In order to engineer unique DNA, you need a lab and strands of someone else's DNA to make altered copies. According to this, Shauna used Dominic's. That's why they're so closely linked on Dominic's lifecheck. The copy is extremely close to his own, but not exact. So she can't be paired as a relative, because it would read as some kind of a clone. Cloning was outlawed nearly eighty years ago. The computer is unsure of how to categorize it, so it just links her name. It's probably why she took Dominic's surname. She knows if she's ever caught, she has to explain that connection. She probably has an elaborate backstory ready to go."

"Yeah, she probably does," Mina agreed. "And it goes like this: A woman of unknown name and origin breaks the law and is desperate for new DNA to avoid doing time for her crimes, so she tosses Dominic into a vat of acid after she cuts off the tips of his fingers and keeps them in a neutralizing solution so she can manufacture altered DNA, and then she can live free and clear of criminal prosecution forever and ever."

Lee owl-blinked at her. "Well, that's…gruesome."

Mina tilted her head up to the ceiling, which was

smooth and white and intact. "Okay, a vat of acid is over-the-top. I admit it. And honestly, that much acid would be hard to find. She could've easily just lasered him right through the eyeball. Or stabbed him in the heart with a regulator pick."

The rookie shook his head. "Actually, I don't think he's dead."

Mina expressed her surprise. "Really? Even though there's no record of him doing anything for the last twelve years? And how do you explain the death certificate being rescinded? I've never heard of such a thing. It's beyond smelly. It's reeking like a sulfur bomb inside a vat of rancid excrement." Suli would be proud.

Lee headed back to the table and sat. "Agreed. There is definitely criminal activity involved. But these kind of DNA manipulations are tricky. They degrade over time because they're no longer attached to the body. It's highly unlikely that this Shauna person has been maintaining dead tissue for years. It could be that Dominic disliked his time in a box and didn't relish ever getting caught again, so he and Shauna came up with a plan. She uses manipulated DNA from him and does all their running."

Mina nodded, impressed with Lee. "I follow what you're saying. So in other words, if a crime is committed, and a third-party DNA comes up, it can't technically be linked to either of them, even though the genetic match would be very close to Dominic's." DNA was either a hundred percent match or was tossed out. That had been the law of the land for over one hundred years. That's why altering DNA was considered a high crime.

Dominic would know that, especially since he'd done time in a box. "They're using this as get-out-of-a-box insurance. Dominic lies low in the outskirts, while Shauna runs around doing what they need to stay in business or whatever, using this magically altered DNA."

"Exactly." Lee's face was concentrated as he typed something into his compucase. "That means that Shauna and Dominic are a team, not...um...a murderer and a victim. Visiting this facility once a month makes sense if that's where they're manufacturing the fake strands. She'd need to get a refill of the topical or whatever she's using. If she swiped degraded DNA, the government would get an alert. It has to be fresh within thirty days. Sooner, for specialty high-value items. She would secure those right after her visit to Honeycomb."

Mina glanced at the screen. Sure enough, Shauna Nesbit visited Honeycomb Gelskin every twelfth day of the month. "She's due for a visit in two days. But even if we can find a way to bring her in for suspicion of manufacturing false DNA, there's no way to link any of those bad deeds to the outskirts. Hauling her in now wouldn't help the residents of Pormal. Or stop Dominic from encroaching, if this is in fact the Nesbit we're looking for. That is, if he's alive and his withered skeleton isn't lying under two meters of loosely packed dirt in a drain field someplace."

"You have a very...vivid imagination." Lee chuckled. "But you're right. There is illegal activity here, as DNA manipulation is a high crime, but there's nothing that would allow us to bring in resources to help the people in Pormal."

"Unless we get a warrant to search Honeycomb and find that, in addition to DNA manipulation, they're storing illegal goods there that are somehow being bartered for profit in the outskirts." It was a long shot.

"A warrant request on what grounds?" Lee asked.

That was the tricky part. "Well, Shauna K. Nesbit is reading as a false identity. And this person who's using this assumed identity is swiping in regularly at a location that could be a lab used to produce illegally altered DNA."

"Yeah, but we don't have any proof. It's just, like, what we *think* is happening."

Proof was, in fact, necessary for a warrant. "At the very least, we could bring her in under suspicion of illegal DNA activity. She's not supposed to exist. Even if we can't enter the building right away, we can get to her. Then, if we can prove Shauna K. Nesbit is not really who this woman is, then we can get a warrant to search Honeycomb."

"That's a possibility. But wouldn't that tip them off? It takes time to get a warrant. Dominic could change course if Shauna's detained. They probably have a backup plan. I mean, I would."

Once again, Mina was impressed. The rookie was picking up on the minutia and processing everything with a critical eye.

Lee continued, "Which wouldn't matter so much if we weren't trying to help the people in Pormal. Dominic and Shauna might decide to do something drastic and come after Quaz and his people sooner. I'm not sure we should risk that."

"Agreed. If we had an official op designation, it would be different. Everything is sped up on a sanctioned case. We're going to have to find a way to make this DNA alias issue with Shauna a real case." In a hurry.

Lee nodded. "Let's keep digging. There has to be more here. Even though the computer isn't finding any data links to Shauna, we can start examining locations where she checks in regularly. Look at video feed, analyze client lists. She could've messed up and given her real name at some point—"

Mina's and Lee's cuffs each beeped simultaneously.

Director McAllister's voice was clipped. "You two in my office. Now. Your next op just came in."

Chapter 11

"THIS IS A prank, right? You're playing a prank on us." Mina stood by McAllister's window, looking out at Atlas Park, a wide embankment topped with a layer of earth and grass that protected the city from the ever-rising water. The angle of the window gave a spec view of the long swath of blue, along with a thick carpet of green dotted with trees, flowers, and the occasional gathering pavilion. People were out enjoying the day. She turned around. "This is a guard-duty designation. A NannyBot could do this job. Arm the bot with a laser, and it'd probably keep a better watch."

"This is not a prank. And you're correct, this classifies as light duty," McAllister conceded. "The federal government has requested our services to protect one of our citizens, so that's what we'll do."

"I've never met anyone famous before," Lee said from the chair across from McAllister's desk. Mina shot him a look. His shoulders hunched. "But I agree with Agent Kane.

This sounds like a job for the PPF, not federal agents." The Police Protection Force handled light-duty stuff like this.

"The PPF have been called in. Repeatedly." McAllister's tone turned exasperated. He wasn't completely on board with this case either. Sometimes, even when he received an order he didn't agree with, it was still his duty to staff it. "It's not...working out, so they've elevated the request."

Mina walked over to stand next to Lee, arms crossed. "Why aren't the PPF handling it?"

"They keep getting turned away."

"The civilian called the threat in herself, correct?"

"That's correct."

"To the PPF?"

"Yes."

"Then once they arrive, she's turning them away?" Mina questioned.

"That appears to be the situation." McAllister folded his hands on his desk.

"Even if she's dissatisfied with the PPF," Mina continued, "or worried they can't handle the job, it's a matter of protocol. The PPF decide what they can and can't handle after examining the evidence. Then they elevate it." Seeing a sparkly, new opportunity to add to their previous conversation, Mina added, "However, altering DNA *is* a high crime. The link we found between Dominic Nesbit and Shauna—"

McAllister cleared his throat. "While I understand your reasonings, Agent Kane, and agree with them for the most part, this is the scheduled operation on my desk.

You two are standing in front of me. All my other agents are in the field. The information you've uncovered on Shauna Nesbit is thin at best, which you are both well aware. You have connected nothing solid to Dominic Nesbit, or any other Nesbit, for that matter, with any links to high crimes in our jurisdiction. It will take time for me to request authorization to proceed with an inquiry about the altered-DNA accusation, which I will do. But in the meantime, while I'm performing my duties here, you two will be keeping watch over Petra Pebbles and trying to untangle the threats she's receiving. Is that clear?"

"Yes." Mina sighed. "What's the threat again?" Mina knew what it was. She just wanted to hear it out loud again.

"That someone is threatening to steal her beauty secrets."

"Does she have proof?" Mina asked. She left off the snark, which would be appropriate to add in now *if* she weren't having a conversation with her director. If Kaylee were here, her best pal would probably compose a song on the spot about the ridiculousness of it all. Mina could hear it playing in her head right now.

Petra Pebbles is short on smarts. She's probably covered in warts. She wants attention but lacks retention. Oh, Petra Pebbles, why are you so...unsmart?

Okay, so Mina didn't exactly have the kind of talent Kaylee did to make up songs. She should probably give her pal more kudos from now on.

"There is proof, but no one has seen it yet," McAllister

replied dryly. "She told the PPF that a device had been delivered this morning containing a threat about beauty recipes. That's all we have."

Mina couldn't help stating the obvious. She was too irritated. The people of Pormal needed real help. This was a frivolous use of her and Lee's time. "Individuals shouldn't be allowed to have access to the federal government just because they want it."

"I don't make the rules, Agent Kane. I simply follow the directives I'm given." McAllister's voice remained calm and measured, fatigue weaving its way through. "You are familiar with the world we occupy. Individuals with elevated currency retain certain...privileges, whether we like it or not. I have not done a lifecheck on Ms. Pebbles, nor do I plan to. But given that her bank account is much beyond borrows, coupled with her status as a vid star, it's clear that she has traded in the gold data chip of prestige to get a case opened on her behalf. We can fight it, or we can accept it. What's it going to be?"

"I understand, and I accept. I apologize. This is just a hard one to digest." For a fleeting moment, she wished she had a porta-grinder. Then she could just flip a switch, and the digesting would be done for her. This was on Quinn. He'd put the image of one into her head, and now she couldn't shake it.

Mina was ready to let it go. This was a dial-in job. Protecting a spoiled vid star over some ill-conceived threat about beauty enhancements was trivial, but maybe she and Lee had earned this break after all of the emotionally exhausting ops they'd had in a row? After all, she had wished for an easy case today. Now she was getting one.

McAllister inclined his head toward Lee. "What about you, Agent Adams? Do you accept this assignment?"

The rookie nodded quickly. "Yes. Of course."

"Good. There's a craft on the roof waiting to escort you both to Bellatone Tower. Petra Pebbles lives somewhere near the top, even though those units aren't specified as residential. She has received some special permits, along with a few others."

"Um." Mina shuffled her feet. She'd been hoping to not have to report this. At least for now. "Just to let you know, Vincent Kramer is also staying at The Bella."

McAllister's eyebrows rose. "I'm aware of that, Agent Kane. Is there anything else you'd like to include in your report?"

"I should've mentioned this earlier, but it slipped my mind." It was the truth. Mostly. "I was caught up in the Shauna Nesbit file, and when I arrived at headquarters, you were in a meeting. But I ran into Vincent Kramer when I went home to change."

"Please feel free to elaborate on your run-in."

She could tell he was fighting back a grin. She wasn't sure she appreciated it, or if she could totally relate to it.

"When I stepped off the tube, I found Vincent Kramer and my mega rep, Suzanne, in my hallway. The mega rep was giving Vince a tour of a residential unit on my floor." Mina wanted to pace over to the window again, but she stayed put. "Suzanne had contacted his office, following up on information I gave her about Vince wanting to secure a residence in The Spire. He felt that playing along would benefit keeping my cover secure." That was a stretch, but Mina wasn't going to go into the real reason he'd been there and the apology that was sitting on her meal counter in the form of a quantum drive with elastomer stuck to the back.

"I see." McAllister's hands, once again, were folded on his desk. "Anything else?"

"I politely invited the colonel into my residence and quizzed him as to why he was standing in my hallway." Mina's jaw was tightening. She actively worked to loosen it. "During that conversation, he relayed to me where he was staying."

"Did he have any other...pertinent information to share?" Which was McAllister's way of telling Mina he didn't need the personal bits, just the French bits.

"He did. The French media is spinning his involvement with Veritus negatively, and Ambrose has ordered him to stay here and work on fixing his image. That's why he's at The Bella. That mega has superior security to any other pay-and-stay in the city."

"I've seen some of the reports coming out of France. They are indeed formulating a negative spin on what should've been, by all accounts, a heroic act on his part. I'll be interested to see how this plays out." Mina heard more than curiosity in her director's tone. That meant there were more details he wasn't sharing about the French Protectorate or the French media or both. "Regardless of Colonel Kramer's current residence at The Bella, you and Agent Adams are scheduled to arrive at the private hub near the top. You've already been cleared. You will use your real names. No altered appearances are necessary. The Bella is discreet, particularly with their high-profile residents, but that may change if you leave the premises. Once on the ground, you'll be escorted to Ms. Pebbles' suite of rooms by one of her employees. If you have any trouble getting through security, let me know immediately." He frowned, his face clouding.

"Should we be expecting trouble?" Mina asked.

"Ms. Pebbles is, shall we say, unpredictable." McAllister leaned back in his chair. "She will find, however, that if she misuses this office, she will pay a steep penalty, including overtime in real currency. That's it for now. You're dismissed."

Once out of McAllister's office, Mina and Lee grabbed their compucases from the conference room. Lee pressed a thumbprint in the smudger for the tube.

He grinned. "It's kind of cool we get to meet a vid star."

Or kind of not.

The era of swooning over vid stars had passed several decades ago. With the corruption and greed running rampant in governments all over the world, people had transferred their glowing adoration and hyperfocus to people they felt could make their lives better and had some measure of power to do so.

That's why top government officials, military higher-ups, and people like Vincent Kramer were followed and swooned over to a degree that seemed, for the most part, too high into the stratosphere.

Vid stars hadn't quite gotten the message, however.

You could still find them strutting around, making big deals about themselves for the benefit of the smaller handful who still bothered to care.

"I'm not looking forward to dealing with a spoiled star who subverted protocol," Mina groused. It was warranted, as far as she was concerned. "Hopefully, once we arrive, we can assess the tiny threat, debunk it or solve it, and get out."

The tube opened and carried them to the top of the building, where a government craft waited, door already open. They both got in, sticking their fingers in helix slots.

"Welcome, Agents Kane and Adams. Destination Bellatone Tower. Do you wish to make any changes?"

"No," Mina replied.

"Travel time to Bellatone Tower is one minute, thirteen seconds."

She turned to Lee. "I've been meaning to ask, but keep forgetting. At Cullen, you always chose to use a hair sample for a DNA verification, instead of a skin scrape, which is the most painless, easiest way to go. Why was that?"

Lee avoided Mina's gaze. "Um. Hair disintegrates the quickest and gives the weakest DNA marker. I was worried that my alias wasn't going to hold. It was my first op, so I figured if the helix triggered the wrong name, I could explain that it was an old hair strand and then offer to give them a new sample. Meanwhile, you would contact Director McAllister to get it fixed." He shrugged. "That was the gist, anyway. I was new and a little nervous. Okay, a lot nervous."

McAllister had installed the rookie on her case, but

had neglected to tell Mina anything about Lee, such as he was incredibly green and in need of guidance. Lots and lots of guidance. It'd been McAllister's way of evaluating whether Lee had good agenting instincts, since Lee had been recruited as a hacker with no previous experience.

Lee could've easily asked Mina about the DNA trigger, and she would've assured him that everything was secure. But he hadn't. Because, in their early days together, she hadn't bothered to build any trust between them. That was on her.

"That makes sense," she replied easily. "Your reasoning was sound. But just so you know, we have several layers of backup if a glitch like that ever happens. It's rare, but not unheard of. First thing you need to do is exactly what you were planning and insist to whoever was extracting the DNA that there had been a mistake. As you're insisting, you send an alert to headquarters. We have a special line for that. You can stream it on your cuff if it makes you feel more secure. They triangulate your location immediately and update the system. Takes about four seconds."

"Thanks." Lee smiled. "That's good to know."

The sim announced, "Landing in thirty seconds."

Mina glanced out the window. She'd been to The Bella a few times, but had never visited this high. This megascraper had some very popular consumer and retail spaces on the main levels. She'd heard all the same stories everyone had about how lux and incredibly lush it was at the top. Extravagance was synonymous with The Bella for anyone in the know.

"I guess we're about to find out how snazzy this place is," Mina told Lee. "And how vid stars act in real life."

"Agent Kane, Agent Adams?" A tall woman with a complicated updo the color of a ripe raspberry stood just inside the automated doors of the transpo hub. Her lip dye matched her hair, and her steeply arched microbrows were threaded with red highlights. She cradled a superboard in one arm and was busy tapping something onto it.

Lee made a low growly sound just under his breath, a mixture of awe and fascination as he gaped around. Judging by the transpo hub alone, this place was going to be completely over-the-top lux, the likes of which neither of them had ever seen before.

The vaulted ceilings were impossibly high and curved. Crisp, white marble polished to a high sheen flowed up from the floor to the walls, no seams visible. The seating area wasn't polymolded printed with colorful gel-cush, like at The Spire. Instead, it was gilded, with curled gold accents decorating the single-person loungers spread throughout the area. Privacy looked to be a concern, so they'd installed an acre of greenery in the form of stylish pots full of tall bushes, flowing plants, and trees with shiny green leaves. There were private holo cubicles, piped with gold trim, so their guests could have a holo meeting in style while they waited for their private, luxury transpo.

Because everything was so large and so spread out, the echo was incredible.

Mina moved toward the woman who'd addressed them, popping her badge up on holo. "You're correct. I'm Agent Kane. This is Agent Adams. And who might you be?"

The woman appeared taken aback. With some mild sputtering, she replied, "I'm Yolanda Terrin, Petra Pebbles' executive assistant." She'd stressed the word *executive* like it held weight with them. It didn't.

"Great. Lead the way."

"First, I need your credentials," she replied crisply.

By way of responding, Mina lofted her wrist higher in the air.

Her holo badge was right there. Lee did the same. They both stared at the woman, waiting.

When she continued to look put out, Mina leaned forward. "Do you have something to scan these with? A thumb tracer? Something attached to that top-of-the-line board?"

"Um," Yolanda said, "that's not really what I'm looking for."

Mina dropped her wrist, hands sliding to her hips, fingertips drumming. "What exactly do you want?

To swab the inside of my cheek? Do you require a detailed history of the last twenty people I've spoken with? A list of all my famous acquaintances? How about a data log of all the schooling I've had since middle programming?"

The woman became flustered. "Well…we just… Usually, the media provides us with complete background—"

"We are *not* the media. Our *background* is our badge. In case you've forgotten, your boss is the one who summoned us here. Apparently, the PPF couldn't give you the detailed pedigree she was looking for. If you ask me for anything other than to scan my badge, we will happily vacate the premises and leave your boss alone to fight her own battles. That's actually preferable—"

"No, no, no. It's fine," the woman insisted. "I don't have a scanner on me. I've never had to deal with a badge other than a press badge, which is different." Damn right it was different. "Follow me, please." The woman took off at a quick clip down the middle of the pristine marble floor. Her clacks echoed like shots bouncing off the thirty-meter-high vaulted ceiling. But no one seemed to notice. She was dressed in a raspberry tuck-pointed suit contoured to fit her body with the kind of precision that came only with custom fittings, detailed design, and exquisite fabrics interwoven with who knew what to give it a high sheen and moldability.

Mina recognized her footwear to be one-of-a-kind Jet Lang creations. She could tell because the heel was impossibly thin and had a tiny ball at the base. They were also raspberry, with buttery jeweled accents. If Petra Pebbles' executive assistant was this done up, wearing more enhancements and a better wardrobe than Mina could ever dream of affording, she didn't relish what was awaiting them upstairs.

Yolanda stopped in front of a bank of tubes. Mina had never seen so many lined up before. There were more than twenty on each side.

Lee leaned in, whispering, "The only time I've ever seen a bank of tubes like this was in a vid. A giant corporation was keeping secrets, and everyone was assigned their own tube. It delivered them to their own secured lab. I didn't think this many existed in real life."

Since tubes operated so quickly, it was definitely overkill. Currency continued to be king.

Yolanda headed straight for a tube in the middle. She stuck her finger in a DNA slot. The tube door whooshed open a second later.

She entered without looking back, assuming they were following. She assumed correctly, and Mina and Lee entered the tube directly after her. The woman was smart not to make small talk. The ride was short and sweet.

The tube door opened directly into an enormous living space.

Mina stood for a moment, staring.

Everything was pink and fluffy. And by everything, she meant *everything*. An occasional glimmer of gold connected a pink lampshade to a pink base, but other than that, it was a migraine of monochrome. It looked as though one of the characters from the tot screencast *Fluff & Friends* had spewed their insides into the space.

The living area dipped down three steps from where they stood. The floor covering was a pink mass of fibers at least three centimeters thick. Mina wasn't even sure what it was made of. It looked like freshly spun cotton candy, an old-fashioned treat served at special childhood events. The furniture was overstuffed to a great degree, all in various shades of pink. Gel-cush pillows were strewn everywhere.

Mina had no idea there could be so many different shades of that particular color.

Only the gigantic solar-catch windows offset the pink carnage. They took up the entire wall in front of them. The ceilings were high. Therefore, the windows soared twelve meters easily. The view was *incredible*. Out of this world. Mina's windows offered a spec view, but these windows seemed to open up to the universe itself. Blues, greens, pale browns, yellows, reds, oranges for as far as the eye could see. The city was spread out below. The buildings and structures looked so miniature that all the colors ran together. The horizon was dotted with shapes that appeared to be islands, even though Mina knew they were likely other cities.

It was truly incredible. Oh, the things currency could buy.

Yolanda held a finger to her lips as she side-stepped down the stairs quietly. Mina quirked a brow. Was this how she typically came in?

Mina watched as the assistant tramped through the

pink cloud and gingerly bent over, settling her hand on the shoulder of someone Mina and Lee couldn't fully see from their vantage point on the steps. The lounger was enormous and the shade of a barely ripe strawberry. You wouldn't think color would have anything to do with occluding the eye, but it did.

More than anything, the monochrome was making it hard to focus on any individual piece of furniture or person.

"What? What is it? Are they here?" A woman with a lyrical voice sat up quickly, reaching for her eye mask, which happened to be pink. No surprises there.

"Yes, ma'am. The detectives just arrived."

Mina made her way down the stairs without being invited. "We're not detectives," she corrected, trying her best to keep the irritation out of her voice. "We're federal agents. We're here to investigate the threat that was made against you." *And, lady, it better be real.*

The woman scrambled off of the lounger. She was tiny. Like, epically tiny. The top of her head came to Mina's armpit. Possibly. She was also strikingly beautiful, in a way that didn't look overly enhanced. People could alter their appearance easily, and they did often, but after that process, they tended to look too perfect or formulaic in some way.

Petra Pebbles had symmetrical features, but not overly so, full lips, high cheekbones, a chin with a perfect dent in it, lush lashes, and a cascade of black hair flowing around her shoulders. Everything fit together in just the right way to make it all work.

Mina was relieved to see that she hadn't diffracted her eyes pink to go along with her pink sleep wrap and nightgown. The woman hadn't even bothered to get dressed.

The vid star rushed forward dramatically, tossing her arms out, her face expressive and full of artfully drawn anguish, her bare feet partially hidden by the cotton candy floor covering. Mina glimpsed a hyperglo toenail blinking pink here and there as she moved.

When she arrived at her destination, Petra Pebbles grasped Mina's arm, a carbon copy of the gesture Suzanne had already made today, and began to pull Mina toward the lounger she'd just vacated. "Thank goodness you're here!" she breathed. "I'm so scared. My life is in danger! And those...those police individuals had no idea what to do. I couldn't trust them. What if they let them in here?"

Let who in?

Mina stopped in front of the lounger, glancing over Petra's head at Lee. Her partner was unsuccessfully suppressing a grin, and from his locked position at the edge of calamity, he wasn't planning on rescuing her from this hell anytime soon.

She cleared her throat. "Please sit down, Ms. Pebbles." She gently peeled the woman's pink-nailed hand off her forearm. "We're here to help. But in order to do so, we need to know exactly what's going on." Since they were coming in with virtually no information, they needed it all. "So start from the beginning. You feared that the PPF would let *who* in? We have our compucases here and are ready to take a look at the drive that was delivered."

"Okay. Okay. I'm sitting." Petra swept back her wrap and sat. A second later, she raised a limp arm toward her assistant like she couldn't muster the effort to lift it any higher. "Yola, please bring me a half glass of chilled lemon bubbles with a shot of ginseng. My nerves are shot." She didn't bother to ask if anybody else wanted anything.

Yola hopped to attention, rushing out of the room. Petra scooped her long, dark hair off her shoulders with both hands and tossed the mass behind her, then straightened her wrap, pulling it across her chest before slumping back into the gel-cush, because life was just so incredibly hard.

She was slight, so she looked like a child, even though she was a full-grown adult. Mina guessed she was around early thirties, but her topical enhancements were definitely geared to lead the viewer to believe she was in her early twenties.

Lee finally ventured into the area, taking a seat beside them in a velvety pink single lounger the color of a guava's insides, opening his compucase on his lap. "Ms. Pebbles, if you give me the drive, I can take a look at it while you fill my partner in on the details of how it came to be in your possession."

Petra glanced at Lee like she tolerated his request, nothing more. She made a show of gathering herself, scootching forward and tucking her legs underneath herself, making sure she was good and comfy before she answered, "Well, I don't have it near me, of course.

Because what if it's contaminated? Or poisoned? That happened to me one time in a vid. It was called the *Spying Squirrels*. Did you see it?" She made a hopeful face.

Neither Mina nor Lee replied.

"Well, the spies all lived in this very tall spire, and they delivered things back and forth using squirrels. I was one of the spies, but you know, the main one." She reached back and scooped her hair forward this time, molding it down the length of her chest, a move Mina figured she made often. "In the vid, I received this encrypted device in the mail, not from a squirrel, because my squirrel had been taken hostage by then."

Mina did not change her expression. It was hard, but she kept her face completely straight.

The vid star continued, "It came in the old-timey mail, like when they used to use paper and everything. I opened it, but I didn't know it was poisoned, and I got this powdery stuff all over my hands." She splayed both of hers in front of her face, waving them around slowly, her expression becoming trancelike as she tracked the movements, clearly channeling her vid character...or someone...or something. At this rate, it would take them an eternity to get the story out of her about the device she'd received. "Then I started convulsing." She began to act it out, heaving her chest, clamping her hands across her breasts.

Mina cleared her throat.

Loudly.

Petra stopped her full-body mime and threw Mina a

questioning glance. As calmly as Mina could, she explained, "It's unlikely that what you received was poisoned. If someone is demanding something from you, like beauty secrets, it's likely that we're dealing with extortion. And when people try to extort, they need the recipient healthy so they can receive the payout they're hoping for. If you could retrieve the device for us, that would be wonderful."

"Yola!" Petra half moaned, half screamed as she collapsed back into the lounger again. "Bring the thingy in here. The tech-chip thing." Like her assistant didn't know the reason why Mina and Lee were here.

What was taking Yolanda so long to get her boss some lemon bubbles, anyway? Maybe Yola took her own sweet time on purpose. And the reason Petra had been asleep on the lounger when they'd come in was because Yola had told her she was going to pick up Mina and Lee an hour ago, then had sat down in that decked-out transpo hub to enjoy a cup of her own ginseng, along with some blissful drama-free solitude.

At least, that's what Mina would do.

Yolanda hustled back into the room in the next three seconds with a glass that looked remarkably like real, cut crystal, judging by its multifaceted angles and the way it sparkled in the light of the magnificent windows. A fresh lemon wedge bobbed on the surface of the liquid as it was transported, one-handed, on a gleaming silver tray. As the assistant neared the lounger, she slid a foot through the fluffy floor covering, tapping something unseen.

The cotton candy cloud broke apart seamlessly, like a

mouth suddenly gaping open, and a sleek, automated table emerged on a thin titanium rod. It rose up out of the pink dust like salvation in the form of convenience. Yolanda dusted off any lingering fibers and set down the tray. Then she swiveled the table and lowered it to rest right in front of the vid star princess in her pink sleep wrap on her pink lounger.

Honestly, if it hadn't all been so painfully orchestrated, it would've been amazing. Mina could totally use one of those tables. She didn't even want to look at Lee. She knew the rookie was overwhelmed.

Petra, very carefully, like she was extracting a precious alloy out of a mountain of slurry, grasped the edges of a tiny square drive, plucking it off the tray. Once it was in the air, she had no idea what to do with it.

Lee shifted his compucase off his lap and hustled over, settling his palm underneath to catch the piece of tech.

A very relieved Petra dropped it into his waiting hand with an exaggerated sigh.

Lee took it back and inserted it into his super-computer, a very sleek pico that could tabulate data at quantum speeds.

Within a second of insertion, Lee jerked up his head.

Mina knew that look. She stood, moving over to his chair. "What?"

"It's vague."

"Lee, what do they want?"

"Ms. Pebbles must grant them access to some sort of secret recipes or they plan to expose her for being...a murderer."

CHAPTER 13

A SOFT *THUMP* sounded, and Mina and Lee both glanced up. Petra had fainted and was sliding off her overstuffed lounger, missing the handy electronic table by a centimeter, then collapsing into the cotton candy, face first.

"Oh my goodness! Petra! Petra!" Yolanda rushed to her side, kneeling and lightly shaking her boss by the shoulders as she turned her over.

Mina ignored the collapsed vid star in favor of gathering more details.

She guided Lee up off the chair, walking him to a nearby table, an incredibly large, glass monstrosity. At least it wasn't pink. Mina ignored the spindle legs that were in fact tinted the color of old-fashioned bubblegum. "Where are the screens in here?" Mina called to Yolanda, who was still huddled next to her boss.

"Can't you see she's collapsed? We need to get a medi-unit in here!" Yolanda was in full panic mode.

"She fainted," Mina assured the assistant. "She's going to be fine. It's not every day you get called a murderer." Murderess? "Her response is fairly appropriate, in my estimation. Now, where are the screens? There are no full walls in here." For the first time, Mina realized they were in a circular unit. Half walls shielded what Mina assumed was the meal-prep area and a sleeping area, but none of these walls would be an expansive enough surface. "We need to get this data up where we can see it and manipulate it."

"Sebastian, engage living-area screens, full display," Yolanda commanded.

The male house sim, in a very prim and proper voice, answered, "Engaging screens."

Directly in front of the amazing windows, screens emerged from the floor, purring up soundlessly, blocking all outside light within seconds.

They were massive.

"Authorize voice access for both Agent Lee Adams and Agent Mina Kane," Mina instructed Yolanda, ignoring Lee's geeky moans. "We need to link our comps with full access."

Screens emerging from the floor wasn't necessarily new technology. Many people had hidden screens. It was the sheer quantity and size of these, not to mention their micro-beveled edges and super-silky nonglare surfaces. Once they had come up seamlessly from the floor, they'd morphed together to form one unit. These alone would cost in the hundreds of thousands of borrows. Since Petra Pebbles was above borrows, they had cost her some serious currency.

Yolanda did as Mina asked.

"Lee, get this information up on the screen. I'm going to make sure Ms. Pebbles is okay." Reluctantly, Mina made her way over to the vid star. Petra was on her back, blinking up from the floor cloud. What *was* this stuff? Maybe elastomer blended with carbon fiber? Just a guess. "Ms. Pebbles, there is a significant threat to you outlined in these demands." This op was becoming a little more serious than guard duty. "I'm going to need to hear your side of things quickly so we can put this together and figure out what needs to be done." Mina reached down to help the petite vid star out of her pink swirl.

Petra latched on to her arm once again. This time, she gripped it like it was a lifeline, climbing her way up Mina. She didn't have to go very far, because she was so tiny, but it was strange. Everything about her was so overly dramatic. Mina wished Kaylee were here to bear witness. Her pal would have some choice words that would likely fly right over Petra's head and sail straight into the galaxy and beyond. Not to mention what the song would sound like. Mina suppressed a small smile.

"You don't believe them, do you?" Petra wailed. "I don't even know who these people are!"

"We don't make judgments. We gather information. First, how did this piece of tech come to be in your possession?" The fact that they were still on step one wasn't lost on Mina. All her internal smiles disappeared.

With her hands still firmly clutched around Mina's forearm, Petra darted a worried glance at her assistant. "You'll have to ask Yola. She handles all the deliveries.

Fans send me so many things, we can't possibly have them all delivered here. We have a special pickup box at MegaMail. It's where all the vid stars—"

"The delivery came here, ma'am," Yolanda answered primly. "The concierge on level one sent it to the concierge on level twenty, who sent it to our personal concierge, Davion, who alerted me. I went to retrieve it at nine a.m. It was wrapped in a pretty pink box with a pretty pink bow. You were either taking a steam immersion, or were having your biotic intake readings analyzed."

The fact that it was wrapped in pink, Petra Pebbles' so ridiculously obvious favorite color, meant that whoever sent it to her knew her predilection for the color, which could mean anyone if Petra wrapped herself in pink all the time. Mina would have to look into it.

"That's right. It came directly here." Petra nodded, unable to shield her confusion. Or unwilling to, since she was obviously a skilled actress. She had no earthly recollection of what her assistant did or didn't do. How could somebody operate so cluelessly? "That's right!" Petra settled the back of her hand on her forehead. "I was getting my biotic readings! You brought it in. It was wrapped up so eloquently. I thought it was a treat." She frowned, dropping her arm. "But it wasn't. It was the opposite of a treat."

"How did you read what was on the device?" Mina asked. The piece of tech obviously required a reading device.

"Oh, I have three or four supercomputers around here

somewhere." Petra made a half-hearted attempt to glance around. "Yola did it. She told me the awful things it said. That's when we called the PPF." Now they were getting somewhere. "But when they were on their way over, I vid chatted with my best friend, Cuticle Cantrell. Do you know her?" Petra gave Mina another earnest look, searching for recognition.

Mina returned the earnestness with a blank stare. This woman had to get to the meat of the story.

"She and I starred in this vid together called—"

"Did your friend advise against dealing with the PPF?" Mina interrupted. And she would keep interrupting.

"Of course! She *loves* me." Petra settled her hands into an X across her chest, taking in a deep breath. "She was in this vid called *Heartbreak Robbery* where the PPF do all this bad stuff. She said the PPF don't handle serious crimes. They just arrest people who use jetties in the pedestrian lanes and people who break into kiosks. They don't do big cases. For those, you need *professionals.*" She'd uttered the word in a breathy, exaggerated tone. Professionals were Mina and Lee, but the vid star failed to make the connection. "She was in this other vid called—"

Mina shot Yolanda a look. "You didn't tell her about the murder part, did you?" If the original report had included the word *murder*, things would've happened differently. The PPF, upon being denied entry, would've contacted the federal government. Murder was not the same type of crime as demanding someone hand over some beauty secrets. But they hadn't. Petra had.

There had to be a reason. Mina was looking right at her.

Yolanda massaged her neck, looking worried, her eyes darting to Petra, then back to Mina. "I...I told her that some very bad people wanted her to give them her beauty secrets, or they would..." Her neck was starting to get red because she was fussing with it so much "Try to smear her name."

"They can't do that!" Petra warbled. "I worked very hard to make my name recognizable. They have no right. It's *my* name." Nothing about being a murderer. Apparently, that wasn't as concerning to her as a smear attempt.

Mina growled under her breath. "Murder is a very, very serious charge. Why would someone imply that you murdered someone?"

"I don't know," she whined. "One time, in this vid, I played a serial killer's muse—"

"This is not a vid you once starred in. If you did murdery things, I suggest we start hearing about them right now." Mina glanced over at Lee, lowering the edge in her voice with effort. "Is everything on screen?"

"Yeah," he answered. "The message is really strange. It's meant to look old-fashioned, like someone cut words out of an old book or something. I'm not quite sure."

Mina, Petra, and Yolanda all moved toward the screen. Petra gasped as she rushed up, placing her hand on it. "This...this is from a vid I did."

Please not another vid. So many vids. So...many.

"It was set back in time about a hundred years, when they used to have something called magazines. They printed them and passed them around every week or every day. I'm not sure. Anyway, they were made of paper, and they contained colorful prints and words on every page, like a book, but more colorful. Anyway, in the vid, the killer cut out words like these and sent them to all his victims. I was his main target, the only survivor. She was an *absolute* heroine. Her name was Maureena Manslooter, and she—"

"So," Mina concluded in a decibel to efficiently stop the purge of vid nonsense, "whoever sent you this knows you enjoy the color pink and knows your vids." Not a huge amount to go on, seeing as how Mina had been here for twenty-three minutes, and she already knew Petra loved pink and was obsessed with her vids. "They are trying to scare you by using things you're familiar with."

"I'm not scared." Petra pressed her hands to her hips, jutting out a leg.

Mina crossed her arms.

The vid star dropped her hands. "Fine. I'm a little scared. But I don't understand what all this is." She turned back to the screen. Lee had pumped up the percentage so the words were huge. She walked along, following them. It read:

You have twenty-four hours to produce your beauty recipes, or we will expose you for what you are. A murderer.

The word *murderer* was in mismatched pink letters falling down the page.

"Recipes are different than secrets," Mina pondered. "No contact information is given, so even if you wanted to, you can't deliver what they want." What they wanted was vague, too. Usually, extortionists were very thorough and wanted their payment quickly. She turned to Lee. "Is there anything else on the drive? Anything traceable?"

"Not that I saw at first glance," Lee answered, heading back to his compucase. "But I'm running a number of searches right now. I can probably find something traceable, at least where the drive was manufactured, where it was purchased, things like that."

Mina decided to redirect Petra back to the lounger, her happy place. She sat her down. Mina stood next to it, trying to be patient. This was no longer guard duty. It was an actual op. "I'm going to ask you a series of questions, and I need you to answer them quickly. No stories. Just answers. Can you do that?"

The vid star's eyes were a little misty, but she nodded.

Yolanda came up behind Mina. "May I sit with her?"

"Sure. Go ahead." Mina waited as Petra's assistant went to her side, looping her arm around her shoulders.

"You can do this, ma'am," Yolanda pep-talked her boss. "These nice detectives will figure it out, and your life will go back to normal in no time."

Petra clutched Yola's hand. "Thank you. I appreciate that. I know I'm hard to work for sometimes, but I'm happy you're here with me."

Mina raised a brow, happy they were bonding, but now was not the time. She ignored the detective comment, because some people could not be trained. "Have you ever killed anyone?" Why not start off with a bang?

The vid star's mouth dropped open, and she began to yammer.

Mina held up her hand. "Very brief answers only. In the realm of yes, no, and a brief explanation."

"Of course not! Why would I kill anyone? I have no reason to kill anyone."

The note hadn't accused her of an accidental death. Murder involved intent and, sometimes, planning. But whoever was making the accusation was also trying to extort something from her. Mina would get to that next.

"What about accidentally? Maybe something happened, an altercation you walked away from? Then later, you found out that the person died? People tend to hold grudges when it comes to death. What about in your younger years?"

Petra shook her head.

"In order for us to figure out who sent this to you and why, we have to pinpoint a time frame. Once we do that, we can start investigating people who were around you during that time. This is what investigating looks like. I need honest answers." *And hurry up about it.*

"There's nothing! I swear. I moved to this city when I was seventeen. Nothing happened when I was younger. Nothing has happened since I've been here."

"Okay, let's try another angle." Mina paced in the fluff. "What are the beauty recipes they are referring to? They must be pretty important to try to extort you with murder."

Petra lofted her arms to the ceiling in a very dramatic motion, the sleeves of her sleep wrap slipping down to her shoulders. "I don't have *any* beauty recipes. Why would I have beauty recipes? I buy high-end products, just like every other vid star on the planet. I need the best on the market, because when I'm on set, I have to look flawless. I don't *make* anything."

Mina shifted her gaze to Yolanda. "Do you know anything about beauty recipes? Nobody uses recipes for food anymore, because we all have meal printers. But everything we print or create came from a recipe, or it would be impossible to know how to make them."

Yolanda shook her head.

"What products does Petra use?" Mina tried again. "Can you go gather up a few samples for me?"

"Yes. Of course. I'll get some right away." Yolanda stood, rushing out of the room, heading in the opposite direction of where she'd gone to get the lemon bubbles.

Mina paced to the table where Lee was still hunched over his compucase. "What've you got? I'm going to have to report to our director very soon. Things on this op have shifted considerably."

"The device has been scraped clean, and by that, I mean someone injected a virus to sanitize it once the data was loaded. It's a powerful one, too, something hackers refer to as an annihilator. It had a six-hour lag, and it's due to deteriorate into nothing in less than an hour. We got here just in time. But don't worry, I've made several copies." He glanced up. "I've already uploaded them to our secure government database and copied Director McAllister."

Good going, Rookie. Way to *not* squirrel away those

nuts. Hackers tended to hoard. Lee was unlearning those skills nicely. It was good hackers didn't crack codes by sending messages by squirrel. Now Mina was thinking in terms of vids. *Ugh.*

"Why wouldn't they send specific directions for Petra to follow? They threatened to expose her for murder, but then they gave her no way to deliver the recipes. Are they assuming she won't take this seriously?" They'd been with the vid star for a half hour. That was an accurate assumption.

"That's a strong possibility," Lee said. "We've seen how she...handles things." His voice was low. Mina glanced over to see if Petra was eavesdropping, but she was engrossed in her lemon bubbles at the moment, likely pondering how she got into this excrement of a mess. "They know enough about her to get the device through to her concierge, and it was wrapped the way she would like it. It's pretty safe to think they knew she wouldn't take it too seriously right away."

"So how are they going to ramp it up to get her attention?" Mina asked. "Another threatening note?" A definite possibility. "We need to, at the very least, get a tracer cam on the concierges, and we need to get authorization to view the vid feed throughout The Bella." She was preparing to call her director on her cuff when Yolanda rushed in.

She carried something aloft in her hand.

"I just found this!" Yolanda called. "It was lying on Petra's pillow. I swear it wasn't there even an hour ago."

It was a tiny pink box wrapped in a silky pink bow.

Chapter 14

"SET IT ON the table," Mina directed. To Lee, she said, "We're going to have to get some specialized equipment in here. While I get hold of McAllister, you keep running scans." To Petra, who had moved to the table, and Yolanda, who looked like she'd seen a ghost, Mina ordered, "Don't touch *anything*. I'm going to contact my director to get some things delivered to analyze this package. Where can I make a call in relative privacy?"

Mina had to ask twice, as both women were clutching each other and murmuring quietly.

"You can use my sleep room," Petra finally answered, gesturing toward the curve Yolanda had just emerged from around.

"I'll be right back." Mina headed in that direction. She passed a partial room divider. All along the corridor were more beautiful windows with spectacular views of the city. So much to see.

Too bad Mina was too distracted to enjoy the view.

She entered Petra's lavish private space and was absolutely stunned to see the absence of the color pink.

No pink. Anywhere.

The entire space was absolutely colorless. No chrome, silver, or any other kind of accents. Just white. It was like Mina had stepped into a purifier. She'd heard of having themed rooms, but this was a stunner. Maybe whoever had sent the package didn't know Petra that well after all, assuming they hadn't been back here.

The room itself was beautiful. No surprises there. One door led to, Mina assumed, a waste room. A huge platform bed took up three square meters in the middle. It was the biggest Mina had ever seen. All snow white.

Mina tapped her cuff with her direct link to McAllister.

"Report, Agent Kane."

"This op has elevated from light duty to extortion with the threat of accusing Petra Pebbles of murder. Agent Adams has sent you the message."

"I've received and reviewed it. What are your thoughts?"

"I'm not sure yet. I'm having a hard time getting a read on Ms. Pebbles. She's...dramatic. But we've just received a second pink box, including what I believe will be another message. It's uncertain at this time, as we will wait to open it until we scan it. Yolanda Terrin, Petra Pebbles' executive assistant, found it wrapped in the same manner, resting on Ms. Pebbles' pillow in her sleep room. I'm requesting a DNA sampling kit, a multisurface helix wand, microgoggles, the works. We need to collect whatever we can from the outside of the package before we open it. Yolanda swears it wasn't there an hour ago.

That means someone was in here without their knowledge. Or someone figured out a delivery technique, perhaps using a bot. Or Yolanda herself could be behind this. If she is, she's a world-class actress." Not out of the realm of possibilities. They had to follow all the leads.

"Everything you'll need will be delivered in the next ten by Agent Darian. After you've done the scans and opened it up, she will bring the box back here to undergo a more thorough inspection and testing. If the package was placed by a service bot, the bot will have a record of the day's activities."

Mina hadn't seen any bots in the residence. "I'll have Ms. Pebbles call someone from The Bella in charge of bots so we can interview them. It's the most logical place to start."

"Agreed," McAllister said. "Accusing a very popular vid star of murder is a serious crime. It seems Ms. Pebbles left off some vital details when she had her case opened with the federal government."

"She did, but it wasn't entirely her fault." Was Mina sticking up for the vid star? Seems she was. "Her assistant took it upon herself to soften the blow and omitted the murder accusation."

"I see. Agent Darian is on her way." Mina was always impressed with McAllister's ability to multitask. "Report back as soon as you open the package."

"Will do."

Mina made her way back to the main living area, where Lee was hovered over the package, a scanner in his hand.

"There are no electrical or chemical currents issuing out," he informed her. "So we can safely assume there's nothing in here that will detonate."

"That's nice to hear," Mina said. "Agent Darian is delivering everything we need. She'll be here in five." Mina addressed Yolanda, who was comforting the vid star back on the lounger. "Agent Anna Darian will be landing shortly. Will you please go meet her in the hub and bring her up as quickly as you can? We're going to analyze this package before we open it. If there's any trace DNA on it, we'll have more clues to work with."

Yola looked to her boss for confirmation. Petra nodded. "Go." The assistant hurried off. Petra asked Mina in a worried tone, "What does this mean? How did that box get in my sleep room?"

"That's what we're going to explore next. Do you own any bots? Or does The Bella provide you with bot services?"

"I don't own any. Bots are provided," Petra confirmed. "I pay top currency for this place, and I have access to anything I need at any time. Chef bots, spa bots, cleaning bots. There's even one who will read a book to you."

Mina kept her eyeballs steady in their sockets. "Let's focus on bots that are on a regular schedule. Do you use any of the same bots daily?"

"Yes. In the morning, Betty One comes in to take my biotic readings and give me a light massage. Betty Three comes in after to do some light cleaning."

"So Betty Three has access to your sleep room area by herself?" Mina asked.

Petra looked momentarily confused, then her eyes widened. "Yes! Betty Three is in there every single morning. She makes my platform for me and cleans my waste room."

"Did she do that this morning?"

"I think so." Petra appeared uncertain. The woman took minimal notice of the world around her. She would make a terrible CIU agent.

"I'd like you to summon her, along with the air breather in charge. I'm assuming they all come from the same place? A bot hub of some kind?"

"They do. The top five floors of The Bella share the same bot pool. But there's plenty to go around. I prefer the Bettys. I like how they look, act, and speak. They're very cultured."

Good to know. Mina's eyes were tired from her constantly checking her eye rolls. Who knew it was more tiring not to eye roll than to eye roll? Bots couldn't be cultured, but they could be programmed to act like a cultured human. There was a difference. "Please get her up here."

Petra leaned over her cuff to make the order as Mina turned back to Lee.

The rookie had stuffed the wand back in his pocket. She beckoned him toward the screens, away from Petra, and kept her voice low. "Did you find anything else?"

"One thing. Along with the virus, the message contained a tiny imprint, like a watermark. Inserting one into a device this small is a specialized process. It's not generated by data or an image. It's a stamping process inside the tech itself, so we can assume it's there on purpose. If Petra had called in somebody else who was competent, they'd probably have found it. Maybe. I mean, if they were good."

"Good like you?" Mina grinned. It was awesome having a hacker as a partner. "What does the watermark look like?"

Lee headed to his compucase. "I took a picture of it." He keyed in a few commands, and an image popped up on the screen behind them.

Mina walked closer. "It kind of looks like a leaf. Or maybe a teardrop?"

"That's what I think, too," Lee said.

Mina called over her shoulder, "Petra, does this symbol up on the screen mean anything to you?"

The vid star glanced up briefly. "Is that a leaf? I don't think so. It doesn't look familiar."

"Not really a leaf," Mina murmured, examining it. "Pump it up forty percent larger." Lee amplified the image. "I think it's a flower petal. The scalloping is really subtle, but you can see more detail at this size."

Lee nodded, coming to stand beside her. "Kind of looks like a rose petal."

"Yes." After all, Mina was familiar with roses now. One small point in the center, with wide scallops on either side. She called over her shoulder, "Why would whoever sent this to you include a rose-petal imprint?"

The vid star shrugged, eyes still on her cuff. "I have no idea. Betty Three and the bot manager are on their way up."

Sebastian, Petra's sim, announced, "Arrival of pre-authorized personnel in three seconds."

Petra hadn't been kidding. The staff here must pop to attention when their wealthiest customers wanted something.

The tube gave one melodic ding, and the doors swished open.

A man in a tidy dark suit and perfectly shellacked hair came out first, followed by a bot who looked too glamorous to be a bot. Long, flowing, platinum hair, features so precise they looked as fake as they were, flawless enhancement applications, likely built in. She wore a black suctioned one-piece uni with white piping and tall, spindly black heels.

This was what Petra deemed "cultured."

The air breather bent his torso downward in a bow to Petra.

He straightened. "Hello, Ms. Pebbles. It's a pleasure to serve you. What can I help you with?"

Serve you? Creepy.

Petra didn't so much as blink. "Hello, Daniel. Thank you for coming so quickly and bringing Betty Three. I've had some unfortunate events happen recently, and this detective would like to speak to you." She gestured to Mina.

"I'm not a detective." Mina came forward, extending her hand. "I'm a federal agent investigating a package that was sent to Ms. Pebbles today, or rather, two packages. We're hoping you can answer some questions, Mr....?"

He reached out to shake Mina's proffered hand. "My surname is Haroldson. You may call me Daniel."

"Thank you for coming so promptly, Daniel." Mina glanced behind her, happy that Lee had had the wherewithal to blank the screens before Daniel and the bot entered. "How many bots do you oversee?"

"Twenty-one," Daniel answered efficiently. Mina appreciated that.

"Is it possible for someone to intercept a bot and ask it to perform an additional task, such as deliver a package?"

Daniel frowned. "I don't think so. The bots use internal tubes that hook up with the private residences, and the entry to the bot hub is secured by DNA and retinal." He gestured to the bot in question. "Go ahead and ask Betty Three what she did today. Her memory bank remains unaltered for thirty days, then it overprints. I could download all the bots' daily interactions, but we try to avoid that to keep the privacy of our guests and residents intact." He bobbed his head toward Petra. "It's of extreme importance for us to protect the privacy of all our clients here at The Bella."

There was no doubt that clients and guests alike absolutely wanted to maintain their privacy and paid a lot of currency to do so.

Mina turned toward the bot. "Betty Three, did you come into this residence this morning to do your daily cleaning?"

The bot nodded. "I was here at eight a.m. sharp. Ms. Pebbles has me clean the private areas of her household."

"Did you deliver a package today?"

The bot cocked her head in a very robotic way before she straightened it. "What do you mean by 'package'?"

Mina gestured toward the table. "Did you place the item sitting on that table on Ms. Pebbles' pillow?"

The bot didn't answer.

"Betty Three, answer the question," Daniel commanded. "Did you deliver that package this morning?"

Betty responded, "Pack...pack...package. Give...give...to...Peb...Pebbles." The bot shook her head, the motion appearing more human this time. "It seems my internal programming has been slightly skewed. Please let me rewind it and play it again for you."

"That's not necessary," Mina said, dismissing her. Having used the hyppie trick recently, she knew it when she heard it. "Mr. Haroldson, we will need to take Betty Three in for a full evaluation. I believe that on her way up, this bot was subjected to bot hypnosis, which is a tool for sanctioned use only by the federal government. So whoever has access to the technology either works for the federal government or has obtained it illegally." Daniel began to sputter, but Mina waved it away. "A federal agent will be arriving shortly. She will give you an inventory data card. The bot will be returned unaltered within twenty-four hours. We will pay a loss-of-use fee up to two hundred world currency for any inconvenience."

The sputtering stopped, and Daniel's face brightened considerably.

Mina had no doubt he would put the inconvenience fee toward his own convenience. She wasn't going to question the way things worked at The Bella, nor did she care.

Sebastian announced, "Arrival of expected guests in five seconds."

Chapter 16

"IT'S CLEAN," LEE announced. "I'm not detecting a single strand of DNA anywhere on this package. They must've used some industrial body covering or put it inside a vac after they handled it. I'm picking up molecules of carbon fiber, elastomer, polyresin, cotton re-creation, to name a few, but nothing human."

"They were careful. Not surprising," Mina responded. "Go ahead and open it." She turned to Agent Anna Darian, who'd helped them on the last few cases. "Can you hand me one of the sealing kits? Once it's open, we'll place it in there so you can transport it to the lab at headquarters. They likely won't find anything either, but we'll follow protocol."

Anna handed her a kit.

Mina opened it as Lee donned protective gloves of his own and unwrapped the bow.

Daniel Haroldson had left. Betty Three was shut down and sitting on a chair, awaiting Agent Darian's order.

Yolanda and Petra stood off to the side, watching the scene unfold.

Lee carefully lifted off the lid. Inside sat a piece of tech identical to the first device.

The rookie plucked it out, running several scanners over it, shaking his head. "It's clear." Then he took it over to his compucase. He used yet another scanner and glanced up once he was done. "This detects a few specific malware strains. It's very specialized. This scanner won't catch all of them, but it will detect the worst ones. It's free of anything that would blow up my system."

Excellent.

He stuck the tech into a small slot on his computer. Immediately, another letter using the same blocky, cut-out letters popped on the screen.

SEE YOU TONIGHT! WEAR YOUR BEST ENHANCEMENTS!

Mina shot a look at Petra. "What's tonight?"

Petra's face brightened like she was about to give Mina the *best* news. "Just a huge, ultralux vid-release party," Petra squealed. "My brand-new vid, *Beyond the Beyonders*, opens tonight. Release parties are so much fun." She clapped her hands like a second message with an implied threat hadn't just shown up on her wall. "For this one, they booked the Ultimax Dome." More high-pitched squealing.

Mina wanted to stick a finger in her ear and rub it.

"Hundreds of thousands of people attend," she droned on. "Both in person and virtually. It's going to be super-out-of-the-strato spec. I'm the lead, naturally. The character's name is Sissy Sisbeck, and she—"

"You can't go." Mina shut her down. "Someone is trying to blackmail you and is willing to publicly accuse you of being a murderer. Even if it's not true, it would be damaging to your career to be accused in such a public venue. Not to mention, it could be dangerous—"

Petra stamped her foot. "Of course I'm going! It's *my* vid. Weren't you listening? I'm the *lead*. I'm the *star*. I'm why people show up. I don't miss premieres. They can make or break a production. I'm going!"

Mina blew out a prolonged sigh. "We don't know who is sending these messages. Physical harm is not out of the question. We haven't even delved into what these so-called beauty recipes are or how you're supposed to deliver them." There was so much wrong with this case. It was a stinky sulfur bomb. Suli could smell it from here.

Dealing with Petra was like dealing with a kindertot, and the level of intelligence was on par.

Yolanda politely said, "If I may interject here. Ms. Pebbles is under contract by several corporations who produce these vids. I believe those contracts stipulate that she can't miss a premiere unless she's...incapacitated because of severe bodily harm and is in a medi-unit, or is...deceased. There are no other exceptions."

Mina crossed her arms. "Whoever is behind these messages knows where Petra will be tonight. There's a good chance they're looking forward to publicly humiliating her, or why would they send something like that?" Mina gestured at the screen. "This is not a typical extortion case. There is no clear sense of direction. No details, no framework. No communication channels have been provided. Anyone who goes to the trouble of doing something like this wants payment quickly and efficiently. This time, in the form of beauty recipes, which is unclear in and of itself. This rings like they understand Petra won't do anything they ask, so they're essentially giving her fair warning." Mina glanced directly at Petra. "Meaning that if you attend this thing tonight, you can expect something big and unpleasant to happen." Mina raised her eyebrows. "I can pretty much guarantee it."

Petra remained the carbon copy of a petulant kindertot. "I don't care. I told you I don't miss premieres. It's release night, which is the biggest night for the life-cycle of a vid. After tonight, no one ever talks about it as much. Other vid stars will be there. It's always a competition. I have a career to safeguard. My fans will be waiting. I worked my entire life for recognition like this, and I'm not giving it up for anything. I didn't murder anyone!" she whined. "I have nothing to hide. As my assistant just explained, if I don't show, and I'm not dead or unconscious in a medi-unit, I will be in breach of contract and owe thousands in currency. I'm going. You can't stop me. If anything, I can just fire you like I did the PPF. Then I can be done with all of this."

This woman clearly had no idea how extortion worked. Asking the investigators to leave wouldn't make the problem go away.

Actually, being fired would be a dream come true for Mina. Even though this had become more than a fluff job, it still wasn't a sure bet to be classified as a high crime. Beauty recipes? Barely threatening notes written in a way that Petra didn't even understand, nor was she even worried about? The whole thing was lacking.

Yet there was still something there.

And Mina was stubborn. She had an op to complete. She didn't like this spoiled vid star overly much, but whatever endgame the writer of these notes intended, it would go down tonight.

Mina caught Lee's and Anna's gazes. The rookie shrugged, and Anna appeared a little shocked, like she couldn't believe what was happening and that this petulant child would insist she knew better than a government agent.

That made two of them.

"What time is this thing at?" Mina had to talk to her director. McAllister would ultimately make the call.

"Ten p.m.," Yolanda replied. "We need to be there by eight."

"If you're coming, you have to dress appropriately," Petra countered, swishing her hand up and down the front of Mina. "I'm not having a bunch of stiffs trailing me like robomanikins. This is a glitzy affair. Lots of sparkle. Over-the-top looks. People count on it. If you go like that"—she swirled her arm in the air—"you will stand out as exactly who you are. The police."

Mina sighed. "We're not the police. We're federal agents. And we know how to do our jobs. I need to check in with my director to see what our orders are. If it were up to me, we would let you go alone and resume operations after this"—super-glitzy, special, indulgent, careless—"event. But it won't be up to me. First, Agent Darian needs to deliver the box and Betty Three to headquarters. Then, Agent Adams and I are going to finish analyzing the second device, which we will do at another location. It's only three p.m. We have time. I'll let you know the plan accordingly. If we're ordered to attend your event, we will pick you up here at seven forty-five and escort you to the Ultimax Dome. You must contact us immediately if you receive any more pink boxes. Or any other boxes or messages in any form."

"We always take lux transpo," Petra said. "A full white escort drone with all the frills. There will be media and film crews awaiting my arrival. I do interviews, pose for image shots with my fans, the works. It's a lava-flow night."

"It will be arranged." Mina was pretty certain her director would want them to see this night through, which would mean catering to this vid star on the government's currency tab.

"Great!" Petra chirped. "Now I have to go get ready." She checked her cuff. "Several bots are due in ten to get me started."

Mina wondered why this hadn't been brought up from the start. She was at a loss, because it was clear this woman was done focusing on crime for the day.

"We'll be in touch," Mina settled on. "I'll need both of you available the rest of the afternoon to answer any questions we might have. It's nonnegotiable."

Honestly, trying to gain anything of value out of Petra at this point—the vid star had formally shifted gears in her brain—would be like trying to milk a meal printer, but they had a job to do.

"Fine." Petra swished her hand. "Whatever."

"I can't believe you're attending a vid premiere," Kaylee said from her position on Mina's sleep room wall. She drummed her hands on her thighs like she was about to announce the winner of an exciting contest or break out into song. "That's *so* funny! What are the chances? We were just having a conversation about vid stars this morning. I don't know whether to be jealous or hyena-cackle hysterically. You're the least-vid-starry-premiere person the world has ever seen. Turn around. I need another gander at the back again." She called, "Harmony! Bring in the snacks. You *have* to see this!"

"I don't need the super-rookie's critique on this abomination," Mina groused. "And I'm pretty sure hyena cackles are winning. You haven't laughed this hard since you took down that guy dressed like an actual clown in the middle of that kid's birth-year party."

"That *was* hysterical. Remember that kid's face? Right before he launched into that screaming fit? Classic. Oh, the wide-eyed innocence of childhood. And that clown was a menace to society. Felt good." Kaylee chortled. "And yes, you need Harmony's critique. She and I are spending quality time, per McAllister's orders, and this puts the Q in quality."

Mina did as her friend asked, and as she turned, the metallic fabric clinging to her body crinkled, making it sound like she was inside a grinder. She was more stable on the metallic scissor-heeled boots she'd insisted on rather than the spindly meter-high heels Jeni Crisfold, her longtime designer at Dutiful Duds, had wanted her to don.

"Holy mother of all comets spinning across the universe!" Harmony shouted as she came into view. "Tell me that outfit is real, and you're not playing a holo trick on us."

"Of course it's real," Mina said. "How do I holo-trick you when you're looking at me through a 2-D screen?" She turned around to face the wall.

Kaylee was guffawing too hard to comment.

"It's just way, way out there." Harmony giggled. "I mean, I've seen vid stars wear stuff like that at these premieres. I just didn't think it happened to normal people. Especially not to federal agents. It's just...weird."

Weird was the perfect word.

And creepy. *Creepy* was a very underused adjective when it came to fashion clothing. But this outfit did creep Mina out.

"I've worn unis and costumes my whole career, and you will, too—it's part of the job," Mina educated the super-rookie in her best mentor-y voice. "But you're right, this one is particularly...weird. I've never worn anything that made this much noise, or was this...puffy and crinkly."

Jeni had done a superb job on short notice. The confection—because there wasn't a better word for it— was a shiny metallic gray with a silver patina. Mina had no idea what it was made out of, as it was both silky and smooth, especially where it molded to her body on top like a skin suit, coming up high at the neck. Then, at the taper of her waist, huge circles began to jut out at odd intervals all the way down to her ankles.

It appeared as though a bubble machine had exploded all over her, and some of the bubbles were midpop.

"Well, your chest area looks nice. Great fit." Kaylee made a purring sound. "But *damn*. That bottom part is total chaos." She was being nice. So nice. "Touch one of those protruding things. I want to see how you're going to sit in that thing."

Mina pressed her hand against one of the globs. It went down easily with no sharp edges, then sprang back once she released her hand, giving off a tiny crinkle of sound. "I have no idea what the stuff is." Mina shook her head. "Jeni is a maven when it comes to design. She assured me that this is an appropriate look for a vid premiere."

"Welp, nobody's going to recognize you, that's for sure," Kaylee said. "Once again, the skin cement is on par. Your face is altered just enough. Those who know you well will be able to recognize you. To anyone else, you're someone totally different. The silver hair mask works magnificently with the outfit as well. You're clearly going to rock this thing out, so okay, jealousy is starting to set in. Why you, of all people? You will so underappreciate this. No marmots gathering nuts anywhere near this thing."

"Marmots?" Harmony questioned. "Oh, is that inside girlspeak for boy, um, parts?"

"Not quite." Mina giggled. "Honestly, if you two want to take our places, that's fine with me. I'm sure Agent Adams will agree."

"We wish," Kaylee said. "But I'm teaching Harmony the seven rules of agenting tonight."

"I thought there were at least ten," Mina countered.

"There are only seven?" Harmony said. "Damn, I'm going to *kill* this thing."

"Not so fast," Kaylee replied. "Each of the seven has a hundred subcategories. Buckle yourself in. It's going to be a busy night."

Harmony's face fell. "Oh. Okay. But I'm a quick learner, so no probs."

"You're not great at everything. I just kicked your butt eating that maple treat."

"Yours was three times smaller than mine." Harmony rolled her eyes.

A girl after Mina's own heart.

"*Pul-eeze*, I ate two while you weren't looking. Snooze around here and you lose maple treats." Kaylee turned her attention back to Mina, flashing a bright smile. "Try to at least have a little fun tonight. Take it all in. Absorb it. It's likely you'll never be invited back."

Mina snorted. "Sadly, there will be minimal fun happening tonight. Lee and I analyzed the messages and a rose imprint all day. We did cross-checks with just about everything Petra could come up with relating to her life and activities, which wasn't much. She had a hard time squeezing us in between her bot appointments." Mina sighed. "We have nothing. No leads. No connections. It's like we haven't investigated anything. This is the weirdest extortion case I've ever been involved with. So we'll be on tonight trying to sleuth it all out."

"Sounds strange. Well, at least you can go in knowing nobody's going to know it's you under all that. Seriously, I know the alt is minimal, but it works. And your surface enhancements, especially around the eyes, are spec. It's like they're popping out of your head."

"Thanks?" Because Mina had been ordered to attend this event by her director, and the media would be present, it was important for her to be unrecognizable. And not just because she'd been spotted out with Vincent Kramer a week ago. In her line of work, since this kind of media event would be viewed by so many, she couldn't risk anyone picking her out as someone other than a hanger-on in Petra Pebbles' entourage. Even though vid stars weren't as popular as they used to be, enough people paid attention.

CIU agents, as she'd explained to Harmony, had to wear costumes often to mask their appearance. It was important that they maintain their cover so they could go into their next op clean.

"I've got to run," Mina said. "I'm picking Lee up in ten. I sent the rookie to Jeni as well, since he can't look like himself either. I'll be interested to see what she came up with."

"Snap some images," Harmony hooted. "Karmaseeker243 all dressed up for a vid premiere. Too bad I can't go on all the hacker boards and shout it to everybody. It would be some serious goss on the threads. Everyone would die. Flat out die." She made a noise out of the side of her mouth and clapped her hands together. "*Splat.* Dead."

Kaylee shot the super-rookie a look and held up two fingers. "That's the fourteenth subcategory under bullet point number two. When you become an agent, you leave your old life behind. Period. End of story. No goss. No boards. No fun." Kaylee shrugged. Mina could see her pal was suppressing a smile, but Harmony couldn't see it from her angle. "See why I don't take on babies? Too. Much. Work."

"Hey, I'm no baby," Harmony countered. "I can follow the rules just fine."

"Like you did today when we stood on that corner and I pointed out that guy? You immediately gawked—"

"I did *not* gawk. I don't even know *how* to gawk. I was simply looking in his general direction."

"I told you not to look. That was the whole point."

"See you two later." Mina giggled. "Try not to kill each other while I'm at this dumb premiere." Kaylee and Harmony completely ignored Mina. It wasn't even worth trying to interrupt, Mina had places to be, and she was content to leave them as two peas crammed in the very same pod. "Veronica, vid off." Mina's best pal and the super-rookie snapped off the screen. "Alert me when the lux personal drone arrives."

"Going someplace special tonight, Agent Kane?" Veronica asked.

Mina laughed. "I wish. It's just for work."

"Maybe this will be the night you meet someone special."

"Are you giving me relationship advice, Veronica?"

"It's just my work."

Chapter 16

"Lee? Is that you in there?" Mina slapped her thigh, the ridiculous bubbles squashing down, then bouncing back up. "You look like you're from a galaxy far, far away. On your planet, are people bipedal, or do they have wheels for feet?" Laughter tinkled out. She couldn't help herself. "I didn't even know your hair could do that. Did Jeni make that happen?"

Once the door to the lux passenger drone closed, the sim purred, "Travel time to Bellatone Tower one minute, forty-three seconds."

"Not exactly," he replied. "After she made me this." He glanced down the front of himself at the metallic one-piece outfit that matched Mina's vibe, except his was green. The outfit had a high, flared collar and a zipper that ran from his neck all the way down to the tops of his megaboots, printed in the same metallic green. The big and clumpy boots had thick toes and even thicker heels, adding at least four centimeters to Lee's height.

Zippers were a rarity. Most people preferred closures that were simple, like hidden mag-strips or gel-seams that glommed together like magic and pulled apart just as easily. "Once I had this on, she called up a friend of hers who works in a salon in the next building. Ferdie did my hair. Honestly, I haven't looked at it since I left. I don't really want to see it." He grimaced.

"Hmm. It's very interesting." Mina giggled for the last time. There had to be a laugh limit, or her partner wouldn't be getting out of this drone. Lee's hair had been temporarily dyed something close to auburn, but more muddy. A lot more. So, reddish brown. Then it'd been scooped up from around his face and shifted back like a giant wave flowing over the top of his head. Mina hadn't even known hair could do that. With the products they had these days, this proved anything was possible. "Shake it back and forth. I want to see if it moves."

Lee did. Nothing moved. It was like a syncrete helmet of hair.

"You don't look anything like yourself, which is exactly the point."

"It feels awful. I can't wait to wash this out. Ferdie gave me some special dissolvers. She said it might take one or two tries." Another grimace. He reached up to touch it.

"I wouldn't do that if I were you," Mina cautioned. "Just leave it alone. It does look cool, though. You look edgy. Like, if anybody disses your favorite vid, you'll set them straight with an open palm."

Lee glanced around the interior of the drone. "Whoa.

This is really nice. I've never been in a passenger-escort craft before."

The lux drone was oversized, the seating a creamy, soft syn-leather, the ultras decidedly low. Various compartments were packed full of treats and specialty items. The walls mimicked fabric in a soft off-white. Everything about it screamed lux.

Mina tried not to grumble as she slumped back in her seat. "It's too bad McAllister is making us attend this thing tonight. After all our research today, there is less than a three percent chance this extortion threat will turn physical. It's Petra's choice to attend, even though she knows there could be a public reveal of some kind. Not sure how anyone could convince people, especially her fans, that she's a murderer. No one around her and no close acquaintances of hers have died. It doesn't make sense."

Lee absentmindedly reached up to scratch his head, then abruptly dropped his hand. He shook his head instead. His hair stayed put. "I think the imprint is still key. I really think Petra should take a second look at it. It could trigger something in her memory. I'm pretty sure whoever inserted it put it there to taunt her, knowing she wouldn't think too hard about it. Which makes me think whoever is doing this knows her well."

"Knows her and has access to government equipment that can perform the hyppie trick on bots."

After a complete system check, it'd been verified that someone had indeed used a bot scrambler on Betty Three. Since the request to place a small gift on Petra's pillow hadn't been something that would harm the vid star, the bot had followed through with it. After all, delivering gifts and packages was something that all of these bots did with regularity.

"I keep wondering how they're planning to expose her," Lee said. "It doesn't make sense that they would demand these beauty recipes, but not give her a chance to produce them. It feels like publicly humiliating her is more the point. The whole thing is amateurish. Maybe this is all just a weird publicity stunt?"

Mina pondered that. "Accusing someone of murder seems like a very unlikely way to garner positive publicity. I mean, scandal is one thing. Everyone loves a juicy scandal. But having your fans believe you're a murderer? Even for a short time? I don't think so. This rings like a humiliation tactic. McAllister should've swapped us out with PPF for the night. They would've done a stellar job and would've been less noticeable. After all, these vid production agencies hire the PPF to monitor things all the time. Instead, we get to look like clowns." Mina sat up and scooted forward in her seat. They were nearing The Bella. "Just in case there are any issues, you brought your stunner, right?" Mina had her gem strapped to her thigh, completely masked by the flouncy bubbles. She was going to enjoy throwing this thing in the grinder when she got home.

"Yeah. There's no pocket, but Jeni added a gel-seam. I have my stunner skin-cemented to my stomach." He looked pleased. "Like you told me to do on the Tedesco op."

"Excellent." The rookie was maturing nicely. Definitely attributable to Mina's awesome mentoring skills.

"Landing at Bellatone Tower in thirty seconds," the sim announced through a perfectly tuned aural system. The clarity was impeccably good.

"They better be ready," Mina murmured. "Yolanda said they'd be waiting and that we shouldn't get out."

Lee glanced out the window. "Is that the media?" He gestured downward.

Mina looked out her side, but she didn't have a clear view. Off to the side, she saw several spotlights aimed at the entrance and a crowd of people corralled behind a plexi windshear.

"She didn't tell us that the frenzy would start here," Mina said.

"Um, I don't think they're here for her." Lee pointed. "Isn't that Vincent Kramer?"

"We have arrived," the sim announced as the door began to rise.

Mina leaned forward, peering through the opening. Shouting erupted.

"Colonel Kramer, are you enjoying your time in the United States?" one person called.

"Is the French Protectorate upset with you?"

"Is this your new permanent residence?"

"Will you be returning to France anytime soon?"

"Are you and Petra Pebbles an item?"

As they came toward the landing pad, Mina spotted Petra and Vince. He was dressed in his standard eurocollared black suit, no metallic anything, no zany hairstyle. Petra hung off his arm while she waved to the waiting crowd. A crowd that was clearly interested in finding out what the colonel was up to.

"He's not getting in this drone with us, is he?" Mina muttered half to herself, half to anyone who would've cared to listen. "I spoke with Yolanda fifteen minutes ago. She made no mention of Vincent Kramer joining us." It was good the lux drone had enough room. It could actually seat ten. But still.

Yolanda entered first. She wore what looked like a bright orange tube. The dress wasn't formfitting—it was literally a tube with stiff sides. Mina hoped she'd be able to sit okay. The assistant's hair was tinted a similar color, wound on top of her head like a snake that had gone to sleep.

"Thank you for securing the transpo. It's much appreciated." Yolanda sat next to Mina, exhaling loudly. Lee moved to the far side of the drone to make room for the incoming couple as Yola said, "They're going to pose for some images at the behest of the media and answer a few questions."

"How did Petra cajole Colonel Kramer into joining her so quickly?" Mina asked.

Yolanda shot Mina a wry grin. "Petra is incredibly crafty when she needs to be. We got word a few days ago that the colonel lives a few floors away, so Petra strategically placed herself in his path several times. They got to talking, and Petra casually invited him to the premiere. He was noncommittal until about fifteen minutes ago. She had me scouting for him in case he showed.

He usually takes his meals in the private dining area reserved for people who live on the top five floors. I spotted him, and she raced down and somehow convinced him to join us. Then she had me call the media outlets." Yolanda waved her hand like this was an everyday occurrence, which Mina was pretty sure it was. They likely filled the media in wherever they were going, all the time. It sounded exhausting. "I'm on a first-name basis with most of them, so it's pretty easy. When they found out the colonel was attending, it became a frenzy pretty quickly. It took them all of three minutes to get here. The media will take images and recordings here, then rush to the Ultimax Dome and do it all over again." Super exhausting.

They continued shouting questions at Vince. He politely answered them, from what Mina could hear, then directed Petra toward the drone.

Mina met Lee's gaze. Vince would have no problem recognizing them in their light alts, but Mina knew he would handle the surprise like a pro.

Lee gave her a shrug. *Well, what are we going to do?*

Mina shrugged back. *I know, but still.*

Vince helped Petra in first.

The tiny vid star was wrapped head to toe in what looked to be feathery gauze. Unsurprisingly, it was pink. Neon pink, to be exact. She had a hat made of the same material perched on her head. Or secured to it. Or molded with her strands. Hard to tell. It all looked like one thing. Her shoes were high and thick, like a sport boot coupled with a heel. A very odd choice. Mina couldn't wait to describe them to Kaylee, though Mina wouldn't have to, because Kaylee and Harmony were tuning in to the media coverage tonight.

As Kaylee had said, *Seeing you glide down the silver conveyor at a vid premiere is worth eight trillion marmot nuts. Not missing it. In fact, I'll likely play it on loop in holo every day. Just so I can start the day off with a good cackle.*

Such a sweet, nurturing friend.

"Hello," Petra greeted them in a cheerful tone as Vincent Kramer climbed in behind her, taking the seat next to her. The craft door eased shut, finally blocking out the sounds of the media. "Everyone, I'd like to introduce my very special guest. This is Colonel Kramer of the French Protectorate." She barely refrained from bouncing up and down. Her voice was doing it for her. "He's staying right here in our very own Bella. He was such a hero taking down Veritus all by himself." Her voice had dipped to rapturous. Mina had to refrain from snorting. "It's so special that he decided to spend his evening with us."

Mina saw the moment Vince looked over and recognized her. The only thing that changed in his countenance was a single flick of one eyebrow and a slight curve to one side of his mouth. The man was a professional through and through.

Petra continued her frivolous introductions. "This is Detective Kim, and this is Detective Lou. They're my personal bodyguards for the night."

Vince locked his gaze on Mina as he leaned forward, extending a hand.

The heat coming from his eyes seared her.

She was suddenly flaming hot under all the ridiculous bubbles.

"It's a pleasure to meet you, Detective Kim." Nothing in his tone gave him away, but he was enjoying the hell out of this. What didn't this man enjoy?

Mina reached out, taking hold of his hand. "It's Agent Kane." She'd like to say when their skin touched she felt an *actual* jolt of electricity, but that would be a lie. The jolt was purely emotional, and the force of it shocked her. She hoped like hell her expression had remained as steady as Vince's.

The colonel turned toward Lee. "Nice to meet you, Detective Lou." This time, Vince allowed for a tiny grin.

Lee cleared his throat. "It's Agent Adams. It's nice to meet you, too."

The sim announced, "Destination Ultimax Dome, travel time two minutes and three seconds. Do you wish to make any travel changes?"

"No," Petra chirped, flicking an adoring glance at Vince. "This is going to be so much fun!"

Chapter 17

THE PEOPLE CONVEYOR that ran along the outside of the Ultimax, a massive arena that could hold over a hundred thousand people at capacity, had been decorated with flashing ultras, some of which beamed all the way into the sky. A long, braided, silver, carbon fiber rope made a makeshift handrail to keep adoring fans separated from the stars they'd come to gawk at. A dye had been added to the conveyor belt itself, giving it a metallic sheen.

Mina knew Jeni Crisfold was synced with the fashion world, but having Mina's outlandish outfit match the dyed people conveyor was right up there at level kajillion. That woman deserved a medal.

Needless to say, Mina felt ridiculous as she exited the drone and fell into line behind the group.

Lee was on the same page, judging by his continual grimace, one he hadn't shed since he'd boarded the drone. They were both uncomfortable as hell. This took "dressing up for an op" to a whole new galaxy, one Mina hoped not to visit very often.

The few who did seem to be having a good time were Vincent Kramer, because he was enjoying Mina's and Lee's pain, and the neon-pink-clad vid star, who was clearly in her element. Petra halted the conveyor every few seconds with a flick of her wrist so she could get her image snapped with a fan or swipe a few digigraphs.

Vince had tried to make small talk in the craft, lightly inquiring—otherwise known as *prying*—as to why two federal agents were accompanying a vid star to a premiere. Mina had avoided the questions like a pro, redirecting without giving anything away. Every time Petra or Yolanda had tried to clarify, she'd cut them off.

Vince might be a high-ranking colonel in France, but he was a civilian here.

Once they'd exited the drone, he'd tried to pull Mina to the side, but Petra had grabbed his arm and dragged him toward the waiting media hounds. Mina had allowed herself a hearty chuckle. Served him right for coming to this dumb thing.

Lee leaned in as they rode the conveyor. "Why do you think Vincent agreed to accompany Ms. Pebbles to this? Doesn't seem like something he'd be interested in attending."

They were a good three meters behind Yolanda, who was a good three meters behind Petra and Vince. Every time the conveyor came to a shuddering stop, Mina had to reach out and grab the handrail so she wouldn't topple over. Her scissor boots were sturdy, but riding a conveyor in them was asking a little much.

"My guess is his superior, Ambrose Bernard, ordered

him to do as many media blitzes as he can fit in. The more positive the publicity, the more it will improve his image in France. There is no doubt that millions of people around the world are tuning in right now because screencasters everywhere are screaming that Vincent Kramer has arrived."

Petra was either brilliant or ridiculously stupid for asking him to come tonight. She could've kept the media coverage lower by not inviting him. Mina could only imagine what Melissa Socorro was reporting right now.

Then Mina's eyes widened. She didn't have to imagine.

As the conveyor sputtered to life again, she saw the intrepid reporter standing just behind a thin blockade, waiting not so patiently for her turn to talk to the guests of honor. Her outfit was outrageous, though outrageous looked fairly normal on her and not at all creepy or weird. She wore a lemony-yellow confection made of bouncy saucers—either that, or Saturn's belt had been made into a dress. Melissa was the nucleus, and the spheres wrapped all the way around her, ranging from small to large as they spun their way to the ground.

There were so many of them, and they were set so closely together, Mina saw only a shadow of the woman's silhouette when she moved. Her hair was done up in huge, open curls secured around her head. Her facial enhancements had been precisely chiseled to make her cheekbones and chin look sharper than they actually were. But with the accompanying artistically drawn lip and eye accents, it all worked somehow.

Petra, of course, halted the conveyor right in front of Melissa.

Mina and Lee edged closer so they could hear the interaction.

Melissa leaned over the flimsy barrier as far as she could go, asking, "You two look positively gorg together! Are you a couple? We *so* hope you're a couple! Who would've thought you'd find love on our shores, Colonel Kramer? It's so exciting. Isn't that right, folks? Our very own Vincent Kramer, freshly returned from France, a hero of the nation and beyond, has found love." She was an expert at pandering to her audience, and her audience loved her for it. The fans gathered behind Melissa began to cheer, coaxing her to ask more inane questions.

Mina studied Vince.

His composure was steady. He didn't look ruffled—that was, to anyone but her. Mina noted the way he adjusted his footing slightly and slid a fisted hand into his pocket, likely so he wouldn't rake it through his hair or possibly punch someone. He gave off a chill air of comfort, but he was incredibly *un*comfortable. Mina felt a little bad for him. Then she didn't.

"Come on. Stop being coy," Melissa pressed. "We just *have* to know if you two are *together* together. You can tell us. We know how to keep a secret." She winked into the minicam drone that hovered in front of her, following her every move. Altogether, three hovered around her, getting all the angles.

Petra began to babble a response, giving Melissa a polite nonanswer, but Mina wasn't really paying attention to that anymore.

Vince had caught her eye behind the vid star as Petra

leaned forward to get closer to the tiny amp mounted on one of the drones, not that she needed to. That mic would pick up anything she said just fine.

The colonel's gaze held Mina there.

It was fire. He was a master at it.

Her body began to spark and tingle, forcing her to amend her earlier handshake thought. Maybe he could actually zap physical charges directly into her body.

Mina finally looked away, breaking the contact, hoping none of the media or anyone else had picked up on it.

This wasn't the time to play googly-eyes with each other. Was there ever a good time for that? Even though the look had made her insides as frothy and poppy as her dress, now was not the time to explore whatever these new feelings were. They *were* new feelings, right? Mina had no idea.

With relief, she noted that everyone was still completely focused on Petra and Vince.

She turned her back on them, nudging Lee to do the same. "Let's stay off the cam feed. At this rate, it's going to take time to get inside the venue, especially when she's stopping this thing every thirty seconds. Once we're in, you stay with her, and I'll take a look around. I'm going to scope out the stage area and the tech rooms where the holo vid will be projected from."

Mina and Lee had both examined the schematics of the Ultimax. Mina knew roughly where to go. For premieres like these, a stage was set in the middle, then the vid was played in holo above it.

It seemed like forever, but twenty-three minutes later, they were finally reaching the opening of the venue.

Several security bot stations were lined up right before the entrance where cuffs were checked for tickets. Mina held hers aloft in holo. After a quick scan, the bot said, "Welcome to the Ultimax Dome. Please enjoy the premiere screening of *Beyond the Beyonders*, starring Petra Pebbles and Ken Nails." More finger references. Kaylee was right. She was always right. "Enter through here, please."

Once inside, Mina and Lee trailed Petra and Vince, who were still being hounded for interviews, this time by fan groups who had won access to speak with the stars.

"Stay here," Mina instructed Lee. "I'll contact you through your cuff if I find anything unusual." She snuck away, heading out of the main vestibule and into the interior, which led to the grounds and the stage.

She didn't get very far before she was stopped by another security bot. "No one is allowed in here until nine p.m. Tickets must be shown."

Mina popped her badge up on holo. "Scan, please." She waited for the security bot to scan her badge.

He took a step back, gesturing inside. "Welcome, Agent Kane."

McAllister had preapproved her and Lee to have access to anything they needed with the company that ran security and any PPF officers who'd been hired independently by the corporations sponsoring the event.

Once cleared, she went through an area where kiosks were set up for people to order a wide variety of printed treats, then passed through another short hallway and found her way to the main floor of the arena.

It was massive.

At least two million cubic meters.

Seating enough for a hundred thousand surrounded her in a huge oval. It would take at least five minutes at a solid trot for Mina to get across the wide expanse. Luckily, she didn't have to go that far, since the stage sat about halfway. She'd start her perusal there.

As she walked, she examined her surroundings. The dome overhead was impossibly high and had been dyed a pale blue color to make it look like the sky. She wasn't sure if the workers readying the stage were air breathers or bots.

After she checked out the stage, Mina would take a trip to look at the holo projectors. The film was being digitally uploaded from a supercomputer that wasn't on-site. That meant, if the person trying to extort Petra planned to interrupt the film somehow, they would have to do it from a different location. But Mina still wanted to see the projector rooms and make sure nobody had messed with them.

With not much to go on, they were kind of shooting in the dark, trying to cover all the proverbial bases.

Mina couldn't exactly trot in her fancy, flouncy, crunchy dress and scissor heels, but she made it to the stage in under a minute and a half. It was much larger than it appeared from afar. It'd been built out of shiny aluminum sheets, likely fortified with some sort of graphene to keep the structure firm. It was at least three meters high and three times that long.

She walked around the side and spotted a door.

The lever moved freely. Ultras were already on. This was a multipurpose area to store supplies, get ready, or queue for an entrance onto the stage. Several small holo cams were mounted on posts and pointed toward square cutouts in the ceiling that would open so a holo image could be shown onstage. These weren't big enough to beam up a vid, but they were the perfect size to enhance an image of a vid star.

Those weren't the only cutouts. Several rectangular outlines were etched in the ceiling, large enough that, when retracted, a person could move through or stage hands could lift things in or out. She spotted a staircase on rollers off to the side, which could be placed beneath any of the openings.

Mina knew from her research that several service tunnels ran underneath the dome. At least one opened up here, enabling people to come and go and receive deliveries of supplies. The tunnels were large enough that wheeled vehicles could be driven right up to the door.

Mina scanned the area.

To her surprise, a piece of the flooring began to retract.

She moved closer, expecting to see a bot pop up or an air breather with supplies. A man with tousled black hair and excellent taste in suits came up slowly, taking his time, fixing something on his shirtsleeve.

Then he glanced up and smiled.

Mina sighed, hands going to her hips. "What are you doing here?"

"It seems I just can't stay away."

MINA TOOK A step back. Even though maybe she'd like him to stay, she couldn't let him stay. "You can't be here. *Shoo.* Go back the way you came."

Vince ignored her, emerging fully into the inner stage, whose flooring was some sort of lightweight composite made to look like granite. Easily movable, but nicely set.

Irritatingly, the tunnel door slicked shut behind him.

He flashed her another grin. "I'm not going back there anytime soon. If I have to, I'll hide out here on my own."

"It's your own fault. You accepted Petra's invitation. What did you think was going to happen?" She smirked as she continued to investigate the space.

Several areas had been cordoned off with movable walls to create private work areas. She peeked her head around one. An automated chair and a table filled with enhancement tools indicated it was intended for quick face and hair upgrades. Another area looked to be a specialized dressing room with a lot of costumes, including some mimicking furry animals, hanging on a rack.

Mina didn't want to know. She really didn't.

Seeing how well the space was utilized, she surmised that the stage had likely been put in place for some other event and kept for the premiere. If they could make it easier on themselves, why wouldn't they?

Vince trailed behind her, inspecting things on his own. It's not like they could turn off who they were. "And about attending tonight. I didn't really have a choice in the matter," he offered. "I'm ordered to do as much media boosting as I can." No surprises there. "But had I known you'd be accompanying Petra, I would've accepted immediately instead of stalling until the last possible moment."

Mina shot him a wry look over her shoulder. "You're not getting anything out of me, so don't ask."

"I've already gathered some details. Petra is quite the talker when it's just the two of us. Extortion, huh? She mumbled something noncommittal about beauty recipes. But that doesn't sound right. When I pressed her further, she shut down."

Mina shrugged. "I'm not at liberty to discuss this case with you. Not even a little bit. Your efforts to ply me are wasted."

"Shouldn't this type of job be overseen by your local Police Protection Force? It seems like overkill to have two special agents follow around a vid star for the possibility of...what? Someone might say something nasty about her because she refused to share a few beauty recipes?"

"Nice try. You may be a colonel in France, but you're a civilian here. And you shouldn't even be here. You should actually go. People are going to notice you're not with Petra, and we can't be seen together. You know that as well as I do." No need to rehash the conversation from this morning. "Unless you're deliberately trying to expose me again?"

"I had no idea you'd be here." He smiled. "It was simply a happy coincidence."

"Where exactly did you think I was going when I took off toward the stage? And don't pretend you weren't looking. You were totally looking." Mina narrowed her eyes lest he try to pretend he hadn't been interested in her whereabouts. He grinned without answering. "How did you know to use the tunnel?" She indicated the opening in the floor that was now firmly, annoyingly shut.

"Ambrose has attended a few events here over the years. Before he goes anywhere, we thoroughly inspect the entire space. I've been through these tunnels quite a few times and know exactly where each leads. I also happen to keep this on me, which is very handy." He pulled a small tool out of his pocket. Mina recognized it as a lock disengager, but it was smaller and Frenchier than hers. "It holds all the codes I've used before. These are far superior to the ones you have here and can penetrate more complex code."

Mina held up her hand and mimicked the words he'd just uttered while opening and closing her fingers and thumb. He tossed his head back and laughed. Honestly, it was a great sound.

"Seriously," he said. "American companies should be more careful. Tech is improving at a rapid rate."

She dropped her hand. Playtime was over. "They probably should. And that's a very handy little tool. I'm sure Ambrose Bernard, leader of the French Protectorate, has many precautions taken on his behalf. The vid star we're keeping an eye on, however, does not. I'm familiar with the schematics and know roughly where the tunnels lead." She just hadn't thought to use one to get here. She probably should have. "Now I have to get back to work, and you have to scuttle along. I'm certain you have more media interviews to partake in before the exciting vid screening begins."

"How about I help you instead? That'll be more fun for the both of us."

"No."

"I'm assuming you want to see all the other areas that contain substantial tech. I can escort you quickly from here to there through the tunnels and tubes. No one has to see us. This dome is enormous and set up nicely with security and cloaking in mind. They host a lot of visiting dignitaries and important people. Plus, I have this." He rocked the lock disengager back and forth between fingers with nicely manicured nails. "Unless you have one?" Both of his eyebrows shot up, then he waggled them.

"No, thank you—"

Voices sounded outside. A group of people were chatting and laughing, moving at a fast clip.

Mina shot Vince a look, part frustration, part amusement.

The guy was fun, but she couldn't risk being seen with him. She made a decision and rushed over, grabbing his arm, tugging him forward, gesturing at the floor. "Fine. Open it. Do it now."

It was a blessed relief when he didn't give a gleeful hoot.

Instead, he pressed the disengager, and the door slicked open.

Mina hurried down the steps, glancing over her shoulder. "Feel free to stay behind. No need to join me."

"Not a chance in hell. I'm coming with you. I'm not relinquishing my tool, and you're going to need it at the other end." He followed her down the steps, the door shutting just as the group entered the area behind them.

Mina was surprised how big the tunnel was, even though she'd known it would be wide enough to allow for the navigation of four-wheeled vehicles. Not big enough for a dronecraft, though. Plus, the blowback from the props would be insane and very unsafe. Four-wheeled vehicles were a rarity, but were used in situations like this. Everything ran on battery or solar. Humanity had done away with fossil fuels more than fifty years ago.

Mina didn't wait for Vince to catch up. She hurried forward, the clack of her scissor heels on the syncrete echoing through the tunnel. That was, until she got to the first junction and had no idea which way to go.

She stopped, crossing her arms, glancing back at Vince, who was taking his own sweet time. "Okay, which way?"

"That depends on where you're going," he drawled.

He was enjoying this so, so much.

"I need to see the hologram-projector rooms. All three."

"In that case, we'll head to the closest one. Head right and down twenty meters. There's a tube stand at the end. We take it up to the top level, and it's right there."

Show-off.

"Got it." Mina made her way right.

Not six meters in, people began to shout above the soft whir of a vehicle. Before she could figure out what to do, Vince propelled her by the shoulders into a small storage area that had several cleaning items leaning against the walls.

Once they were tucked away out of sight, Mina whispered, "You can let go of me now." Vince dropped his hands. Mina was thankful they were in a shadowed area so he couldn't see her face, which felt flushed. "I feel the need to reiterate that it's really not a good idea for us to be seen together. Not only will Petra be missing you, but the media is not just going to simply forget that you're here. The reason there are so many of them is because you decided to join the party."

"I wouldn't call this a party. Parties are fun. But I understand. I'll just accompany you to the rooms, then we can part ways," he assured her. "I'm not here to compromise your identity. I take your job very seriously, as I do mine. I was just incredibly happy to see you. You make everything more bearable."

Well, okay.

"I also needed a break from all the cam drones and mics shoved in my face." He frowned. "When I signed on to the French Protectorate, I never thought the job would entail any of this. I'm not a front-and-center guy. Being behind the scenes is my strength. Everything I do, every piece of me, is focused on making the people of France, and my fellow guardsmen, safe, and none of that has anything to do with this." He gestured in the vicinity of where Mina assumed Petra and company were still congregated. Then he raked his hand through his hair. Mina closed her eyes for a teensy second. "I made it worse by trying to take on Veritus by myself. That never should've happened. I should've called you immediately once I suspected who you work for. I can't apologize enough." He looked hopeful. "Have you had a chance to watch the recording I left for you?"

Mina shook her head, bringing her finger to her lips. A vehicle passed by their space. No one took notice of them.

"No. I haven't had time," she whispered. "But I will. And I'll consider the apology. I know you're not a bad guy, Vince. You and I share the same core values. We grew up together and happen to have been thrown together in this craziness, but once things settle down and life goes back to a more normal variation, I'm sure we'll vid chat again." Comfort clothing required. Lots and lots of comfort clothing.

Vince's face brightened. "We will? You're interested in chatting again?"

"Yes. Now let's go. I need to check out these cams, check in with my partner, report to my director, and you need to be back in place, all before the festivities begin."

The tubes expedited travel time greatly. One of the tunnels even had a conveyor. Mina managed to check out all three locations within fifteen minutes. Nothing amiss with any of the hologram projectors. Each room also had a security bot installed in front of the door with instructions not to let in anyone without authorization.

Mina and Vince stood in a tunnel underneath the main congregation area.

"Once you get back up there, distract Petra," Mina said. "She's going to be wondering where you were. Ply her with niceties."

"I will. But are you sure I have to go back?" he joked. "Being covert is what I'm good at. I could just slide out, and I guarantee you no one would see me leave."

"Too late for that now. You have to fulfill your duties. I don't even want to know what else you promised Petra." Mina meant it as a lighthearted comment, but when Vince's face fell, she quickly formed a rebuttal. "I didn't mean that you *promised* the vid star anything." She was suddenly flustered. "Never mind. Even if you did, it's fine." She shook her head. "Just go, already! We've wasted too much time here already. Anyone could ride down in that tube and see us standing here." They were right in front of a tube station that would whisk Vince to the lobby.

The plan was for Vince to take the tube up, and Mina was going to walk back to the stage.

The colonel hit the lock disengager, summoning the tube with the embedded code. Then he held the tech out to her, surprising her. "I'm trusting you with this. Feel free to return it in person."

Mina opened her palm, and Vince set it down, his fingers lingering. "I probably won't, but thanks. I'll take good care of it. You know, you could've just given this to me earlier."

"Where would the fun have been in that?" The tube door slicked open, and Vince stepped inside. He gave her a three-finger salute. "Thanks for making my evening entertaining. There's another tube station down around the first corner." He gestured to Mina's right.

"Got it. Make Petra believe you had some French Protectorate business to attend to. No one healthy would be in the waste room that long, then give her your undivided attention. She'll forget you were gone in no time."

"Yes, ma'am." The door closed.

Mina hurried down the hallway, feeling grouchy that she was in this dumb dress, but grateful Vince hadn't commented on it. After a short bend, sure enough, there was another tube station. Mina hit the disengager. Nothing happened. She hit it again.

Nothing.

They must've changed the codes to these particular tubes. She made her way back to the tube Vince had just used. She'd give him some time to regroup with Petra, then use it herself.

She leaned against the wall and tapped her cuff. "Lee, what's your status?"

No response. She tried again. She took a few steps away from the wall and searched around. This place was made of thick syncrete, so there apparently was no signal in or out. She'd have to wait.

A full minute later, she held the lock disengager up to the tube and depressed the button. Nothing. She inspected the useless lock disengager, muttering to herself, "This is probably coded to your DNA." How could Vince not know that? Better question: Why hadn't she asked? "I guess it's back to the stage for me."

It took Mina longer than she wanted to get there. After the disengager failed again, and she did some thorough pounding, the door slicked open. Mina stared into two confused faces. She announced, "I'm with Petra Pebbles," as she paced up the steps. She tapped her cuff, and the holo ticket marking her as security came up. "I was just checking out the tunnels to make sure everything is locked down and lost my keycode." She muttered the last bit, hoping they wouldn't catch what she was saying, nor would they ask her to explain.

A second later, an amber star floated above her cuff.

It was from Lee.

She turned her back on the two workers, who hadn't requested any additional explanation from her, and moved to a more private spot. She tapped her cuff, bringing it up to her lips. "What's going on, Lee?"

"Where have you been?" His voice was steady, but she could hear some minor panic brewing. "I tried to get a hold of you a few times."

"The tunnels are constructed of thick syncrete. No signal gets through. Give me a report."

"Petra's sister is here."

"Petra doesn't have a sister."

"I know."

The very thorough lifecheck they'd performed earlier today on Ms. Pebbles hadn't revealed any siblings. Overall, the lifecheck data had been slim compared to that of the average person, so Mina would wager the vid star had hired a pretty good hacker to clear it all out. That meant there was baggage she hadn't bothered to divulge.

"Who spotted this so-called sister?"

"I'm not sure. The details are sketchy. I don't see how I missed it, but there's a lot going on with the fans and the interviews. Yolanda came to get me after the fact. Initially, they grabbed a security bot and went after her, but she disappeared. I searched a bit with Yolanda, but she was nowhere to be found." Lee's tone conveyed his dismay.

Strange. They had two federal agents at their disposal. Why not alert one of them? "I'm on my way. I'm underneath the stage."

"Stay there. We're making our way out there now."

"Okay. With this new information, be prepared to escort Ms. Pebbles from the dome. I'll talk to Petra when she arrives. For all we know, she knew her sister was coming and deliberately didn't tell us."

Lee's voice came out snippy. The rookie was very unhappy. "It's going to take a laser rod with a hot tip to get her to leave."

"Maybe so, but we can apply the tip if necessary."

CHAPTER 19

MINA WENT OUTSIDE to wait for them. The lights had been dimmed and the atmosphere had changed to a party vibe. A low, steady rumble echoed around the stadium as people began to take their seats. She positioned herself so she faced the direction Petra would be coming from.

It was easy to spot the vid stars.

Large ultras tracked their single-file progression. Petra tugged on Vince's arm with one hand and waved to the crowd with the other. Like no time had passed. Mina was going to have to find a way to intercept her before she made it to the stage so they could decide how to handle the situation with this sister sighting.

McAllister wasn't expecting frequent updates on this op since there was a very low threat of violence. But if something unexpected happened, like a long-lost sister popping up to cause trouble, Mina would contact him.

For now, Mina took in the scene as she waited.

Automated chairs had appeared out of the main floor,

popping into an array of shiny, uniformed rows, decorated with colorful gel-cush. The stage seating was decidedly more lux, gleaming white with glittery cush, standing proud like thrones for royalty. Appropriate for stars who thought the royal designation applied to them.

There weren't many other decorations, as Mina assumed the vid stars themselves provided the main sparkle.

She tried not to be impatient, but they were taking their printed-sweet time walking across the floor, which was its own kind of stage. Petra had taken full advantage of her primary place in the spotlight next to the colonel. A crowd of media followed them at a distance, tiny camera drones swooping all around them, flashes popping on and off. It was quite the spectacle.

One Mina was ready to part with as quickly as possible.

She searched for anyone in the immediate crowd who could pass as Petra's sister. The vid star herself seemed completely unconcerned. It was hard to imagine that someone who might be declared a murderer in front of hundreds of thousands of people, both here and on-screen, could be this unaffected.

Maybe Lee was right, and this was just one big giant publicity stunt? To what end? To garner attention? To relieve boredom? To boost coverage, negative or not?

Mina mulled it over. Something felt off. And when that happened, she always trusted her gut. Something was going to happen tonight. She just wished she knew what it was.

When Petra and Vince were within three meters of where she stood, Mina gave a discreet wave. Vince, who had eyes on Mina, which he had to quit doing, immediately tried to redirect Petra toward her.

The vid star resisted. Vince's eyebrows rose as he gave the woman on his arm a questioning look.

Trailing behind the two of them, Lee wore his perpetual grimace. The rookie didn't like the feel of this op either. Petra met Mina's head flick, indicating she wanted to talk, with a frown. The vid star shook her head slightly, as she and Vince continued forward. It seemed as though Petra thought that if she spoke to Mina at this moment, she wasn't going to like her options.

It didn't matter. Mina needed to confer with her about this sighting and what it meant. It might be totally benign. Petra might love her nonexistent-in-the-government-system sister and had invited her here. But running away wouldn't solve anything. It was better to be clear on this new development so they could check it off or be wary of it.

Then, just like that, Petra let go of Vince and darted up the large staircase that led to the stage.

The crowd went wild.

Several staffers corralled Yolanda and Lee, moving them toward an area at the foot of the stage, while encouraging the colonel to join Petra onstage.

At first, he shook his head, then seeing it was useless, he gave a small shrug and walked up the steps.

The sound of the crowd crept toward deafening.

Next came the vid co-star, Ken Nails. He was alone.

He took his time ascending the stage, waving to the crowd, likely rewriting that their reaction was for him. A few others followed. Melissa Socorro was last, heading up the stairs like she was a queen. Vid stars weren't the only ones who thought they were royalty.

Her voice boomed loudly the instant her Jet Lang-clad heel hit the stage. "Welcome, everyone! This will be a night to remember!"

Mina wasn't surprised she was the MC for the evening. She was the perfect choice.

Yolanda and Lee sat down in the seats reserved for them at the base of the stage, and Mina joined, taking her place next to her partner.

"I'm letting her stay up there until I get more information." Mina gestured where Petra was now perched. "She ignored me. It was a stupid thing to do. I can't protect her if she doesn't cooperate." Mina leaned in, speaking directly to Yolanda. "Petra doesn't have a sister—at least not on file. I need to know what happened. Did you see this mystery woman first? Or did Petra?"

"I didn't think she had a sister either." Yolanda shrugged, her face earnest. "Petra spotted her. She was angry. She grabbed my arm and pointed her out. Said her sister was messing up their agreement by showing her face here and that I needed to have her thrown out."

Agreement?

Yolanda continued, "But by the time I got there, with a security bot in tow, she was gone."

"Why didn't you alert Agent Adams?" Mina asked,

keeping the disgruntle in check for now. "A federal agent was positioned five meters away from you for this reason." That's literally the *only* reason they were here. To help with a problem. This was a problem.

She averted her eyes. "It all happened so fast. I'm sorry. I'm not used to operating like that. I'm always the one who takes care of everything. But I told him right after I rushed back, and he went with me to continue searching for her."

Lee nodded, but the grimace stayed. Mina didn't blame him.

"What did she look like?" Mina asked. "What is she wearing? I need a full description of her outfit, the color of her hair, any defining features. Was anyone with her?" This op qualified right up there with one of the strangest Mina had ever been assigned. Frivolous, yet not. Trying to get information out of the two of them was like slogging through quick-drying syncrete.

"Yolanda told me she was in a dress the same color as Petra's," Lee answered as Yolanda nodded. "And that she was about the same size, but her hair was short and blonde."

"The same size? Are we talking twins here?" And if so, why was the vid star working so hard to hide it? "Yolanda, how many years have you been with Petra?"

"Two. Well, almost two. She goes through assistants pretty quickly."

Unsurprising. "Has she ever mentioned her parents?"

"Never. That subject is taboo. She claims she has no connection to them."

"What about siblings? Any kind, sisters or otherwise?"

Yolanda bit her lip. "Not specifically. I did overhear her vid chatting with someone a few times. I didn't try to listen in, I swear. But she was very angry. Whoever she was talking to, it felt personal. But she talks to her production staff similarly, so I'm only guessing."

"Go on," Mina encouraged. It was the only line they had. They might as well hear it all.

"Well, she said things like, 'I'll never give you control,' and 'Your threats can't hurt me,' and 'We had an agreement, and you're breaking it.' She was definitely fighting with someone."

"Good. What else?" Mina coaxed, upping the volume so Yolanda could hear her over Melissa Socorro, who was ramping up the crowd by encouraging Petra and Vincent Kramer to answer personal questions. "I need as many details as you can remember. Names, locations, anything else that comes to mind. If you felt these chats were intimate, they probably were. After working with her for two years, you understand your boss and how she interacts with people. Think back. It's important."

Yolanda nodded. "Okay." She closed her eyes. They popped open a moment later. "I remember something! She said something about recipes. It was a long time ago, when I first started working for her. I'm only remembering it right this minute. I've been so stressed all day. I'm sorry."

Mina made a short roll of her fingers to get Yolanda to keep talking. She didn't want to interrupt her.

"It was something like, 'That place is mine.' She was

really angry, almost screaming. Then she said something like, 'I allowed you inside because we have an agreement, and you stole those recipes. They're not yours, they're mine. Auntie left that place to me.'" Yolanda scrunched her eyes closed, in an effort to recall everything she'd overheard. Mina appreciated it. "Then maybe something like, 'I don't care what you have planned. You can stay in the outskirts for all I care.' I'm not really sure of the exact words, but it was something like that."

Mina held up her hand. "The outskirts? What specifically did she say about the outskirts?"

Yolanda shook her head. "Nothing else. I came in right after that, and she shut the vid down. But when I was helping her get ready for an event later that day, she mumbled something like, 'I wish you were dead.' I questioned her about it, but Petra waved it away and said she was just rehearsing lines. When she's in a vid, she says them out loud all the time, so it could've been that. But it was right after that chat. So I'm not sure." Yolanda's shoulders were hunched, her knees were locked together, and her hands were laced together so tightly the pressure points were white. She was appropriately stressed. She seemed sincere, but Mina wasn't entirely convinced. This was a pretty detailed accounting of several one-sided conversations overheard from her boss. They wouldn't have confirmation until they quizzed Petra. "I should've given you all this information today when you were at the residence. If I'd made myself think—really sit down and *think*, I know I would've remembered sooner. I should've pulled you aside. But I was so worried about Petra and the threats and finding that box. I'm so sorry." She wrung her hands together some more. "I hope I don't lose my job over this." She bit her lip.

Lee asked, "How about single words or phrases that you couldn't place or didn't understand in that context. That would be helpful."

Good thinking, Rookie.

"No, nothing like that. Wait." She shifted in her seat, leaning in closer. "There was one word that stood out. She said it repeatedly, and I was always confused. It was the word 'Rose.' I think it was a name, not a flower. She said, something like, 'You should be grateful I let you use the place, Rose.' Does that help?"

Mina and Lee exchanged glances. Hard to know.

Instead of consulting with Lee, because vid premiere, Mina ran it over in her mind.

If Petra had a secret sister who was trying to extort her, why would the sister come here? How would she benefit from exposing something about Petra in front of all these people? And what exactly were the beauty recipes? That was at the heart of all this.

Lee whispered, "I don't think the Rose mention is a coincidence. The watermark imprints are rose petals."

"Yes, that's true," she whispered back. "But this is not coming together for me. Something's off." Mina kept her tone low and in Lee's ear, which was hard to do since Melissa Socorro was still riling up the crowd. The aural sound system in this place was top-notch. "If her sister wanted beauty secrets, and they were important enough to threaten to expose her as a murderer, why wouldn't she just show up at her residence and demand what she wanted? Doing it here is complicated." Mina gestured toward the stage and the mass attendees. "Siblings are less likely to resort to extortion without trying other means first. Meaning, Petra would already know her sister wanted something from her. Extortion or blackmail is usually the last option for family members, because the victim and perpetrator share a past together, and why get messy if you can bully your way to what you want first? If it's her sister doing all this, I feel like Petra would've divulged already. She seems to have no loyalty to her family and went to great lengths to wipe away any personal connections in the system." Mina glanced at the stage. Melissa was still performing for the audience. Mina didn't want to think of her fee for one of these things. The woman probably had a drawer full of real, not printed, gemstones. "None of this makes much sense."

Lee nodded. "I agree. It's not coming together for me either. Maybe the sister is jealous? Maybe she wants to be her? She's tired of all the attention Petra gets and wants some for her own? Maybe the threats are to get Petra to acknowledge her in some way."

"Wants to *be* her?" Mina narrowed her eyes, thinking back to the rectangular cutouts she'd seen in the stage floor when she'd been under it. Mina had no idea if any of them corresponded to the seating that was up there now, but she had a sudden urge to find out. She leaned over, her voice not above a murmur, "Stay here. I'm going to check something out under the stage. Something's up.

We're not understanding what it is, but we can't just sit here and wait it out."

"I'll go with you." He started to get up.

Mina shook her head. "No. Keep your eyes on Petra. I'll position myself under Petra. That way, we'll have her covered. Then, when this is over we get her out quickly."

"Okay."

Mina slipped off her seat and skirted the edge of the stage, sticking to the shadows. Most of the ultras beamed down on the stage, leaving an edge of darkness around the perimeter. She was certain the majority of the crowd was focused on Vincent Kramer, which she had to admit made it easier for her to keep a low profile.

She reached the door, but the lever wouldn't turn. It was locked. That was strange as this was a communal space. She reached into her pocket and pulled out Vince's fancy French lock disengager. It hadn't worked at the tubes or the tunnel door, but it was all she had at the moment. Trying to kick in a door would be too noticeable. She pressed the button.

A soft click sounded.

Mina grinned. For whatever reason, the device worked this time, and she was relieved. She eased the door open and slipped through.

Chapter 20

As Mina entered the space under the stage, she didn't even have time to comprehend what was happening in front of her as the ceiling opened, and Petra tumbled through. The chair the vid star had been occupying on the stage had essentially dumped her through the hole like she'd been sitting at the top of a chute.

Petra landed on her feet, then collapsed onto her backside with an *oof.*

A woman, who was dressed in Petra's exact neon pink outfit, strode confidently over to the vid star, from her place by the wall, where she'd likely been the one to engage the trapdoor. She held a huge syringe aloft in one hand.

Mina didn't have time to think. She ran, plowing into the woman before she could stab Petra with the needle, sending them both flying.

The crowd roared above them.

Melissa Socorro was saying something about technical

difficulties and then relaying a joke about amusement park rides that had the audience laughing. It sounded like a rumble of barking dogs.

"Don't *touch* me," the woman raged beneath Mina. "I'll kill you. I've killed before." She fought, kicking and clawing at Mina's arms and face.

Mina held her down, cursing the fact that she was wearing this awful dress and hadn't had time to get out her gem. She hardly thought that anyone would try to do something like this in front of a hundred thousand witnesses. If Mina had been smart enough to access her gem ahead of time, a nice, tiny hole through the foot would have stopped this woman in her tracks. Literally. As they tussled, Mina was vaguely aware that Vince had jumped through the hole in the stage after Petra.

"I'm a federal agent. You're under arrest. Drop your weap—"

The syringe stuck deeply into Mina's side. It hurt like hell. Luckily, she knocked it out as she rolled in the opposite direction.

Dizziness hit immediately.

Mina grabbed her throat, gasping for air. The woman broke away, crawling out from under her as the door opened, and Lee and Yolanda rushed in.

"I stationed two security bots outside, and I'm making sure nobody else enters," Lee called.

Go, Lee.

The woman appeared above Mina, a snarl on her extremely pretty face.

It was Petra, but blurry.

Mina blinked a few times, finally able to catch her breath, and watched as the woman swiped away blood from a cut on the side of her mouth with her forearm, smearing it across her face. "There's nowhere you can take her I won't find her. This isn't over. I'm not giving up my chance."

Yolanda, surprising everyone, did not run to Petra, but instead to the mystery Petra faux twin. "Shauna, are you all right?" Yolanda fussed over the woman, trying to fix her hair and straightening her torn dress.

"I'm fine. Get off of me." She swatted Yolanda's hands away.

Lee rushed forward, taking in the interaction, surprise finally replacing his grimace. "What are you doing, Yola?" He gestured to where Vince was hovering over the vid star. "Petra's over there."

Mina couldn't speak, but inside her head she was screaming at Lee to take out his stunner. He hadn't heard Yolanda call the woman Shauna. Mina tried to form words, but her throat felt too full, and her head felt like it'd been inflated with helium. She might actually be floating on a cloud somewhere in outer space. It was so peaceful out here.

She watched helplessly as Yolanda stepped in front of Shauna. The woman in the neon pink dress had to be Petra's twin, unless she'd had enhancement surgery to look just like her. But not even the most professional reconstructionists could get that close. At least Mina didn't think so.

Mina's brain was trying to convince her that Petra had

somehow broken into two perfect halves of herself. It made total sense. Just look at them. Same, same.

She shook her head. It felt like the whole world was rotating back and forth on its axis.

"Step back, or I laser everyone," Yolanda said in a voice that cut through Mina's outer-space-cloud-riding haze. "We're leaving through the tunnels. No one's coming after us. If you do, we'll take out anyone who gets in our way, including innocent people who are down there right now."

Mina heard Vince, but couldn't see him, because her eyes were locked on Yolanda's laser like it was an eyeball magnet. "Go ahead and leave. But these agents will find you. There's no doubt about it. Much easier if you both surrender right now."

Both women laughed.

Sounded like braying donkeys mixed with yipping marmots. Did marmots yip? They did in Mina's brain. And they were loud.

"Yeah, right. We'll just surrender," Shauna spat. "Do you actually live in reality? Or are you so blinded by your imperial power that you don't understand how the real world works? I'd rather die than go into a box."

For the first time, Mina saw that Shauna had exchanged her syringe for a blaster. Not surprising, considering. "We'll be leaving, and once we're gone, nobody will find us. Our hidey-hole is secure and out of reach of *your* government. But I'll be coming back for my dear, dear sister. Very soon. You can count on it."

The two women turned, disappearing down the stairs and into the tunnel.

Vince rushed to Mina's side and scooped her up, making Lee's surprised wide owl eyes go more owly. Mina hadn't known that was possible. She couldn't look away, but then she remembered she didn't want to be in Vince's arms like this. Did she? She managed to get her limp wrist raised up just enough to slap it against his chest. "What are you doing? Put me down."

Those were the words she'd uttered in her head. She was pretty sure what came out was, *Shush err yeee doinn? Puuu my dooon.* There might've been some drool. To her relief, Vince understood drugged-up Minaspeak and set her in the nearest chair.

Lee was at her side in the next instant, leaning over to inspect her eyes. "What happened? Did she drug you?"

Mina nodded vigorously, meaning her head flopped up and down a few times. Then she angled a weak arm toward the syringe on the floor and said, "Have the security bot outside analyze the contents. Then have them call in a medi-unit." There were at least two units in the dome tonight, as was mandatory with a crowd of this size. "Once they know what it is, they can counteract it."

The rookie looked worried. Really worried.

He shot a look around the room as he called, "What did she just say? Did anybody understand her?"

Mina huffed, getting ready to try to say it all over again when she noticed Vince trotting toward the door with the syringe in hand. Apparently, he understood out-of-it Mina extremely well. Either that, or he was smart and intrepid. Probably that. He had lots more experience than the rookie. Poor rookie. He was doing his best.

Wasn't he? Hard to know when the earth was still rocking.

The colonel whipped open the door, signaling a security bot to come inside right as Melissa Socorro stuck her head through the ceiling. Mina wondered what had taken her so long.

"What's going on down there? Petra, why aren't you back up here? Are you hurt?" Melissa's wild curls looked hilarious upside down, and Mina started to giggle.

Nobody noticed, because all eyes were on the vid star, who rocked back and forth on the ground, hat gone, hair falling around her shoulders, appearing like she'd seen a ghost. Or maybe she was on the same ride as Mina. Petra shook herself out of her daze after what seemed like five hours, but was likely only one second, and glanced at Melissa's funny-looking head as she tried to stand.

She cried out in pain, gripping her leg. Apparently, her sturdy shoes weren't sturdy enough.

Mina was about to order Lee to get that medi-unit in here when she heard Vince order the bot to do the same. "Analyze the contents of this and alert the nearest medi-unit. We need medical attention in here immediately." Then he walked briskly over to address Melissa Socorro's upside-down face. "Ms. Pebbles will be out of commission for the rest of the event, as will I. Make excuses for us and start the vid. I'm sure you're competent enough to get the job done. In fact, act like this was supposed to happen and connect it to something in the vid."

Melissa's mouth opened in protest.

Vince said one word, but he said it like he meant it. Smartly and intrepidly. "Now."

Melissa popped out of sight immediately.

A moment later, her voice soothed the roiling crowd as she explained that Petra popping out of sight was, in fact, supposed to have happened, and they were ready to start the vid!

Roars of approval followed.

Honestly, Melissa Socorro could sell anything. And thank goodness for that.

Mina wondered if she had a pet marmot. That would make sense, after all.

Mina's head felt like it was being pressed together between two sheets of titanium locked in a vise the size of a megascraper. But at least it was clear, bright pain. All the fuzziness was gone. She could lift her limbs. The medi-unit had just left on Vince's orders. Lee had finished his report to Director McAllister. Their boss had wanted to send in another team, but Lee had convinced him that everything was under control, and they didn't want to make this any more of a spectacle or endanger any civilians as the woman had threatened to do if anyone came after them.

Petra had wept on and off and, following her modus operandi, hadn't managed to answer any questions at all.

It was time for Mina to get her head back in the game, even though it felt like the sun had exploded inside her skull. She stood, wincing a little. Her side was still sore from where the syringe had gone in. The medi-worker had told her she'd been very lucky she'd received only half a dose of the industrial-strength tranq. The full dose could've—likely would've—killed her.

Her dress was ruined. Half the bubbles on the bottom had popped during her scuffle with Shauna. She leaned over and tore off a wide swath of her skirt and tossed it aside. She was a little unsteady on her legs, but not too bad. Not enough to take off the boots. She made her way over to Petra. It was time to figure out what was going on.

She stopped in front of Petra's chair, hands on her hips, mostly so she could massage the spot where she'd been stabbed by the syringe. The medi-workers had rubbed some numbing agent on it, but it was still sore.

"Why didn't you tell us you have a sister?" That seemed like a fair and easy place to start. "Or that you've been vid chatting with her, or that she was trying to extort you? Honestly, we could've solved this already. At the very least, we would've been more prepared for what just happened." It was hard to know exactly, but there was a high likelihood they would've been ahead of things had the vid star come clean.

Petra immediately stopped crying, her sad face morphing to furious, her fists balling at her sides. "What are you talking about? I don't have a sister!"

Well, that would explain it, then.

She continued, "Why do you think I am an inconsolable mess? I just saw a woman who has gone to great lengths to look just like me, and she took off with *my* assistant after she tried to fill me up with whatever she shot into you." The vid star jumped out of her seat.

The medi-unit had used a portable limb pod on her leg, and since Petra had suffered only a hairline fracture, they'd knitted it together in a matter of moments. Lucky her. Mina massaged her side again. "You let her get away, and I'm missing my vid right now. We're here because you failed to do your job! You were supposed to stop this from happening in the first place!" She jabbed her finger at Mina, then promptly burst into tears again.

Mina took a deep breath. Then another one.

Yolanda had invented the entire sister story, and she'd done it very convincingly. Mina and Lee had mostly fallen for it. Mina had had a few moments of doubt, but ultimately felt the assistant had been sincere. Yolanda was a very talented actress. Something the vid star would not be enthused to hear at the moment. This was on Mina. She'd been so focused on the greater possibility that Petra had been lying, due to her skimpy, and obviously hacked, lifecheck data, instead of factoring in that the liar could've been Yolanda. Not her best agent work to date.

"Let's get a few things sorted out," Mina started. "We didn't focus on your assistant because she covered her tracks very well." Petra's wailing increased, so Mina spoke louder. "When we received confirmation that Betty Three had been tampered with, it redirected our suspicions off Yolanda. Although we'd considered her to be a suspect for planting the boxes, going to such great lengths to scatter the bot data seemed unlikely. It was a very smart thing to do, then when she introduced the fictitious sister, we were more easily led to believe someone else was after you. She was also smart to bring up a sister angle because she knew another Petra sighting could be reported by security, as Shauna was walking around the dome dressed like you. Therefore, if their plan to drug you and replace you didn't work, Shauna could escape, and Yolanda could blame the attempt on this crazed person she *thought* was your sister. But Yolanda panicked when she saw her real boss was in trouble. She made a mistake. She broke character. And it's a good thing she did." None of this had made Petra any less weepy. Vince handed her a piece of fabric, likely culled from the costume room. She mopped her face. "Now we have something solid to work from. We'll find out who they are, and we'll bring them in. They will spend time in a box for what they did."

Lee stood next to Mina. "We've been doing our job to the best of our abilities with very little help on your part. We had very little information to go on from the start." The rookie was chastising the vid star, but he was doing it nicely. "We asked about your family and asked you to confirm their status, and you were too busy getting ready for this event to answer our questions. If you had confirmed you had no siblings, a sister sighting would've raised the proper alarms." This was true. They had asked the vid star various things throughout the day, and she'd evaded them. Petra quieted some. "Right after you tumbled through the stage, Agent Kane was here. She took your look-alike down quickly and efficiently. And she was able to do it because she has excellent instincts."

Thanks, Lee. "Those instincts saved your life. In the process, she took the syringe meant for you, which could've killed her, and if she hadn't taken it, you would be dead instead." Petra was more petite than Mina, and the dosage had been weighted by kilogram.

Everyone was quiet for a moment.

"I know," Petra replied weakly. She turned her gaze on Mina. "I'm sorry. I'm just so emotional. I do appreciate that you risked your life to protect mine. No one has ever done that before. I'm happy to be alive."

"It's part of the job," Mina said. "One I take very seriously." Mina tried to be gentle like Lee, since Petra had responded to it well. But her nice wasn't *as* nice, but she was trying. "Your assistant played the long game with you for two years." She held up two fingers. "And if Yolanda and Shauna had succeeded in replacing you, your former assistant would've vouched that Shauna was you until her dying breath. She has all your codes, all your information, access to your residence and beyond. You would've been erased. But the good news is"—it was more than time for good news at this point—"they're not nearly as intrepid as they think they are. They've admitted their plan. Now that we know what it is, there's no way they can succeed. We can have your DNA tested every hour if we need to. That will sink in for them eventually. What we need to do now is figure out where they are and round them up."

Lee turned to Mina. "You keep saying Shauna? Did she tell you her name when you were fighting?"

"No. Yolanda called her that," Mina said. "You were too far away to hear. Yolanda probably let it slip. She made quite a few mistakes by worrying about the wrong boss." Or the right one in her mind. "Works in our favor, but my guess is Shauna is not too happy. Keeping Yolanda on the inside would've been key to continuing with their plans. They can't now. It's all over."

Petra had, for the most part, finished her tearfest. Mina was grateful. "I don't know any Shaunas. Why is that name important?"

Lee shook his head. "Honestly, I feel like it's too much of a coincidence for the two cases not to be connected." He'd addressed Mina, specifically.

"I'm listening." Mina wanted to hear what was going on in the rookie's mind. She knew it would be good.

"If Shauna, whether she's Shauna Nesbit or not, had succeeded in replacing Petra," he started, "she would've needed her DNA to fool any swipes for the foreseeable future. Shauna Nesbit has been working a DNA alias successfully for over twelve years. It might not be the same person, but it seems likely. I mean, if you're extremely successful at something, why not try and up the prize? Impersonate Petra and take what's hers. If they brought Petra back to Honeycomb, assuming that's where the lab is located, they could freeze as much real DNA as they wanted to." He shot an apologetic look at Petra, who in turn looked horrified. "If Shauna's threat not to give up is real, they could try again. They went to all this trouble to make Shauna look exactly like Petra. Why give up now? They're so close."

"What you're saying makes sense. I don't believe in that much coincidence either." Mina turned her attention to the vid star. "Have you ever heard of the company Honeycomb Gelskin? If you do, it's very important that you to tell us everything you know."

She nodded quickly. Mina was enjoying this new, cooperative Petra. "Yes. My aunt Esther owns it. It's where I get all of my top-of-the-line skin enhancements. She's the best! Such a sweetie."

"Your aunt?" Mina said. "She didn't come up on your lifecheck."

"I paid to have a hacker erase my history years ago." Petra wouldn't meet Mina's gaze. "I had a very tough... family life. I didn't specify which family members should stay or go. I just told them to wipe it all but the very basics. The stuff you have to have to get bank borrows and stuff."

Not a surprise. "When's the last time you talked to your aunt?"

"Actually spoke to her? As in vid chat? More than fifteen years ago. But she sends me packages all the time."

 Chapter 21

"WHAT KIND OF packages?" Mina asked, placing her chair right in front of Petra. Now that she was talking, Mina wanted to hear it all. The vid was playing above them, but it was easier to hear than when Melissa Socorro had been speaking.

"Beauty stuff, mainly. She realizes how big of a star I am and how much upkeep that takes. She's such a love. She's the only one in my family I'm in contact with." Sounded like they were barely in contact.

"Do you ever vid chat her to thank her?" Lee asked. They needed to know if Petra had laid eyes on this woman or spoken to her in person.

"No. But I do occasionally record something and send it. We don't have a personal back-and-forth. That's not our way. She's still in contact with people back home, and I prefer to stay out of it."

Mina had to let Petra know. "There haven't been any DNA swipes for Esther Rizzo anywhere in little over twelve years."

Petra appeared stunned. "What does that mean?" Her head bounced between Mina and Lee. "Does that mean she's dead?"

"It means we have more to investigate," Mina said gently. "But if she's not running Honeycomb, someone else has been sending you those packages."

Lee asked, "Do you open the boxes yourself? Or did Yolanda open them for you?"

"Yolanda retrieves all my packages. She brings them into the residence and usually opens them in my presence. It's what I pay her to do." Petra's voice cracked a little. "At least, it's what I *used* to pay her to do."

"Was there ever anything inside the packages that seemed odd to you? The first note you received mentioned beauty recipes. Yolanda and Shauna wanted you to hand over something they couldn't get on their own. And they called them beauty *recipes*. That's extremely specific."

Petra shrugged. "Not that I can think of. It was mostly enhancement products like lip dyes, sculpting cream, crease reversal, elastomer second skin. Things like that."

"There has to be something else," Mina said. "Something Yolanda didn't have access to in your residence or somewhere you keep personal things. If she could get to it, she would've just taken what she wanted."

Petra closed her eyes, trying to concentrate. *Go, Petra.*

When she was ready, she opened them. "The only things in the packages that had recipes were the ad plates. You know the ones? They try to get you to buy their products. Full sound, sometimes a vid, usually snappy music. The ones from Honeycomb sometimes included beauty recipes on the front, like how to mix two colors together by hand, the old-fashioned way, to get the perfect color, or how to mix a hyperglo nail color with some kitchen ingredient to make a fun goo for kids to play with. Yolanda always wanted me to toss them, but I liked them. My aunt Esther included them in my packages because she knew I loved them as a kid. I used to collect them from all over." Something Yolanda and Shauna might not have known if they'd been the ones to add them in. "They had an imprint of a rose petal up in the corner, because my aunt's middle name is Rose. They made me nostalgic, so I kept them." Petra's eyes widened like she was finally beginning to understand that this was all real and connected to her.

Mina nodded, encouraging her to keep putting the clues together.

"The imprint! The imprint of the rose petal. That's it. They must've wanted those ad plates." She frowned. "But why would they want the ad plates? They weren't *my* recipes. They were just recipes for homemade things."

"That's what we intend to find out," Mina said. "Once we get them in our possession, we'll figure it out. You must've placed them somewhere your assistant couldn't get to them." It wasn't a question. Because, as previously stated, if Yolanda could've just taken them, she would have.

Petra nodded quickly. "They're in my private safe. It's where I keep all my special memories and lots of coin. Just in case. It's a rotary. Too many hackers out there.

I was in this vid called *Bank Credit Crooks*, and the hackers cracked open all the safes and stole all this widow's currency, including all the death benefits. I was the widow, but I was only twenty-three. It ruined her life, and she was forced to live in the *outskirts*—"

"Did Yolanda ask specifically about the ad plates?" Mina guided the vid star back on track.

"She did!" Petra seemed shocked with each revelation. Mina was glad the revelations were coming, but she wished that'd happened a lot sooner. But here they were. "Come to think of it, she's asked me to see them a few times. I've always been busy, and honestly, I thought it was a weird request. I have private stuff in the safe about my family, too. Nothing I want made public. Because of that, I never give out the combination to anyone. Private things should be kept private. But it never occurred to me…" She took in a long breath and met Mina's gaze. "I guess that's my problem, right? Not thinking about the right things."

"You're thinking now, and that's what matters," Mina said. It was pretty magnanimous of her considering, but the vid star had been through a lot tonight. Someone she'd trusted had almost gotten her killed and replaced, and that had to sting. "We're going to need to get our hands on these ad plates as quickly as we can. I'll send a couple of agents to your home, so you're going to need to give us the combination to your rotary."

Petra's face fell. "Can't I do it? Can't you just escort me in, and I'll retrieve them for you?"

It would be risky to take Petra back to her home with

Yolanda having access to everything. Before Mina could make a decision, Vince leaned over and draped his arm around Petra's shoulders and gave her a stabilizing hug. "How about I go? You can trust me not to rifle through things. My entire job as the colonel-in-arms of the French Protectorate is to keep secrets, and I keep them very well. I will only grab the ad plates, and I'll ignore everything else."

"I'm not so sure that's going to work—" Mina started.

Petra clapped her hands, looking incredibly relieved. "Yes! That's perfect. I *do* trust you."

Mina tried not to make a face. She really tried. "I shouldn't have to remind you, Kramer. You're a civilian—"

"A civilian who's cleared at The Bella already. I have access to all the floors. Trying to get your agents in would take time. Petra can clear me remotely in her system. It will be less hassle all around. And we all know that having me go is much safer than Petra herself going, with Yolanda and Shauna still on the loose."

Petra grasped Vince's arm, her face pleading with Mina. "Please let him go. I trust him above anyone else."

Mina did not roll her eyes, but she did shut them. For a full two seconds.

When they popped back open, she was ready to go. "Fine. Kramer, you get the ad plates." No use wasting air over this any longer. The only thing that would stand in the way is if her director said no, but she didn't think McAllister would. "The next thing we have to decide is where we're going to take Petra." She aimed this discussion at her partner, even though Petra and Vince were in on it. "We can't take her home, that's been decided. Since this case now includes a possible link with Pormal, I say we place Petra with Norm and Harri for safe keeping. Then, when we arrive, we can have an audience with Quaz and see if he can connect some of these data strands together so we can start to weave together what happened here tonight. He mentioned today there was something big going down, and if we're correct about this Shauna being Shauna Nesbit, that means she's in a partnership with Dominic Nesbit, and this event could be what Quaz was talking about. Stealing a vid star's identity and currency would certainly qualify as big."

There were certainly a number of Shaunas in residence in this city. Seeing what Quaz had to add to the investigation was imperative.

Mina continued, "While that's happening, McAllister can try and secure a warrant for Honeycomb. Shauna attempting to murder Petra should be grounds enough to get a warrant granted immediately. He will have to extrapolate that they are the same woman." McAllister was extremely good at things like that. "But if he's successful, things will start coming together."

Lee nodded, appearing thoughtful. "That makes the most sense. Since Pormal is near the outskirts, which is where the Nesbits are likely located, Shauna and Yolanda would never dream that Petra would agree to go there. It would be very out of character for her. She'll be safe with Norm and Harri."

"Pormal?" Vince asked.

"It's a place on the edge of the outskirts," Mina replied. "We're working on another case, which is not *exactly* a case yet, and it seems these two might be interconnected."

"I'm not trying to pry," Vince said. "It's just an unusual name."

"Well, actually…" Lee hesitated, looking at Mina. Mina raised her eyebrows. She had no idea what the rookie was going to say. "The colonel has been cleared to help us in this case. Full details." Lee shifted his gaze to Vince. "Our director only requires that you sign the appropriate digital data agreement, which covers all of the agency's nondisclosure and privacy mandates."

Before answering, Vince shot a pointed look at Mina.

"It's up to you." Mina shrugged. "Your help would be welcome."

Vince smiled. "I accept."

"Great," Mina said. "You're hired. Now let's get back to figuring out how we're going to get Petra out of here and to the secure safe house in Pormal." She glanced at the vid star. "Have you followed along? We have a place that we think will keep you very safe while we try to track down Yolanda and Shauna. Until we have them in a box, they're still a threat to you."

"I think so," Petra said tentatively. "I'm not sure what Pormal is, but I want to be safe."

"A friend of mine is already in residence. He's very nice. And an ex-marshal, who is also a friend, is there guarding him. You'll be in good company."

"Okay." Her voice wavered a little, but held.

"Excellent." Mina turned to address Lee. "You and Vince figure out the best way to get us through the tunnels unseen and into a craft. Vince knows the routes. I'm going to report to McAllister so he can hopefully start the warrant process for Honeycomb and give me his approval on moving the vid star to the safe house and Vince's involvement." She reached into her pocket and drew out Vince's lock disengager. She dropped it into his open palm. "By the way, this didn't work for me at the tubes after you left, but it did open up the outer door here."

He looked at it quizzically, flipping it over in his hand. "That's strange. It's not coded specifically to me. It's just a copy I keep on file. It's possible that when Shauna was moving through the tunnels, she changed the codes as she went." That also meant Mina and Vince might've just missed her. Things would've gone down a lot differently if they'd captured her before Petra had dropped through the stage.

"Which begs the question as to why someone like Shauna has internal access to codes at the Ultimax Dome," Mina pondered. "There's a lot here that we still don't know. Hopefully in a few hours, we'll have more pieces of the puzzle, and an image will start to reveal itself."

"You've always loved solving a good puzzle," Vince said with a chuckle. "You have the same sparkle in your eyes as you did when we were solving those holoseek games together as kids."

"I do not," Mina argued.

"You do, too." He elbowed Lee. "Don't you see it?"

Lee had the decency to not even pretend to look at her. "Um."

"The look in my eye is sparkle-free."

"I actually see the sparkle." Petra giggled, then her face became contemplative. "Wait, you two knew each other as children?"

Mina chose not to answer that. Instead, she said, "It's not a sparkle. It's determination. There's a difference."

MINA DIDN'T HAVE to worry about getting a message to Quaz. The second the door of the craft opened, Mina spotted Suli. The young girl stood with her top lip curled like she was suffering through a massive stink bomb that had just been dumped on her head. It kind of had. She thought she was done with them, and yet here they were once again. Mina hoped she could turn that lip curl into a smile at some point, but she knew the kid would be a tough sell.

Once out of the craft, she walked up to the child. "We've got another occupant for the safe house, and I need to speak with your father as soon as possible." Lee and Petra stepped out of the craft, moving off to the side. The door closed, and it took off with Vince still aboard. He was going to retrieve the ad plates. Petra had made all of the arrangements while they were inside the craft. Mina gestured upward. "When that drone comes back, I want you to escort the guy inside to wherever I am. Can you do that?"

The girl crossed her arms. "Nope."

They didn't have time to banter about this. Channeling Kaylee, Mina bounced down into a squat, which didn't have the same effect as when Kaylee had done it, since Mina was in this ridiculous half-ripped dress. Suli eyed it with a smirk, her lips still fully curved downward. "I know I look like an idiot, but it can't be helped," Mina began. "Your dad asked me for help, and I'm here to give it. If you don't follow my directions, you're going to cost us a lot of time we can't afford to waste right now. I need you to lead us to the safe house and then go alert your dad that we're here." Mina didn't even consider barking. It would've sounded ridiculous coming from her. "Then come back here and wait for the craft to return."

Suli was completely unimpressed. The kid even rolled her eyes. "You're not here to *help* us. You just want a free place to stash your trash." She raised her chin, holding her ground. "Your stinky, rotten, smelly, sulfur-laced *garbage.*"

Mina sputtered as she stood. "That's not true. First of all, we're paying for the safe house. Good, solid currency, which you're in short supply of, and that will help—"

Petra walked up to the young girl, seeing that Mina was failing hard at convincing her to do anything she wanted, and offered, "If you do what this nice agent is asking you to do, I'll give you a personalized digigraph. You can show all your friends, and they'll be positively jealous. I only give them out on very rare occasions to very special people."

Or a crowd of media hounds and whoever shows up at your premiere.

Mina appreciated the help, but she knew the offer wasn't going to fly.

On cue, Suli snarled, "Who in the *hell* are you? And what is that stupid outfit you're wearing?"

Petra gasped, tossing a hand over her heart. "This is an Arvin Archibald! People beg him to be their clothier. It's an honor to wear his designs. He only offers his services to four other people currently, and I happen to be one of them."

"It's horrible. And I don't want your *digigraph*. I don't want anything from you, whoever you are. What I want is for you to get out of here. You're stinking up the entire—"

"Hey, little monster, it's time to back off," a familiar voice chimed. Kaylee came around the corner a beat later, dressed head to toe in syn-leather. She had a laser hooked to her waist, a small duffel slung over her shoulder, along with her ever-present take-no-prisoners attitude.

Mina watched Suli's eyes expand. She didn't know if the kid was experiencing awe or fear, but Mina knew Kaylee would accept either. Her fellow agent stopped in front of the group.

"Hiya," she said to Mina. "I'm the only one who knows her way around this godforsaken place, so I'm it. Again. I left the baby at home. Her first op will not be near the outskirts. She's far too fresh." She turned her gaze on Suli, frowning. "Speaking of not so fresh, it's time to get your act together. If not, you're going to be trading your current digs for a couple of carbon fiber panels twined together with a foot of microthread you bartered off of some old woman with no teeth. That's what living in the outskirts is like. No more comfy walls. So I suggest you do what this nice agent is asking you to do. Then we can all get back to saving your scrawny backside, along with all your family and friends." Kaylee stood, legs splayed, arms crossed, going look-for-look with the kid. "What's it gonna be? Are you going to be the one to tell them it's all your fault they have trade resources with a woman with no teeth and have carbon panels for homes now? I bet they won't be too happy. Maybe they'll show their displeasure by—"

"Fine!" Suli shouted, accentuating her word with a stomp. "I'll take you. But this is the *last* time." She swiped her hand through the air. "No more people are going to use us for their gain." Words that had most likely come directly out of her father's mouth.

She stormed ahead.

Mina fell into step with Kaylee. "Thanks for," she gestured ahead of them, "whatever that was. You have such a way with children. Harmony is in for a real treat."

"It's all in the technique." Kaylee nodded toward the Pormal child, who was probably trying to figure out if she could outrun them. She couldn't. "She's totally using all that." Kaylee waved a hand. "Anyway, fill me in. All I have are sketchy details." She glanced over her shoulder to where Lee and Petra trailed behind them.

Lee was comforting the vid star as she became newly acquainted with her reality. She was no longer in the

Ultimax Dome being cheered on by tens of thousands of fans, and a preteen had just burned her.

"I thought she'd be taller," Kaylee said.

"She makes up for it in attitude. I'll give you a quick rundown on what's happened since right before the vid premiere." Mina had already filled in Kaylee on what had gone down this afternoon. "Yolanda, Petra's executive assistant, turned out to be the extortionist, along with a woman named Shauna, who we think might be Shauna Nesbit, who's potentially involved in a full DNA alias scheme linked to Dominic Nesbit and therefore possibly linked to what's going on here. Shauna tried to take Petra out tonight. She's had extensive enhancements done to look just like her. I mean, they're *identical*. But I got in the way." Mina thought about rubbing her side, but the pain had pretty much disappeared, as had the pain in her head, which was helpful. "If it's the same couple, there's a strong possibility they're hiding out in the outskirts planning Petra's demise and their overthrow of Pormal."

"Jeez, is that all?" Kaylee snorted. "Possible case overlap? A rare, but wonderful, thing." She glanced over her shoulder again. Mina knew her friend well. Kaylee was trying to get a read on Petra. "They wanted to kill the neon pink princess and this Shauna woman was going to replace her?"

"That's the current line of thinking," Mina confirmed. "We won't know until we track them down. Lee thinks that maybe, because they've been perfecting this DNA alias thing for so long, they got cocky. To add to all this, Petra's been getting deliveries from a beauty manufacturer owned by her aunt Esther called Honeycomb Gelskin. We think they've been hiding something in ad plates that were included in the deliveries. Yolanda couldn't get her hands on them in the residence because Petra had locked them away in a rotary. We'll know more once Vince comes back with them."

Kaylee shook the duffel hanging over her shoulder. "That's why I brought this. We're going to need some tools." Then she mused, "Kramer to the rescue again."

"He's not *rescuing* anything," Mina insisted. Again or not again. "He happened to be there because Petra invited him, not me. She had no idea we have a past." She did now, though. Mina stepped up her pace, as Suli was indeed trying to lose them.

Kaylee stared up at the dark windows as they passed. "So what's the deadly duo's endgame? Sounds muddled to me. Were they really planning to off a vid star with federal agents literally sitting right next to them? Yolanda's worked for Petra for a couple of years. That's more than enough time to put a decent plan together. Instead, the whole thing sounds like a middle-school-programming vid production gone all kinds of wrong."

"Agreed. It does feel muddled. I don't think Yolanda was counting on federal agents. The PPF were summoned several times, but were turned away by Petra because she got word from another vid star that they were incompetent. Her advice came from the astute Cuticle Cantrell. These people act like vids they star in are real life and not completely fictitious."

"Have you asked her why their names are so ridiculous?"

"Haven't had a chance." They rounded a corner. The dead end looked familiar, even in the dark. A dimly lit ultra hung above the door.

Suli opened it with a huffy growl, and they all went in.

Once inside, Petra gasped, "What is this place? *Ew.* I can't stay here. It feels like a prison."

"It's not a prison," Mina offered. "There's no other place more fortified than this until we figure out what's going on. It's better down below."

Petra peered around. "Are we in the *outskirts*?" Mina heard her weepy voice creeping back into her words. "People are not kind to celebrities in the outskirts. I don't feel safe here."

"This is *not* the outskirts," Suli announced before anyone else could explain. "You're lucky to be here, lady." She jabbed her finger at Petra, who was wise enough to keep quiet. "I'm doing this as a *kindness*. Something people like you never understand. All you care about is your fancy clothing and your stupid life, while we survive here on scraps. No more complaints, or you're out. And nobody here is going to stop me."

Kaylee bobbed her head. "I guess my work here is done."

Mina chuckled. "If only."

Petra quieted down, only a few small sniffles escaping as they followed Suli underground.

Once they arrived at the bottom, Mina knocked on the door twice, calling, "Norm, it's me." She would've alerted the ex-marshal earlier, but there was no signal in or out, which was a good thing, but it made stuff like this harder.

"Hold on a minute." Mina heard Norm disengage the locks on his side. "Almost...there." The door opened, and Norm took in the crew. "Well, looks like we have company." He took a step back to let everyone through.

Harri jumped up and rushed forward. "Does this mean I'm free? Can I go home?" Then his eyes found Petra. "What...is a vid star doing here?"

"It's a long story," Mina said as she brushed past him and into the room. Everyone else followed, except Suli, who remained in the doorway. Mina turned back to her. "Please go get your dad."

"He's coming. Word travels fast around here."

"Then go wait for the drone to return and bring the passenger here. No questions asked."

Suli was about to say something snide. Mina could tell because her mouth was in the process of scootching up on one side. Then her eyes darted to Kaylee, who'd set the duffel down and was gently stroking the gem at her waist. Suli stomped her foot and turned around, racing back up the steps.

Kaylee unzipped the duffel and tossed Mina some syn-leather. "When McAllister told me you were coming from the premiere, I figured you'd need this."

Mina gratefully grabbed the new clothing. "You're a goddess. Can't imagine running through the outskirts in this thing." She glanced down at her raggedy, torn-up dress. Jeni would be so disappointed.

"We're going to be running through the outskirts?" Norm inquired.

"Not all of us have to do that, right?" Harri asked with a quake.

"Don't worry, Harri," Mina assured him. "You're going to stay here and keep Ms. Pebbles company." To Norm, she said, "I'll fill you in on everything once Quaz and Vincent Kramer arrive. No sense in going through all of it twice."

"Vincent Kramer? Here?" Norm shook his head. "Well, that's a new one. I thought it was an anomaly with all the Veritus stuff, but I guess the guy's sticking around, huh?"

"Something like that," Mina muttered.

"Oh, he's definitely sticking around." Kaylee grinned as she nodded. "Most definitely."

"He's sticking around to protect me," Petra boasted. "I'm the one who invited him to my premiere. He's been such a gentleman. He jumped through the stage to help me and stayed by my side when they knitted my fractured ankle back together. In fact, he's picking up things at my residence right now, including clothing. He's amazing." It seemed as though Petra was finding her old self again. Not being the center of attention was a new concept for her. One she apparently didn't care for.

Kaylee chuckled. "Of course he is. He's definitely here just for you. That tracks." She dipped down into the duffel again, pulling out more tech and setting it on the table next to her.

"Are you a detective?" Petra asked. They hadn't been introduced. "I'm assuming you are, based on your clothing." Then she glanced at Mina and Lee. "But you guys weren't wearing that kind of tough-looking outfit when you came to my residence today. I mean, if you had, I think I might've taken this all a little more seriously. She looks," the vid star waved her hand around, "like she knows what she's doing."

Mina was incredulous. Petra was basing the entire investigation on what they'd worn today. While the vid star had donned a pink sleep wrap. Mina was about to say something, her blood churning up to a good froth, but Kaylee stepped in, flashing a solid grin Mina's way, mouthing *I'm tough* then waggling her eyebrows.

Kaylee turned back to the star, reaching her hand out to the vid star. "I'm a federal *agent*. We're not detectives." Petra shook her hand. "You can address me as Agent Poston. It's my job to help these two very talented, and sometimes underdressed, agents find out why your assistant is a bagless hag."

Petra smiled, brightening. "I was in this vid once, called *Shadowland Shadows*. I was the heroine. I always am. Anyway, she was forced to take shelter in a tiny crawlspace, or the shadow monster would devour her. She was stuck in there for three weeks until, of course, her lower half was eaten. But she survived, because she was a fighter." Petra's retelling of this ridiculous tale was enthusiastic, but thankfully she didn't try to act it out. "While we were filming, I had to stay in the crawlspace for up to thirty minutes *at a time*. If I can do that, I can do anything, including staying in this...kind of prison." She seemed incredibly proud of herself for putting those two scenarios together. "I mean, that's what my character would do, and I am my character."

Kaylee raised a single eyebrow, shooting a glance at Mina that conveyed she wasn't going to touch that. Mina shook her head and looked at Norm, feeling she'd done enough. Lee appeared to be intently inspecting the bare-bones meal printer.

Norm straightened, clearing his throat. "You don't say? Why don't you come over here and sit on this very clean lounger and explain the rest of the vid to me and Harri? It sounds very interesting. We'd love to hear all about it. I'm sure it's prepared you for hardship very well."

With relief, they watched Petra latch on to Norm's arm and start chattering.

Kaylee pulled Mina aside, her voice low. "I'd rather be tucked in a single sleeping pod with the little monster than be trapped in here with her for the night. So if nothing goes down that needs my attention once Kramer gets back, you're on your own."

Mina darted a glance at the animated Petra doing what she enjoyed most—talking about herself. "I don't blame you. That makes two of us. If it comes to that, I'll have to take my lumps." This was her case after all. "What I really hope is we can find a way to help the people of Pormal. There's a solid chance we can do something tonight."

"Once Kramer gets back, we'll know more."

THE GEARS BEGAN to churn above them, signaling the opening of the floor door to reveal the staircase. It was too soon for Vince to be back. Mina drew her gem, so did Kaylee. Mina assumed it was Quaz, as Suli indicated he'd come on his own, but it was better to be prepared.

A knock sounded. Quaz's voice ordered, "I have Packard with me. Open up. We need to talk."

Mina hung her gem back at the hip of her newly donned syn-leather outfit. It was a little snug, as it was Kaylee's, but it would hold. Syn-leather had a bit of a stretch to it. Thank goodness.

Mina signaled Norm to open the door. He'd set the protocols to his own bioreads once they'd left earlier that day. He hauled it open with a grunt.

Once inside, Quaz's gaze landed on the lounger and the vid star. His eyes widened as they shot to Mina. Even though his daughter hadn't recognized her, he certainly had. "Why is she here? I didn't give you permission to bring someone else in, especially not someone so high-profile. This is a dangerous game for me, and I'm not getting anything substantial in return. I want you out of here. Now."

"Is keeping Pormal out of the outskirts substantial enough?" Mina asked, moving forward. "I wouldn't have come back unless what we're investigating was linked specifically to you. That's not how I operate. I'm back because this vid star is connected to the business with Nesbit. When I left, I told you I'd look into his file. I kept that promise. Dominic and a woman by the name of Shauna Nesbit came up linked. The assumption is she's using part of his DNA as an alias." Simplified, but close enough. "And in a lining-up-of-the-sun-and-moon kind of way, we were assigned to protect Ms. Pebbles this afternoon. Then a woman named Shauna tried to kill her. It might not be the same Shauna, but there's a high likelihood, as we're assuming that she wanted to use Petra's DNA for yet another alias or even a full identity swap. Shauna missed her mark, but attempted murder still qualifies as a high crime." Mina had the syringe to prove it. "Killing someone is not taken lightly in our city, especially when the victim has amassed a crater full of currency and maintained a long-standing place in the public's eye." Mina inclined her head.

Quaz inclined his right back, indicating that he knew very well that the government would be paying close attention to this case now because a high-profile vid star was involved.

Mina continued, "What I need from you is every piece

of information you have on the Nesbits. Where they live, what kind of goods they're moving, how often they move around town, everything. Ms. Pebbles has received deliveries from a place called Honeycomb Gelskin over the last couple of years, which included ad plates. We think there might be a link to those plates and Nesbit's plans to overtake this area." The moment Mina had uttered the word *Honeycomb*, Quaz's demeanor had changed. "What is it? What do you know about Honeycomb?"

For a moment, Quaz appeared undecided about whether to confide in Mina. After all, she was an outsider who worked for a government he didn't like or trust.

He also wasn't that fond of her. That was okay. Mina didn't take it personally.

Kaylee sensed it, too, because she was excellent at her job. She moved forward and said, "Like I finished telling your daughter a few minutes ago, you can give us everything we need to solve this, or you can find yourself living under a few sheets of carbon in the outskirts. We're trying to protect you and your kid from calling the 'skirts your new home. This is your chance. Your only chance. I suggest you take it."

He nodded as he walked farther into the room. He was contemplative as he stroked his face. Packard stayed by the door, eyes assessing.

Quaz finally blew out a breath. "Fine. I'll talk. Honeycomb is the name of Nesbit's operation. Honey, for short. It's been kept secret for a long time, but I've got a few loyals who keep an eye out and report back.

I don't have specifics on what goes on behind closed doors—I've heard only rumors—but Nesbit's been building up his operation for years. When Barker was here, he cut into his resources, and that set him back. I don't know anyone named Shauna, but I do know Dominic has a female partner. Goes by Thorn. And when she goes out, she's covered from head to toe. Every time."

Mina took everything in, rolling it around in her head. "That makes sense. She's likely covered because she looks exactly like Ms. Pebbles. And when I say exactly, I mean *exactly*. She's had extensive, very costly work done by someone who has access to top-of-the-line face-altering technology. If it's the Shauna we're looking for, the task she was supposed to complete tonight failed." Mina processed a few things, thinking. "What's are the rumors about Nesbit? Is he manufacturing weapons? Tech? Chemis? Doing illegal-goods transfers?"

"He has weapons, but he's not making them. Word in the 'skirts is that behind those doors is a fully operational laboratory."

"A lab."

"The rumor is identity stuff."

Right on track. "Full identity swaps so people can get out?" Full aliases were tricky, because they needed to be bank-legitimized to create a borrow stream for the new user, or they weren't any good.

Quaz shook his head. "Pretty sure Nesbit doesn't want anybody to leave. He wants the population to grow, which is why he wants to co-opt us. Not only does he want our people to work for him, he wants the empty buildings so shops can be set up." Quaz gestured above his head to indicate the area where they were currently. "We don't have much in the way of resources, but we have a lot of empty space."

"Shops?" Mina thought she was on track, but this was a sharp turn.

"Yeah. Not sure exactly, but I think the people who get new identities are supposed to bring goods into the outskirts legally, so he can resell them or barter with them or something." Quaz scratched his head. He was low on details, but anything he could contribute at this time was worthwhile.

Legally was not the right word. Creating a DNA alias was a crime. Buying things with borrows obtained using a fake identity was also a crime.

Packard cleared his throat. Quaz shot him a look, then nodded. The former military man clarified, "His runners are going to use altered helix strands to swipe as legal and bring product back to sell."

"That doesn't make sense." Mina began to pace. "Even though they might have new DNA," usually applied as a topical cream or stamped onto a rubber coating one wore over a finger for a swipe, "these people are essentially fake. They won't have bank borrows attached to those aliases. They won't have backgrounds that would stand up to any kind of lifecheck. They won't be legally registered and therefore won't qualify for credit. The most successful DNA aliases are full-strand steals harvested from a living person who's either killed or kept cloaked. Then the alias becomes an assumed identity, and the new person inherits their bank account and is able to go around swiping as that person." Technically, fetuses could be registered, so parents could take out borrows against the cost of having the child, but once a baby became viable, it was registered in the government system based on DNA. A newly registered baby couldn't suddenly become a thirty-year-old swiping to buy a piece of expensive tech. Mina glanced at Lee. "We didn't have time to investigate Shauna K. Nesbit's bank borrows, but we did see that she'd been swiping in a lot of locations. It didn't occur to me that she shouldn't have access to bank borrows if she's a partial-strand alias. But she must have access to borrows or she couldn't shop."

Lee nodded. "Half-strand aliases have been talked about on the boards for years. They're complicated and much harder to maintain than an identity swap. She would need a pretty solid hacker to get her qualified for borrows so she could go undetected for as long as she has. Twelve years is an incredibly long time not to be flagged, which means someone is also paying down her debt."

Mina turned to Quaz, who looked uncomfortable with where all this was going. This was a greater threat than he'd anticipated. Which wasn't good news for the people of Pormal. "Does Nesbit have solid connections and resources in the city?"

Quaz shrugged. "I don't know. I've only seen him face-to-face a couple of times. But in the 'skirts, he brags a lot. He has connections. I don't know who they are, but I'm sure they have resources. I didn't think this operation would be this big, but it plays. At least with his ambition."

Packard nodded, adding, "A few guys I know were approached recently by Nesbit. He wants them to go into the sector and come back with goods. Says they'd be untraceable with real borrows. He's calling them helix hackers. Nobody's buying it, since nobody's ever heard of something like that being a real thing."

Mina took a moment to wrap her brain around this new information. That meant this operation had the potential to be enormous. Which would better explain why Shauna, or Thorn, or whoever she was, was so emboldened. She had powerful people outside of the outskirts backing her.

"So the plan is to make the outskirts a wealthy business enterprise?" Mina asked the room in general.

"An untapped resource," Norm commented from his place on the lounger. Beside him, Harri and Petra were quiet. "This wouldn't be the first time corporations have tried something like this. During my lifetime, there's been a few attempts to monetize the outskirts, but they were always shut down quickly. Banks and bankers have very few scruples, if any. If they see an opportunity to make currency and have someone like Nesbit slide it to them under the meal printer, they jump at it. Happens all the time in the city. It was my job as a marshal to accompany these lowlifes to trial. And more than a few times, they got off. Corruption stems from the banks. It's the root of all the greed."

"Nesbit plans to be king of the outskirts, that's all I know," Quaz said. "He wants currency to burn, power, status, control, everything. And he's going to take out anyone who stands in his way. And he'll keep doing that. Nothing will stop him unless he gets put in a box. Everyone here is going to pay the price for his ambition. I don't understand how the DNA thing tracks, but it sounds right."

Mina and Kaylee exchanged glances.

Kaylee whistled. "Whoa. What you thought was a low-level guard-duty op just turned out to be a stratospheric-level federal-high-crime op. Honestly, other than taking down a killing ring like Veritus, it doesn't get bigger than knowingly manufacturing bank borrows for DNA aliases with plans to make under-the-counter profits from the 'skirts. It sounds like it's right out of a vid." She glanced around the room, hands on hips. "Which seems to be a theme around here."

Light footsteps sounded on the steps. Quaz hadn't reengaged the trapdoor. A second later, Suli rushed in. She was out of breath. Loud, heavier footsteps came next and Vince entered the room behind her.

Suli had given him a run for his currency, literally. The kid didn't know who he was. But her father and Packard did, both of them taking a few steps back.

Quaz's eyes shot to Mina, then back to Vince. If he'd been startled to see a vid star sitting on his lounger, he was comet-blasted to see the colonel-in-arms of the French Protectorate standing there. He lifted a shaky finger. "What's he doing here?" Then he slowly raised both his hands in a surrender pose.

"Put your hands down," she told Quaz as she rushed to Vince's side and grabbed the bag he'd used to gather the evidence from Petra's safe. "He's with us. Ms. Pebbles invited him to her event." To Vince, she asked, "How many are in here? Is this all of them?"

"There were seven in total. I took everything in the safe."

"I thought there'd be more than seven." Mina shot a look over her shoulder. "Petra, are there only seven?"

The vid star made her way over, peering at the ad plates. They were thick. Usually, ad plates were thinner. "I have no idea," she said. "I never counted them." Typical. "What do you think is inside them?"

"Hopefully, we're about to find out," Mina said.

Lee and Kaylee already had their heads together at the table, pulling out more tech from Kaylee's duffel. Lee set Kaylee's compucase on his lap. She granted him voice control. Everybody moved in as Mina set the plates on the table in front of the rookie.

"My guess," Lee started, "based on the information we just received from Quaz, are that these plates contain some kind of encrypted data. Either names of people who are involved in this new operation, or possibly the names of banks. Maybe detailed bank borrow credit lines? Or possibly Petra's entire background, including her bank account information and personal information." Petra gasped. "They can't start their alias business without whatever's inside these. It was obviously pretty important to them. Dominic or Shauna, or both, have made contacts over the years to make this entire thing operational. Maybe the banks created these and sent them to Honeycomb, and then they were sent to Petra because deliveries can't be sent to the outskirts. Or maybe Shauna needed a place to stash them away from Dominic?" Lee shrugged. "Just an idea." He turned one over in his hands. "We won't know until we find a way to open them."

Vince's eyebrows rose. "It seems you've uncovered quite a bit of information since I've been gone."

"Yes," Mina agreed. "According to Quaz and Packard"—Mina gestured toward the two men—"who run things in this part of town, Dominic and Shauna Nesbit have been busy. They've set up an operational lab to manufacture DNA aliases in the outskirts. But the object is not to sell the aliases. It's to buy products with legitimate bank borrows and bring them back here to upsell for a profit. Now, like Lee said, we just have to figure out how to open these things and see if we're correct."

Kaylee, Packard, and Norm had each picked up one.

"No seams that I can see," Norm grunted. "Made pretty solid." He rapped on it with his knuckles.

Harri picked one up and squinted at it. "The ad plates the Pleasure Emporium use are skinnier. And these are much heavier." He lofted one up and down in his open palm. "At least three times more."

"Let's try NeuDAR," Lee said, plucking up the right device. "See if we can get a clear image of what's inside." He ran the small wand over it.

A few beeps sounded, then a low, continuous noise, then a few more beeps.

"What's the reading?" Mina asked, glancing over his

shoulder into Kaylee's compucase, where an image was beginning to show on the screen. "I've got to get a report to McAllister. He should already have a team on-site at Honeycomb if the warrant came through. He's going to be waiting." Not so patiently, Mina assumed.

"I'm not seeing anything inside that's not supposed to be there," Lee commented as he continued scanning, squinting at the screen. "These things have very simple parts. A battery source, which I see. A microconnection to the screen, which is also here. And a small bank for memory. If there's another device stashed in here, I'd see it. It's clear."

"How can that be?" Kaylee said, bending over to look at the screen beside Mina. "These are the things Yolanda was after. There has to be something stuffed inside these biscuit-thick plates."

Petra said, "I've watched all the ads multiple times, and some of them are pretty weird. They talk about strange things like math problems and temperature settings. Not very beauty-related, if you ask me."

Everyone in the room turned to stare at Petra.

Lee was the first to speak. "Um. Well, how about we watch one of them now?"

Mina tapped the face of the ad plate she held in her hand.

A woman who looked remarkably like Petra, but not quite, with red hair and ample enhancements, faced the camera with a product in her hand, her smile syrupy sweet. "This is the new just-on-the-market Polyresin Data Distributor 101537!"

It was a simple, small, rectangular box of polycarb, by the looks of it.

"And it's only found at Coronado and Bale. It contains four special ingredients…"

Those were street names. "Lee, find out what's on Coronado and Bale," Mina ordered as the woman continued.

"The first ingredient is a colossal one…"

"She could be referencing Colossal Bank," Kaylee said. "Maybe they're in on it?"

Strong possibility.

"…and the key elemental ingredients are three, twenty-six, fifty-six, seven, and nineteen—"

"Periodic table references," Lee said. "She just spelled Life Bank."

Leave it to the hacker. *Go, Lee.*

Several big banks were predominant in the city and around the world. Colossal was one, Life Bank was another, as were Tantamount, Parlay, and Future.

The woman on the screen, who had to be Shauna midmetamorphosis into Petra, continued, "Stay tuned after the ad to hear from Tarren Bollow for more details on how you can get one of these all for yourself."

Lee looked up from Kaylee's compucase. "Static map of Coronado and Bale shows residential and one small accounting firm called Bennet Brokers. I can't hack them or, um, get in legally until I get a signal, but I'm assuming the numbers 101537 would reference a specific account or file number."

"I'm having a problem with this. These clues are too easy," Mina said. "Anyone with a few brain cells critically examining these could crack that code. And it doesn't explain why these ad plates are thicker and heavier than other ad plates. I'm not buying that there isn't something inside. We need solid evidence to get a warrant to bring these two in. Living in the outskirts, they're outside the city's jurisdiction. We need something definite and irrefutable that connects them to high crimes involving banks to get a SWAT team in tonight and get them to Government One for a chat."

It would be a longer process to bring them to justice. It would not happen in a single evening. But they could pick them up. The quicker, the better.

Vince reached into his pocket. "This might help."

Mina crinkled her brow. "Another disengager?"

"Not quite. I agree that there's something inside. My guess is whatever's holding that plate together is magnetic. They look like they're made of a lightweight polysteel composite. Easy to make in a standard mold injector, no need for a printer. If you wanted it sealed, but want to be able to open it later, you install an alternating pixelized set of magnets with intervals of strong negative poles. One of these"—he rocked the gadget in his hand—"repels the strong negatives, and the maxelized seam is forced apart."

Lee nodded along enthusiastically. "Yes, that makes perfect sense." Maybe to those with highly formed geek minds. The rest of them remained clueless. "Normally, no one would ever want to open an ad plate. They're consumed and then ground up for elemental reuse. But using a maxelized seam makes complete sense for this. An easy way for it to appear closed, but able to open. Let's give it a try."

Kaylee handed Vince an ad plate, and they all watched as the colonel pressed his tool into the top of the plate. In less than a single second, the bottom clicked off, dropping into Quaz's outstretched hand.

Suli, who peered around her father's side, blinked twice. "What's all that?" She pointed to the spherical data sheet embedded in the plate. The tiny, wafer-thin circles would each be full of data. They hadn't been detected by Lee's scanner because the sheet had been embedded into the polysteel and read as one unit.

"It's the evidence we need." Mina turned toward the door. "I hope there's something in that duffel to interpret sphere data. I'm going up to report to McAllister. Once we have names and players, send someone up. The Nesbits are going to be rounded up tonight."

Chapter 24

"I'M NOT A baby! You can't make me stay!" Suli raged, her face scrunched up, her fists slamming into her sides, right foot stomping.

Quaz looked helpless as he rose from his position in front of his daughter. "She'll just follow us. There are small places she can sneak in over the wall." He gave her a stern look. "Even though that's against our code, and you're not allowed. If you did that, you'd get hurt." He shook his head, addressing Mina. "In this community, we stick together. Other than physically confining her, which I won't do, there's no way to make sure she stays here."

This was highly unusual, and Mina wasn't sure how to proceed.

She glanced at her cuff. "We're due in position in ten. We're backup in case they try to vacate on foot. SWAT will take care of infiltration and acquisition of the targets." She glanced at the stubborn kid, who had her arms crossed, ready to stick out her tongue. Mina refrained from sticking hers out, because adult. "I've never in my entire life brought a child into a potentially dangerous situation. I'm fairly certain if she accompanies us, we will be breaking several child welfare laws."

Quaz shrugged. "Your laws don't exactly apply to us, do they?" He was right. The government doesn't enforce anything here. But still.

The leader of Pormal had dressed appropriately in a battered carbon protection vest and old combat fatigues. Mina had informed the three men who were accompanying them into the outskirts that they could not weapon up, which they agreed to without complaint. She appreciated that. Packard and another man, who went by the name of Ronnie, stood a meter behind Quaz. Pack's clothing was decidedly newer and military-issued. The three had insisted on the need to give an accurate firsthand account of what went down. Without firsthand accounts, rumors went wild, tempers flared, and battles broke out. Everyone involved wanted to keep that to a minimum.

As to not give anybody any warning they were descending, no other civilians in Pormal or the outskirts knew what was about to go down.

"She's with me," Kaylee announced, jerking her head back, indicating Suli should come and stand beside her. "Your only job is to stick by my side like a clingy ball of elastomer and do what I say the second I say it, or else you're going to pay a heavy price. Are we clear?" Suli didn't move. Instead, she darted a look at her dad. Kaylee growled, but didn't bark. "He's not in charge, *I* am. You stick by *me*. If you figure out how to pay attention, you'll see that I'm giving you a gift. I'm about to show you how this is done, and then you'll know. Either that, or I'm cuffing you to the cooling unit." She grabbed a pair of e-restraints from her pocket. "See these?" She bounced them up and down. "They shrink to fit little monster-sized wrists."

No need for another growl. Suli hustled forward and took her place next to Kaylee.

Mina gave her friend a questioning look, then shrugged. "I guess that's the best we've got. We can't have her tailing us on her own. Keeping her safe is your top priority over everything," she said to Kaylee, "including taking down the perps if they try to make a break."

"Understood," Kaylee answered, crossing her arms.

Since this was Mina's op, and she was responsible, she addressed the kid, "If you so much as twitch in the wrong direction, I will make sure the city sends a NannyBot here. Have you ever seen one?" Suli's eyes widened. "They make you do schoolwork all day long."

"You can't do that! Nobody comes in here without my dad's permission!"

Quaz didn't reply, but his expression was bemused. He knew his daughter had to stay in line, or she could be hurt—or worse, killed. Life here was much different than in the city. A whole separate world. One, apparently, where a small child could accompany federal agents on a tactical mission.

Mina straightened up, addressing the group. "Okay,

let's head out. Once we're in place, the alert goes out. SWAT is on drone standby. We need eyes on the building before they're deployed. Lee, please tell me that tiny heat sensor will penetrate the walls. Kramer, if something happens to you in the outskirts, this government is not responsible." The colonel had, of course, insisted on coming along.

Norm had stayed back with Petra and Harri, even though his inclination had been to join them. But ultimately, Norm was damn good at protecting, and he'd agreed to stay behind. Mina needed him in place in case people in the 'skirts decided to retaliate, which wasn't out of the realm of possibility of what could happen tonight if things didn't run smoothly.

"I added extra power to the scanner," Lee answered. "It should detect heat signatures as long as the walls haven't been reinforced to more than a meter thick."

He held the scan gun up. The screen was set and ready to go.

"I made a vid declaration and sent it to the appropriate places," Vince confirmed, locking a blaster onto his hip. The man was the colonel-in-arms of a large military. He got a weapon.

"Great. Then we're good to go." Mina made a motion with her arm. "Quaz, Pack, and Ronnie, lead us in. Once we're on the ground in the 'skirts, we have limited time. Word that we're there will travel like a comet streak. We have to make it to our targets before the comet strikes earth."

The group started off at a trot.

Quaz and company, going back to the pre-Barker days, had delineated Pormal from the 'skirts with a long line of broken buildings with high walls in between made mostly of discarded syncrete blocks with jagged metal and plexan fixed on top. This border could be breached, but it kept the majority out.

Once Mina and her group crossed over into the outskirts, they were going to attract attention no matter what, but at least the three men in the lead would be recognizable. The idea was to spark curiosity, not violence.

Luckily for everyone, the building the Nesbits occupied was only a hundred meters past the Pormal barrier. Once SWAT descended, McAllister would land with backup so they could all get out safely in case a crowd gathered.

The group stopped in front of a building that appeared better off than most, and Quaz retinal-scanned in. They had extremely minimal tech options here, so they used them wisely.

While they waited, Vince leaned over and whispered, "You connected all the complicated carbon threads and wove them into a solid net in a very short period of time. It's always impressive to watch."

Mina shrugged. "Yolanda was the giveaway. Everything else was a coincidence, which I'm thankful for, because it's allowing us to help these people."

"I don't believe in coincidences that big."

Mina quirked a brow. "How so? I came here to meet Norm to talk about Harri. Then Quaz pulled me in, which wasn't in the plan. Then later, Lee and I were assigned a case no one previously knew about. It had to be a coincidence. Sometimes that happens, and here in the US, we count them as happy chances."

"In some cases, perhaps. But Norman Webb is wily. Stories about his prowess have filtered across the sea to France. It wouldn't surprise me in the least if he knows more than he's shared. Harri said they stayed at a pay-a-day. Why here? How was he able to book a room so late? There has to be a previous relationship there." Vince was definitely thinking like the critical military operative he was.

The door opened in front of them, and they followed Quaz through.

Mina trailed the group for a second, thinking. There was a chance Vince was right. Norm could've facilitated things so they'd end up here, or close to here, to help these people. The spider, a retired marshal who was over eighty years young, had maintained a solid list of connections both inside and outside the government. Mina knew better than to think she would be able to get anything out of him that he wasn't inclined to share. He would tell her, or he wouldn't.

They cleared another door, this one fortified with titanium rods and locks, and entered the outskirts at a jog.

The topography changed immediately. Debris blanketed the ground, and makeshift shacks made of carbon fiber sheets, just like Kaylee had described, lined wide streets. Faces stared back at them from inside. Mina didn't glance at the kid, but she knew Suli was taking it all in. There was a high likelihood her father had never brought her in here before, but she had gotten glimpses of it over the wall through the years. If Harmony was considered too young at twenty-one to be a part of this, Suli was an infant.

But here she was. Mina knew Kaylee wouldn't let anything happen to her.

The few people they encountered on the streets shifted away, sliding into the shadows like they'd never been there. Several places seemed to have patrons inside, judging by the glowing interior ultras and noise emanating through the walls. They were likely swilling and imbibing, using trade to get what they could.

Packard slowed, allowing the group to pass, taking up the rear.

However many people disappeared in front of them, more would gather behind. Pack would make sure they stayed well behind, and if he couldn't, he'd let them know.

Mina trotted up to Lee. "All set?"

No use having SWAT land if no one was home. If body heat registered, there was no way to know for sure if the body-heat sigs Lee captured on his gun would be Dominic's and Shauna's. But even if the Nesbits weren't in residence, the federal government would take whoever was there in for questioning. But getting it wrong would mean the Nesbits would be clued into what was happening, and they could burrow, which wasn't the outcome they were looking for.

The group had discussed it at length and figured with Shauna and Yolanda being exposed, the safest place for them to rabbit would be back here until they could figure out how to carry out the removal and impersonation of Petra Pebbles.

"I'm ready," Lee replied. "Are you certain McAllister has secured the warrant?"

Mina nodded. "No question. The data we got on the spheres is irrefutable. Add that to what they found at Honeycomb, and it's a lock." They didn't technically need a warrant to infiltrate a place in the outskirts, but if they wanted it to stick in the courts, since it involved a whole bunch of bankers who dwelled in the city. They would do this by the book.

It turned out that Honeycomb Gelskin had contained a lab in a corner of its processing area. On first examination, it appeared that DNA manipulation was happening, but further investigation would be necessary. The owner, Esther R. Rizzo, Petra's aunt, hadn't been seen in years. The company was run by bots, and a competent air breather named Hayes Reed made sure it all stayed on track.

He'd told agents that a woman who went by Mrs. N had been allowed to enter the facility once a month since he was hired, but Hayes wasn't sure why. He'd never spoken to her. She usually went into the lab, but sometimes she went into the offices upstairs.

The lab equipment had been confiscated and was being analyzed at headquarters for Shauna's alias DNA, Esther's DNA, and DNA that they assumed would reveal

Shauna's real identity. The results would be available by morning. The warrant to pick up the Nesbits had been requested right after Lee, with the help of Vince, had managed to capture the sphere data, which indicated that at least a dozen individuals in high-ranking jobs at three banks were involved in this alias scheme, not to mention Bennet Brokers and a couple other private companies.

This had become a big-time connected case.

The appropriate federal departments would be called in, and all the players involved would be charged with multiple crimes. But first, all the participants had to be rounded up and brought in, which was happening all over the city at this very moment. They would then be interrogated by the appropriate departments, and more evidence would be gathered, which would happen over the course of a week or more.

This would likely be as far as the CIU went.

The only thing Mina knew for sure that would happen tonight, if they managed to bring the Nesbits in, was that Pormal would sleep more soundly, and hopefully for many, many days after that.

Quaz turned down a new intersection and lifted a fist above his head, swinging it forward. The building ahead looked exactly like Quaz had described it. Lee waved the gun in front of him as he ran. This had to happen fast.

"Almost close enough," Lee panted. "I got one! Two, there are two." He moved the scanner higher. "Three. Four. Four people inside."

"That's good enough for me," Mina said as she tapped her cuff.

Chapter 25

SWAT WAS EFFICIENT, as always. Four crafts had descended thirty seconds after Mina had sent the alert. The residence had been infiltrated in the next thirty. They were due to bring out the perpetrators in the next minute or so.

The area surrounding the residence had been cleared, but Mina knew a kiloton of eyes were watching from afar. This was going to be a huge story in the 'skirts. The government rarely sent agents in, and if they did, they went in undercover, like Mina had in the past.

This was a spectacle. Ultras blazing, props whirring, dozens of feet on the ground.

Quaz and his crew stood off to the side, observing. They would be the truth tellers. Maybe this would benefit the people of Pormal and open some trading avenues. Who knew?

Another craft sounded from above, whooshing in quickly and landing six meters in front of them. Director McAllister, along with four other agents, exited.

"I just had confirmation that four adults, three matching the descriptions of Dominic, Shauna, and Yolanda, have been apprehended. DNA identification is forthcoming," he announced as he moved forward, the other agents fanning around the perimeter of the residence. "They will be taken back to Government One and held, pending further investigation, along with seventeen others taken into custody across the city. All based on the data you collected. Nice work, agents. This is not the first time that an operation like this has been attempted, but it's the first time it's ever gotten this far. Agents Kane, Adams, and Poston, you managed to stop this before it became operational, and the government is grateful for your hard work." His gaze landed on Suli, who was peeking out from behind Kaylee's leg.

He said nothing. He merely looked at Kaylee.

"It's a long story, sir," Kaylee said. "This child is under my protection for the time being. I will be escorting her and her father back to her home, with your permission."

"Of course," McAllister said. "I have two crafts waiting to take the group back, first to the safe house location, then home. I'll expect a full report in the morning. Interrogations will start tomorrow. The DGS, High Crimes, along with Identity Fraud & Misuse and Banking, Borrows & Credits, have all been called in. They are currently fighting for lead."

Lead would be able to control the investigation and usually went to the department that could make the largest charges stick to the perpetrators, guaranteeing maximum time in a box.

McAllister continued, "This will likely be as far as we go."

Not a surprise. The CIU collected evidence, its primary goal was to facilitate other departments in taking down crime at the highest levels, while doing so undercover.

A commotion came from the outside of the residence. SWAT was on its way out, but Mina couldn't get a clear read on who was with them. She said to her director, "I would like to request that Agent Adams and I be able to interview Dominic Nesbit, Shauna Nesbit, and Yolanda Terrin tomorrow morning, as they are still relevant to our extortion case with Ms. Pebbles, which I would like to close personally. Petra is anxious for answers. She has also requested permission to go home as soon as possible. I feel, in light of these three perpetrators being taken in tonight, it's safe enough for her to do so." Mina nodded to her right. "Colonel Kramer has offered to escort her back to her residence, making sure she gets home safely, as he's also staying at The Bella. We can alert their internal guard squad to keep watch over her residence for the evening, as an added precaution."

Vince made a small sound, but kept quiet otherwise. Mina hadn't cleared the request with him, but it made the most sense. Less time with Petra meant more sanity for Mina.

"I also need orders for Harri Hampburg, who is currently still residing at the safe house."

"You're in luck with that, Agent Kane," McAllister said. "Not more than an hour ago, a statement came in from Bliss Corp claiming that Mr. Hampburg's firing had been a mistake. Not only do they want him back, but they want to elevate him to a senior position. This is not unlike how we thought it would play out." McAllister's face clouded. "It will be up to Mr. Hampburg, of course, but I would advise against accepting the job. My response will be forthcoming and will include the threat of a federal, and public, investigation if anything were to happen to Mr. Hampburg now or in the future, accidental or otherwise."

"That's good news." Mina nodded. "I'll fill him in. I'm also making a few inquiries of my own. I'd like to help him find a landing place outside of the city."

"I realize you feel responsible for your friend, Agent Kane," McAllister said. "But had Mr. Hampburg stumbled upon these Plush issues himself, being close friends with the victim, he would've been in grave danger. Without federal intervention, things would've been much worse. Now he is, and will continue to be, a government asset." He turned toward Vince and held out his hand. "Thank you for assisting my agents tonight. Your quick thinking and tech assistance have been noted and will be passed on to the Protectorate. I have data docs for you to sign, typical of the agency nondisclosures. Secrecy is the utmost importance in my department. I'll send them over to The Bella tomorrow."

Vince shook his hand, giving a quick bow of his head. "It was my pleasure. I will sign anything you send. Secrecy is a daily part of my life. Watching your agents work has been nothing less than miraculous. They did an amazing job."

Way to polyresin it on, Kramer.

"You run a very smooth, competent department," Vince went on. "My hat's off to the work you and your agents do."

McAllister nodded. "I'm sure you see your fair share of undercover work." Another agent came up to McAllister and whispered something in his ear. He looked up. "You're all dismissed. And, Agent Kane, it's a yes to the interrogation. You've earned it, and it will be essential to close your investigation. I'll see that it's a priority. Plan to arrive at Government One at seven a.m. on the dot." He turned and walked away.

Mina made her way to Quaz, Packard, and Ronnie.

Quaz stepped out from the group. "Are you going with them?" Overhead props sounded.

"No. It's being taken care of," she assured him. "The Nesbits are secured and being brought in for questioning. A full investigation by multiple departments will be launched. We do the legwork that leads to arrests."

Although the last few ops had said otherwise, that's how it was supposed to go down. Rarely had Mina experienced as much action as she had in the last few weeks—not that she minded. This was infinitely better than sitting inside a telework cubicle for eighteen insufferable months, like she had on the Cullen op. The only action she'd seen there had been a gratifying punch to the throat and securing some e-restraints on a greasy hacker.

Two drones dropped out of the sky, landing in front of them.

Mina glanced at Quaz. "Our primary job now is to get you guys back on the other side safely and get our people back where they belong. The Nesbits won't be bothering you anytime soon. Once I have information to share, I will personally deliver it, along with currency payment for the safe house stay." After it was cleared by her director. "Let's board these drones so we can all go home. It's been a long night."

* * *

"Watching Kramer take off with the princess was epic," Kaylee snarked tiredly, her head pressed against the gel-rest. They were on their way back to their residences. It'd taken a while to get everything sorted out, but everyone was now heading in the appropriate directions. "I'm pretty sure he shed a tear."

"He had it coming." Mina stifled a yawn. "I'm just glad Harri got to go home. He was so relieved, he was the one with tears."

"I can't believe Petra's and Shauna's cases were so interconnected," Lee said from his position next to Kaylee, across from Mina. "I've never been a part of something that came together like that. It was kind of cool."

"Yeah, about that," Mina said. "Vince put a few strands in my ear about the possibility that Norm could've been orchestrating some of what went down today. I plan to get to the bottom of it after we interrogate the Nesbits, clear everything with Petra, and pay Quaz for the safe house and give him the information he needs. So, like, fourth on my to-do list tomorrow."

"That old spider is sneaky," Kaylee agreed. "I lean toward Kramer's assessment. I mean, things can line up like a row of trees in an arborist's regrow zone once in a yellow moon, but they never look this pretty."

"Speaking of pretty," Mina said. "You're now Suli's real-life superwoman. How you handled that little girl was nothing short of freakishly impressive. I have a whole newfound respect for how you're going to hone your new rookie. Harmony's in for a treat if she pays attention."

"Oh, she pays attention, all righty. She's a super-absorbent-freakishly-porous-sponge. I've got plans for her. She's going to be one of the best of the best. Just you wait."

Mina giggled. "Did you just rub your hands together like a supervillain?"

"Maybe."

"That means you're going to have to change your stance on how you feel about mentoring," Mina pointed out.

"No, I'm not. She's just special."

Mina snorted. "Either way, Harmony's got it made. Sorry, Lee," Mina told her rookie. "I can't possibly live up to the greatness that is Kaylee when it comes to mentoring. You're stuck with middling second place."

"No way," Lee said. "You're good at it. Like, really good."

"Shucks, Lee," Mina replied. "Hear that, Queen of Mentors? I'm really good."

The drone sim intoned, "Landing at Highland Court in twenty seconds."

Kaylee chuckled. "That's me. I always get a kick at hearing my building's name. So old-timey aristocratic." She scootched forward in her seat. "And I wouldn't say you're *really* good. You're passable. You taught me a few good tricks along the way, I'll give you that." The drone landed, and the door opened. Kaylee got out, ducking her head back in for a quick second. "And if you don't do something about that doe-eyed puppy soon, he's going to give up on you. By-*eee*." Then she was gone.

The door closed, and they took off again.

Lee scratched his head. "I've been going over this case in my head. A lot of it still doesn't make sense. Like, why would Yolanda and Shauna go to all the trouble of sending the extortion notes to Petra? And why would they do something as big as trying to kidnap or kill a vid star in front of federal agents? It's all so risky and ill-advised."

"Greed," Mina answered. "Greed is a huge motivator. Maybe they got carried away. Maybe they didn't have an excellent plan to begin with. Or maybe they had a falling-out with Dominic. There are so many factors to consider. As agents, sometimes we apprehend masterminds, and sometimes we scoop up a couple of misfits trying to pull off something bigger than they can handle. You're new, so you haven't experienced it all yet. But being ill prepared and screwing up is more common than you'd think. Being a criminal is hard work and takes thorough planning. Being a screwup is easy and is how many perpetrators get caught. After the interrogation, we'll have a lot more answers. Things will come together. Get some sleep and come tomorrow with good questions. I'm counting on you. Then, once we have the answers, we'll make a trip back to Pormal. Suli is going to get her reward." Mina had been thinking about what would be appropriate payment for the kid.

"Do you really think Norm had something to do with all this?"

"It's definitely a possibility. Obviously, he couldn't have orchestrated it as well as it went down, but he could've picked Biters as a meeting place so we would have to talk to Quaz as a favor to him for hiding them the previous evening, knowing that the people of Pormal needed our help. That's not so far out there. I don't think he knew we'd be assigned to Petra's case, but it's not implausible that he hoped we would. He has reliable intel on the inside. He could've got word that the vid star had requested a case be opened, but then he would've already understood that the Nesbits were linked to her in some way. If he kept all of that from me, he risks breaking the trust that we've built over the years. I'd like to believe he wouldn't do that. But I fully intend to ask him."

"Will he tell you?"

The sim announced, "Public landing at Sullivan and Twelfth in twenty seconds."

Lee glanced down at his hands, embarrassed that he wasn't being delivered to a hub, but rather an intersection of streets.

"He might." Changing the subject, Mina asked, "Your big move should happen in the next day or so. Are you ready?"

Lee brightened, smiling. "I will be. I don't have much to pack, and I've already contacted the mover-drone place."

"Great," Mina said as the drone landed, and the door opened. "I'll meet you at headquarters tomorrow at six forty-five. Make sure you're there on time so we can go over the interrogation plan. I'll send you a ping as a reminder in the morning."

Lee hopped out. "Okay. And for what it's worth, I agree with Kaylee." Even in the dark, Mina saw a streak of red flare across his cheeks. "Vincent Kramer is a really good guy. He'd be lucky to have you. Oh, and I wasn't lying about the mentoring. If you were a hacker, you'd be at super already."

Mina opened her mouth to respond, but the rookie had already disappeared.

The doors closed, and the sim said, "Next stop is The Spire, landing hub level twenty, arrival in one minute, seven seconds. Do you wish to make any changes?"

"No."

The drone took off.

Mina was dead tired, and her feet ached like crazy. She couldn't wait to get her boots and Kaylee's too-tight syn-suit off and crawl into her platform and wrap herself up in her sheets. That sounded like heaven.

The craft arrived quickly. The moment she stepped through her door and the ultras snapped on, she remembered Vince's apology drive sitting on her meal counter.

"Welcome home, Mina," Veronica said. "You have no current messages, six previous messages from a certain nameless individual." There was that excrement list again. "Would you like me to start the soaker? Or prompt Eggie for a meal?"

"No," Mina said as she walked to the meal counter. "Is there a place to insert a quantum drive in this residence?" She didn't really want to pull out her supercomputer if she didn't have to.

"Yes," Veronica answered. "There are several. One in each room. These readers can take up to ten drives at a time, all different types. Which one would you like to open?"

Jeez.

It seemed Mina needed to do a little more investigating into what her residence had to offer.

"Let's do my sleep room so I can get ready for bed, which is number one on my to-do list." As Mina headed down her hallway, she heard a mechanism being activated. The ultras popped on as she crossed the threshold, Veronica anticipating her arrival.

Right next to her platform, an integrated tech box had extended from the wall. Mina peeled the ball of elastomer off the back of the drive, grinning as she remembered Vince's plan to stick it to her door. If he'd thought he could evade Suzanne the mega rep for any amount of time, he was dead wrong.

No one was that good.

She clicked the quantum drive into place, and the box retracted into the wall.

A second later, her wall screen popped on at one hundred percent. Mina began to tug off her pants, but the sound of a young Vince stopped her.

Mina moved closer. The old vid playing on her wall had been taken during their childhood together. It showed Mina's old room, messy and well lived in, her small sleep pod off to the side, clothing from the previous day draped over one end, toys and games spread out across the floor. She'd loved that room. So many happy memories.

She and Vince were planning something behind the cam. The two of them were giggling, voices high-pitched and excited. She had no immediate recollection of the specific moment, just that it brought her back to one of the many times they'd spent together playing games.

"Here, let me do it," Mina ordered. Typical.

"You can, just let me get it ready first," Vince answered, not sounding irritated in the least that Mina wanted to take control.

Endorphins began to bounce around inside her body.

"My uncle brought this over from France. It's called a holo box."

"Are you sure it's safe?" Mina asked. "My mom says we have to make safe choices."

"Of course it is. Do you trust me?" His sincerity was front and center. She loved the sound of his young voice. It was clear and melodic, just like it sounded now, but deeper.

"You're my *best* friend. I will always trust you." Mina's voice didn't waver. She was absolutely certain of her trust in her friend.

"This is going to be fun," young Vince said. "Here, let me set it down." He walked in front of the cam, his dark tousled hair in front of his face, his clothing just a bit big, a wide grin on his face. He set a shiny silver box in the middle of Mina's floor, then walked back behind the cam. "Now just press that button, and you'll activate it."

Just before young Mina hit the button, present Mina remembered exactly what happened next, and she clapped her hands together, murmuring, "Oh, Vince."

"Here it goes," young Mina exclaimed.

Three little flaps opened on the box, and three microcams rose up and began to oscillate.

Then, like the best magic trick in the world, her little-girl sleep room filled with holo butterflies.

The excitement she'd felt in that moment was eclipsed only by the excitement she felt reliving it all over again.

This was one of her most precious memories.

Mina watched as young Vince and Mina ran around, cupping their hands together as they pretended to try to catch the butterflies. Their joy was unbridled. Two young children with no worries, their lives ahead of them for the taking.

After a few moments, the vid cut to adult Vince.

He sat on a lounger, his hair mussed like he'd been raking it through his fingers over and over again. He likely had. "You trusted me then. You always trusted me. Completely. And I broke that trust." He clasped his hands in his lap, staring directly into the cam. "I felt like my decisions where the right ones regarding Veritus, without bothering to consult you. Something you would never, ever do to me. As your mom said, we have to make good choices, and I made a terrible one. I'm not sure how you'll be able to find a way to trust me again, but it's my greatest hope that you'll consider trying. Spending time with you has always been one of the great joys of my life. Then and now. These small moments, caught on old cams, have gotten me through some of the toughest years of my life."

Man, that's a lot.

Mina's mother had old vids, though Mina had never asked to upload them. Not to say her childhood hadn't been an extremely happy one. It had, especially with Vince in it. Mina just wasn't someone who held on to the past.

But reliving it now, the recollection of seeing those butterflies for the first time, the joy that she'd shared with Vince—it meant something.

"If you choose not to forgive me, I understand," Vince continued. "It's asking a lot. I just hope that you remember the good times we had together. And that I trust you as much as you trusted me when we were young. I care about you, Mina. If we can repair that trust, you have my solemn oath that I will never, ever make a bad choice when it comes to you again."

The vid snapped back to the butterflies.

Mina felt herself go teary, so she stood and began to undress. The voices of young her and young Vince stayed in the background, giggling.

"You win, Vince," she whispered. "How can I possibly say no to that? Even though having you in my life will complicate it to an insanely high degree, you win."

Veronica cut in, startling her. "Does that mean we're taking Vincent Kramer off the excrement list?"

Mina chortled, donning her sleep gown and climbing onto her platform. "I guess it does. Ultras off. Wake-up at five thirty a.m."

"Confirmed. Good night, Mina. Pleasant dreams."

"I'm sure they will be. Replay vid."

Sneak Peek

CODE TEAL

A MINA KANE NOVEL: BOOK FIVE

AMANDA CARLSON

Chapter 1

Mina checked her cuff for a second time. She stood on the roof of Government One waiting on her partner, Lee Adams, to arrive. It was six-forty a.m. They had five minutes to get to the interrogation rooms. "Where are you?" she muttered.

"What's that?" Agent Darian asked from position a few meters away. She was there to escort them in. Government One was a maze of checkpoints and security scans. It was easier to have someone with clearance on the inside to lead them down.

"Nothing," Mina said, managing to keep the grumble out of her voice. Barely. "Just wondering where my partner is. He should be here by now. I sent him a reminder ping this morning. He pinged me back." Mina shielded a hand above her eyes as she scanned the sky. It was mostly dark, the horizon just beginning to brighten. The start of a brand-new day. Why Mina was blocking the nonexistent light out of her eyes, hoping to spot something that wasn't there, remained to be seen.

No craft. No Lee.

Mina dropped her hand.

Anna Darian moved closer. "Can I ask you something while we wait?"

Mina's eyebrows rose. "Sure." She forced herself not to check her cuff again. She didn't want to NannyBot the rookie. Even though he might need it. Mentoring was constant, like a mother chasing after an errant tot.

"What's it like to be involved in an op like the one you had last night?" Agent Darian blinked rapidly, her excitement at the forefront. She'd obviously been briefed on the basics of Mina's case by their mutual director of the CIU, Duncan McAllister.

Mina didn't know a lot about Anna Darian, other than she was personable, competent, and smart. They'd work together a few times, Agent Darian providing fieldwork assistance. But as far as Mina knew, this agent had never been assigned her own case. She was usually found at headquarters.

What did it feel like to be involved in a big case?

Mina had never analyzed it before. It's just what she did.

"I'm not sure," she started. "It feels great when all the pieces finally fit into place. You know you're helping innocent victims, and at the end of the op the perpetrator goes into a box where they can't harm anyone else. That's the height of what matters to me." Mina shrugged. "So I guess I'd say it's pretty fantastic."

Agent Darian nodded along.

During this last op, Mina had been able to help the people Pormal, a group of individuals without access to bank borrows who lived on the border of the outskirts. It'd been a happy chance, as it wasn't inside her jurisdiction. Most ops don't go down like that. Mina and Lee had been assigned to investigate an extortion allegation against a vid star, and the two cases had overlapped in the best way possible.

Although, at first, Mina thought it'd been a coincidence. But Vincent Kramer had given her the idea that Norman Webb, an ex-marshal, might've been more involved than she'd originally thought.

She was planning to get to the bottom of that very soon.

Agent Darian hemmed for a second, while Mina searched the sky again. "But what about, like, going into the *actual* outskirts. That had to be scary, right? Were you worried anything was going to happen?"

"Happen, as in bodily harm? Not really. We had escorts and SWAT doing the actual round up. Our time on the ground was minimal. We were in and out in about twelve minutes. Not really much time to be worried."

Anna shuffled her feet, kicking a nonexistent pebble in front of her. "I don't think that'll ever be me," she lamented. No hint of a whine. "I don't have the courage it would take to do something like that. Or to jump off a twenty meter hydro ship into the harbor. Or to be in the same room with a serial killer. You've done all of that, in like, a week."

Mina heard wistfulness, but not envy. "You're in your

second year at the agency, correct? Once you pass that phase, you'll enter the field more. It takes a while to get comfortable making hard decisions, but then it becomes second nature." She glanced to the sky again. Where was Lee? Her impatience tingled all the way down to her toes as a euroboot began to tap on the syncrete roof.

Agent Darian blushed, shaking her head. "No, I've actually been here for four years. McAllister has offered me time in the field, but I've refused. I'm really great at researching, data filing, and assisting agents like you. But my stress levels would be through the strato if I did what you do on a daily basis. Even though I love being part of the agency, and it's been a dream to work here, I'll never be that kind of agent."

Mina wasn't sure if that statement needed a reply. She settled on, "If you change your mind, you can always start small."

With relief, props sounded in the distance.

They watched as a government drone entered the airspace, no eye shielding necessary. They wouldn't know if it was Lee until it set down.

"Maybe," Agent Darian replied.

"I cut my agent teeth on catching petty thieves. Kiosks are notorious for break-ins."

Kiosks were usually small, one room shops that printed specialty items that contained hard-to-find trace elements. Those trace elements were essential to get the flavor and consistency perfect. Kiosks had been a part of their world for at least fifty years, and since they were usually standalone structures, they got broken into a lot.

Like, a lot.

But luckily, kiosk owners had gotten good at hooking up vid and audio feed surveillance, on at all times. Tracking down the unlucky assailants had never been overly difficult. Just time consuming. And those crooks were usually nonviolent. Most of the time petty thievery landed under the jurisdiction of Street Crime, but CIU agents were called in when they were overwhelmed.

It was a good place to start.

Agent Darian bit her lip. "Honestly, I'd jump into the field if I was lucky enough to be assigned a partner like you."

"There are plenty of agents out there like me," Mina replied.

"Oh, there's not." She shook her head aggressively, but the blonde knot at the base of her neck remained unmoving. "I can assure you."

The government drone set down, and a harried Lee hustled out.

Mina was relieved to see him in more ways than she could count. She sympathized with Agent Darian, but counseling her on her career path was not Mina's strong point. Or even a weak point. It was more of a moot point.

Lee appeared more rumpled and owlish than usual. But maybe not? He so often looked like that. "Sorry I'm late," he huffed, coming to a stop in front of them. "Right before I was ready to leave, I got a visit from my landlord. He sent a bot. It took me a while to get rid of it."

Mina gestured for Agent Darian to lead the way. "Bots do what you say. They're unconfrontational for a reason."

If humans had to deal with confrontational bots, they wouldn't exist. As it was, people were highly suspicious of them anyway.

"I know. But this one...wouldn't leave." Lee coughed, clearing his throat by thumping on his chest a few times. It'd been a *morning*, apparently. "I had to short-circuit its power. I didn't know what else to do."

They DNA swabbed at the sky screen enclosed entrance and followed Agent Darian to a wall of tubes, where they offered their helix strands once again.

"Expedited entrance, interrogation level, no stops," Anna commanded.

The tube doors whisked open and they stepped inside.

A sim intoned, "Expedited request accepted. Please grip the handrails. The ride may be unstable."

Mina grabbed onto one of the protruding polymolded handholds. They were about to plunge down two hundred and fifty stories in about five to seven seconds. "What you mean you had to short-circuit it?" Mina asked Lee as the tube started its descent.

"I have a special tool. It's a remote power blast. It affects the bot's circuitry and takes them a few minutes for them to recover. Kind of like the hyppie trick, but it's not a memory thing, it's just a power thing. While it was sputtering, I snuck out." Lee frowned. "It told me I owed a bunch of currency and said I wasn't allowed to leave until I paid it." He glanced at Mina, eyes blinking. "Do you think that means I can't move into my new high rise?"

Lee had just been assigned new government approved housing, which was a big improvement over his current living situation. He'd been occupying a super tiny, two room, outdated residence since his mom had left him alone at age sixteen.

Mina was about to scoff at the mere thought, but seeing the genuine concern in her partner's face, she held off. Being basically abandoned at the age of sixteen, Lee hadn't learned how to function inside their bureaucracy. Her mentoring process wasn't just about making him a good agent, it was about educating him about their world. "You will absolutely be able to move into your new high rise. We'll just have to figure out what this bot is talking about. You've been living there for, what, six or seven years? Why would they only mention something now? They have to legally inform you of amounts owed, minimum once a year. When you enter into an agreement or Terms of Residence, borrows are deducted directly from your bank account. If you don't have approval from your bank, you can't get a residence." That's how people ended up in Pormal and the outskirts. "Do you have monthly borrows deducted out of your account?"

Lee scratched his head, his other hand gripping the bar next to hers. The ride hadn't been bad. Just a little stomach wobbly. The tube was already slowing. "No. Nothing comes out of my borrow account. I have to talk to my mom. I thought everything was taken care of by my father's death benefits. I guess not."

The sim and announced, "Arrival at underground level five. Have a nice day."

The door whooshed open and they stepped out.

"Try not to worry about it," Mina suggested. "It'll work out." To Agent Darian, she asked, "Is McAllister in the building?"

"I'm not sure," Anna replied, moving to the right. "He was off site at an investigation bright and early this morning. I know he wanted to make it down here at some point. Follow me."

They wove their way through winding corridors, stopping at various checkpoints to give more DNA and complete retinal scans. They passed through another secured doorway, and as the doors opened inward, Mina spotted guards standing sentinel in front of four doors down a long hallway.

This was the place.

Last night, SWAT had apprehended four individuals at a location in the outskirts. Dominic Nesbit, Shauna Nesbit, Yolanda Terrin, and Jesse Guthrie, according to the intel Mina had received this morning. Shauna had tried to kill, or at least subdue and kidnap, Petra Pebbles, the pink-is-her-favorite-color spoiled-above-borrows vid star who they'd been trying to extort.

Mina had taken the industrial strength tranq meant for Petra, getting less than half the dose through a syringe jabbed painfully into her side while she was wrestling on the ground with Shauna. Luckily, it fell out quickly. Or she wouldn't be standing here.

"I want to start with Yolanda Terrin," Mina told Agent Darian. "Is there a completed DNA match for Shauna yet?" They were relatively certain that Shauna Nesbit had been using a DNA alias made from Dominic Nesbit's strands, and she wasn't actually Shauna Nesbit at all.

"Nothing conclusive," Anna answered.

"What?" Mina shot a look at her partner. "How can that be?"

Lee shook his head, his expression equally dismayed. "DNA inside the body can't be manipulated," he said by way of explanation. "I mean, it can, over a lengthy amount of time, involving the natural process or sped up slightly by a chemical process. But even if it shifts a little, you'd still get ninety-nine percent of the sequencing. It should show up with lifecheckable descendants, even if she paid a hacker to wipe her background completely clean. We should have a definitive as to what her real identity is through blood samples."

Agent Darian nodded, looking impressed by Lee's knowledge. That made two of them. "I totally agree with you. But the results say inconclusive. You're free to peruse the data. I'll shoot it to your cuff. It just came in about ten minutes ago."

"That means something major is happening here." Mina asked Lee, "What do you think the chances of getting a nonconclusive DNA result from a blood sample are?"

Lee shook his head. "I would've said zero. That it was a complete impossibility. But it looks like it happened. I'll assess the data while you start the interview. Maybe something will pop for me."

"Good plan," Mina said. "I'm talking to Yolanda first. Join me when you can."

Agent Darian gestured to a door on the right. "She's inside there. She's pretty haggard. Been here all night.

Crying off and on. Refused food."

"Who's running lead?" Mina asked.

"Hasn't been decided yet, but if I had to guess Banking, Borrows & Credits will get it. Their agents were in last night, and they were righteously angry. This was a big operation, lots of their people involved on the inside. A couple corridors over we have seventeen bankers and brokers in holding rooms. Had this plan launched, it would've been a fast moving asteroid, hard to stop. Lots of currency lost. You know how they feel about lost currency."

"The BB&C equates loss of coin akin to murder," Mina replied wryly.

The rough idea of the scam, as Mina understood it, was that Dominic Nesbit and his cohorts were going to provide people in the outskirts with DNA aliases and fake identities, send them into the city to purchase goods funneled through fake bank accounts, and then resell or trade whatever they brought back for a profit. The outskirts didn't run on borrows, it ran on hard coin and items of value. Often extremely inflated because things were so hard to get.

The gains would then be split between Nesbit and the bankers and brokers who'd set up the fake borrow accounts. The banks would take the losses, because the payments from these fake aliases would never be paid back, and bankers would prosper with direct payouts from Nesbit. Once an account was flagged as illegitimate, the corrupt banker would just create another, tagging another fake DNA alias.

Mina knew exactly how banks felt about being stripped of currency.

Because of that, they would fight for max time in a box, which was equal to what Mina wanted. The more time the Nesbits spent in a box, the more time the people Pormal were free of them, as Dominic Nesbit had planned to enlist the people of Pormal to do his dirty work and steal their meager resources. Whoever took lead would run this investigation. They would allow and disallow access.

McAllister had wrangled this interrogation first thing in the morning so Mina and Lee could shore up the extortion case against Petra Pebbles. They owed the vid star that much. Not to mention, Mina wanted to know exactly why the Nesbits had been trying to murder Petra and assume her identity.

There was a lot to unravel here.

Just as Mina was going to head through the door, nodding to the guard, her cuff beeped. It was a holo alert.

"Engage," Mina ordered.

Director McAllister popped up, hovering above Mina's wrist. "Remains of a human body have been found."

Nothing is completed without a great team.

My many thanks to:

Awesome Cover design: Damonza
Digital and print formatting: Author E.M.S
Copyedits/proofs: Joyce Lamb
Final proof: Marlene Roberts

*Head to my website to sign-up for my Book Alert
newsletter to receive new release info in your inbox so
you don't miss a thing!*

About the Author

Amanda Carlson is a graduate of the University of Minnesota, with a BA in both Speech and Hearing Science & Child Development. She went on to get an A.A.S in Sign Language Interpreting and worked as an interpreter until her first child was born. She's the author of the high-octane **Jessica McClain** urban fantasy series published by Orbit, the **Sin City Collectors** PNR series, the contemporary fantasy **Phoebe Meadows** series, the dystopian **Holly Danger** series, and the futuristic thriller **Mina Kane** series. Look for these books in stores everywhere. She lives in Minneapolis.

FIND HER ALL OVER SOCIAL MEDIA

Website: amandacarlson.com

Facebook: facebook.com/authoramandacarlson

Twitter: @amandaccarlson

Instagram: @author_amanda

www.ingramcontent.com/pod-product-compliance
Lightning Source LLC
Chambersburg PA
CBHW050805190726
48285CB00005B/1800